By HARVEY SWADOS

HARVEY SWADOS

A STORY
FOR TEDDY

-and Others

SIMON AND SCHUSTER
NEW YORK

FOR JENNIE AND KAUFMAN, TOO

CONTENTS

A STORY FOR TEDDY

W<small>HAT IS IT</small> that drives us to consider the girls of our youth, those we enjoyed for a day or a month, those whose scruples we strove and strained to overcome, those who scorned us, those who fled? I am not sure, since even the easy nostalgia arising from the memory of success must give way to other emotions when defeats and not victories come to mind. In the case of Teddy, it was an accident, a typically New York accident, which brought her back to me not long ago, but it is only as a result of my own deliberate life as a writer, and the painful, endless effort to understand, that she has come back with such clarity that I can close my eyes now and see not merely as much but more than I saw twenty years ago.

When I try to recall how I first came to know Teddy, I think back to a double date early in the war, arranged by an acquaintance. Teddy was his date, but my own I cannot visualize in any way—she was surely one of those girls who sit near the telephone, waiting to be fixed up by an attractive cousin. Teddy must have been that cousin. Within an hour of our having met, while the other two danced (we were in some collegiate hangout in Yorkville), I was urging her to go out with me.

Teddy colored. With her fingertips she pushed her ginger ale glass toward my bourbon glass. "You're pretty fast."

"I have to be."

Teddy was not very strong on repartee, and I fancied that I was ruthless. She was just eighteen, went to college at night, was taking courses in child psychology, and worked by day as a steno for some agency that helped soldiers' families, like Travelers Aid. She lived with her little brother and their widowed mother in an apartment house in a remote fastness of the Bronx. All that mattered to me was that she was lovely.

As for me, I was twenty-three and terribly world-weary. I had worked as a copy boy on the old New York *Sun* the year between college and the Merchant Marine, long enough to learn my way around town. I had only three months before finishing boot camp and shipping out, and I was anxious to waste as little time as possible.

Teddy was not sharp and competitive, like the girls I had known at Ohio State and around Manhattan. She was simple, unambitious, and vulnerable. She made no pretense of being smart or well read, but she was gentle and modest and virginal, and utterly unsophisticated—you might have thought she was the one from Ashtabula instead of me. Her skin was clean and glowing, her blond hair tumbled over her forehead, her lavender eyes were soft and troubled.

I picked up her small, defenseless hand, ostensibly so that I could admire her charm bracelet, from which dangled a little Scottie and a windmill with revolving sails; she had gotten it from her father for her fourteenth birthday. Squeezing her still childish fingers, I said, with a self-pity that was realer than she could imagine, "I've only got my weekends—and not too many of them—before I ship out. Won't you meet me next Saturday? In the afternoon, as soon as I can get in? Say at two-thirty, under the clock at the Biltmore?"

All that week I thought about Teddy. In the clapboard barracks where, like college boys all over America, I was learning with a thrill of despair that my fellow citizens from farm and factory were foul-mouthed, ignorant, and bigoted, it was difficult enough to remember that girls like Teddy still existed. Teddy, snub-nosed and sincere, in awe of me because I came from out

of town and had hitchhiked to California and back, and eager
to help me forget that hell-hole where I alternately sweated and
froze; such a girl took on the proportions of a prize, one I had
been awarded without even being fully eligible.

When I pushed my way into the Biltmore lobby through the
swirling Saturday crowds, I was struck speechless at the sight of
Teddy, already waiting for me. Not only was she unaware that
she had breached the code by arriving early, but she did not
even seem to notice how she was being sized up by a group of
nudging sailors. She was nervous, yes, but only—I could tell—
because she was looking for me. The tip of her blunt little nose
was pinker than her cheeks, and she dabbed at it with a handkerchief that she took from the pocket of her fur-trimmed plaid
coat as she squinted this way and that, searching for me. I realized for the first time that she was nearsighted.

I hung back for just a moment, then stepped forward and
called out her name.

With a glad cry she hastened toward me. "I was afraid I might
have missed you in all this crowd."

"I was afraid you wouldn't show up at all."

"Silly." This was a word Teddy used often. But she was
pleased, and as she pressed my arm I could smell her perfume,
light and girlish. "What are we going to do?"

I wanted to show her off. Outside, I led her over to Fifth
Avenue, then north, and we paused now and then in the faltering late-October sunlight to look in the shop windows. With
Teddy at my side I felt once again a part of the life of the city,
secure for the moment at least, as I had not felt wandering for-
lornly with my false liberty, or hanging, miserable, around the
battered ping-pong tables of the USO, waiting for nothing.

At 53rd Street we headed west and stopped at the Museum
of Modern Art. The bulletin board announced an old Garbo
movie. I turned to Teddy.

"We're just in time for the three-o'clock showing."

"Don't you have to be a member or something?" Teddy
looked at me uneasily.

I was still learning how provincial some of these New York

girls could be. I led Teddy through the revolving glass doors and took unhesitating advantage of my uniform to get us two tickets; skirting the crowd waiting for the elevator, we skipped down the stairs to the auditorium.

The movie was *The Story of Gösta Berling*. I remember very little about it other than the astonishingly plump whiteness of the youthful Garbo's arms, for I was burningly aware of Teddy's forearm alongside mine. After a while I took her hand and held it through the picture. As our body warmth flowed back and forth, coursing between us like some underground hot spring, I peered covertly at her. She was staring intently—too intently—at the screen; and I knew, as I knew the thud of my own pulse in my ears, that I would never be content with simply sitting at her side. I would have to possess her. Somewhere near the end of the movie, reasonably certain that no one would be observing us, I raised her hand to my mouth, palm up, and pressed it full against my lips. At that she turned her head and gazed at me tremulously.

"You mustn't," she whispered.

She meant the contrary, I was positive. Giddily, I allowed her to retrieve her hand, and when the picture ended I slipped her coat over her shoulders and led her up the stairs to the main gallery.

"I'll show you my favorite picture here," I said. We stood before the big canvas that used to be everybody's favorite in those old days before everybody went totally abstract. It was by Tchelitchew, it was called *Hide and Seek*, and it's too bad it didn't get burned up in the fire they had not long ago. It consisted mostly of an enormous, thickly foliated tree, like an old oak, aswarm with embryolike little figures, some partly hidden, some revealed, some forming part of the tree itself.

Teddy appraised it carefully. Finally she said, "You know what it reminds me of? Those contests I used to enter. Find seven mystery faces hidden in the drawing and win a Pierce bicycle."

I was nettled. "Did you win?"

"Sure. But instead of giving me the girl's twenty-six-inch bike, they'd send me huge boxes of Christmas cards to sell."

By the time Teddy and I were walking south on Lexington, with the wind comfortably at our backs, we had exchanged considerable information about our childhoods, none of hers important enough for me to recall now except that her father had dropped dead in the street during his lunch hour, in the garment center, two years earlier.

"Where are we going?" she asked, clinging to my arm.

"I thought we'd eat in an Armenian restaurant. Unless you don't care for Armenian food."

"I never tasted it. Not that I know of."

No other girl that I knew would have admitted it. Not in that way. We hastened to 28th Street, to a basement restaurant with candlelit tables and a motherly proprietress.

I thought I was doing not badly at all. Over the steaming glasses of tea and the nutty baklava Teddy's eyes glowed, and she held my hand tightly on the crumpled linen cloth. Her face was still unformed, but I observed, for the first time, that her cheekbones slanted, almost sharply, beneath the soft freshness of her delicate skin, and in the shadow cast by the uncertain candle there was a suggestion of a cleft in her chin. I couldn't wait to be alone with her, and I judged that the time had come for me to tell her about my friends in the Village who sometimes loaned me their little apartment for my weekend liberties, as they had this weekend.

"Phil is in four-F with a hernia, but he's nervous about being reclassified, so he's been trying to line up a Navy commission in Washington. Charlene—that's his wife—just found out she can't have children. She's planning to start her own nursery school in Washington if Phil gets into Navy Intelligence."

"If they're your friends," Teddy said gravely, "they must be nice."

I winced for her. Now I know a little better; don't we all flatter ourselves by thinking that way of our friends, when all too often it is simply not true? Phil was not nice; he was a climber.

His ambition, combined with his terror of death, drove him to get that commission.

But to Teddy I explained, earnestly and wholeheartedly, "Phil is an anthropologist, and Charlene paints. They've been to Mexico, and their place is full of things like beaten silver masks and temple fragments."

"It sounds lovely."

"Let's go. It's not far—just down on Jane Street."

Teddy was not quick, but she was not stupid either. "Will there be anyone there?"

I knew at once that I had moved too fast. And lying could only make things worse. "They probably won't be back from Washington before tomorrow."

"In that case I think I'd better not." Teddy flushed, and forced herself to look at me. "You're not angry, are you?"

"I wasn't planning on assaulting you," I said, trying hard not to sound sullen. "I mean, the place isn't an opium den."

"I know. It's just that I don't think it would be a good idea."

When we were out on the street once again, walking west into a fall rain as fine as spray from an atomizer, Teddy stopped suddenly before a darkened courtyard and looked up at me anxiously.

"I didn't mean to hurt your feelings. I guess I'm just not very sophisticated about those things."

Pressing her against the wrought-iron picket fence before which she stood, her head tilted, trying to catch some light in my eyes or across my face which would tell her what I was feeling, I folded her in my arms and kissed her for the first time.

I kissed her again, and a third time, and maybe I wouldn't have been able to stop, but Teddy passed her hand across her forehead to brush back her damp hair and said, laughing somewhat shakily, "Don't you know that it's raining?"

So we went on to the Village Vanguard, and then to Romany Marie's, where Teddy assured me, after she had had her fortune told, that this had been the loveliest evening she had ever spent. Like a dream, she said—the whole day had been like a dream.

At about two o'clock in the morning I offered to see her home. She insisted, as we stood arguing by the mountain of Sunday papers at the Sheridan Square newsstand, that she wouldn't think of my riding the subway all the way up to the East Bronx for an hour and then all the way back for another hour. Not when I had to get up almost every morning at five-thirty, do calisthenics, and practice lowering lifeboats into the icy waters of Sheepshead Bay. I yielded, but not before I had gotten her promise that we would meet that afternoon at the Central Park Zoo, where she had to take her younger brother. I stood at the head of the subway stairs and watched, bemused, as she tripped down them, as lightly and swiftly as if she were still a child, hurrying so as not to be late for school.

At the zoo I found Teddy as easily as if we had been alone in that vast rectangle of rock and grass, instead of being surrounded as we were by thousands of Sunday strollers. She was standing in front of the monkey cages with her younger brother, Stevie, a solemn-looking mouth-breather with glasses and the big behind that many boys acquire during the final years of childhood. She whirled about at my touch, her face already alight with pleasure.

"Did you sleep well, Teddy?"

"Like a baby. Such sweet dreams!" And she introduced me to her brother.

What he wanted was to attend a war-bond rally at Columbus Circle, where they were going to display a Jap Zero and a movie star. I think the star was Victor Mature; in any case, on the way to see him and the captured airplane I pulled Teddy aside and asked her if we couldn't cut out for a couple of hours and run down to Phil's apartment.

She stared at me. "Honestly, I think you have a one-track mind."

"Phil and Charlene are in from Washington," I explained hastily. "They'd like to meet you."

"But I'm hardly even dressed to meet *you!*" In dismay she

pointed to her loafers, her sweater and skirt, her trench coat, but I succeeded in persuading her.

While we stood in line to see the airplane, Teddy asked Stevie if he'd mind if we left him alone for a while. He barely heard her. He promised to wait for her through the Army Band concert, and we hurried off to the downtown bus. All the way to the Village Teddy kept me busy reassuring her that we wouldn't be barging in where we weren't wanted.

Phil's place was strewn not only with the various sections of the Sunday *Times* but with a crowd of weary weekend loungers who hadn't been there when I left that morning: an unmilitary Army officer and his hung-over girl friend, a dancer in blue jeans from the apartment across the hall who was studying the want ads while she picked at her bare toes, a nursery-school-teacher friend of Charlene's who was arguing heatedly with her in the kitchen about child development. The radio on the bookcase was blasting away with the New York Philharmonic.

Teddy sat primly on a corner of the studio couch with her knees pressed together and a paper napkin spread over them, sipping coffee and nibbling on a Triscuit and speaking only when spoken to. Phil got me off in the john at one point and said, grinning and shaking his head and winking in his nervous way, "You'll never make that girl."

I was annoyed, but I wasn't exactly sure why. "What makes you say that?"

"Aside from the fact that she's a virgin and terrified of you and your highbrow friends, she's too clean. I'll swear she uses those soaps they advertise in *The American Girl*."

"How would you know about *The American Girl?*"

"I've got a little sister."

I thought of the contests that Teddy used to enter—Find 7 Hidden Faces—and I found myself hurrying back to her side with her trench coat.

"Yes, let's go," she said. "I'm getting worried about Stevie. If my mother knew, she'd kill me."

"I wouldn't let her do that," I replied manfully.

"I'd like to see you stop her," Teddy said to me over her shoulder on our way out. "You don't know my mother."

I didn't know quite how to answer that, so I busied myself with finding a cab—no mean trick in those days, when they weren't allowed to cruise. I didn't want to know her mother, but on the other hand I wasn't about to come out and say so. When we were settled in the taxi that I had gone several blocks to find, Teddy said mournfully, "Your friends are very talented people."

That made me a little suspicious. "Most of them aren't my friends. And besides, who's talented?"

"Well, take that Army lieutenant. He's an artist. He told me so."

"Rollini? He paints camouflage on the sides of airplane hangars. I don't see that that's such a big deal."

"You know what I mean. I just don't think I fit in with those people. I can't do anything special." She gestured helplessly. "Look at me."

The cab swung sharply onto Sixth Avenue, and Teddy was flung into my arms. I kissed her while her mouth was still open to say something else.

"Wait," she panted, breaking free. "I want to ask you something." She huddled up, very small, out of my reach in a corner of the cab. "Do you really like me?"

"Like you?" I asked. "My God, you're the most beautiful girl I've ever known. All week in those cruddy barracks I keep telling myself—"

She interrupted my protestations. "That's not what I mean. I wasn't fishing for compliments. I didn't ask you if you thought I was pretty, I asked you how much you liked me."

Teddy knew as well as I how hard that would be for me to answer. Maybe that was why she didn't stop me when I reached out for her once again, wanting to substitute caresses for words. Only when we were within a few blocks of Columbus Circle did she part from me again, her forehead wrinkled and her lower lip trembling just the slightest bit.

"I just don't understand," she said wonderingly and not very happily. "It's all wrong."

What was I going to tell her—that I wanted to make love to her? She knew that already. Before I could say anything we were caught up and blocked in the traffic of the bond rally that was on the point of breaking up. Teddy darted out of the cab door, calling over her shoulder, "I'll write you!" as she dashed off in search of Stevie. While I stood there in the eddying crowd, paying the driver, the band broke into "Praise the Lord and Pass the Ammunition," and I saw Stevie the mouth-breather, standing with his jaw agape and staring at the trombones through his eyeglasses.

Before the week was over I had my letter from Teddy. I am not going to try to reproduce it here. I will only say that it can best be described as a love letter and that it was so gauche, so overwritten, so excruciatingly true ("I am simply not used to going out with boys like you") and at the same time so transparently false ("my brother Stevie thinks the world of you") that it was immediately, painfully, terribly clear to me that I would never be able to answer in kind, and that there was no sense in my deluding myself into believing that I would. I hope it does not make me sound completely impossible if I add that her words not only released me from thinking seriously about her; they also made it all but impossible for me to think of anything but conquering her.

What inflamed me all the more was that shortly after I found Teddy's provocative letter on my bunk, my entire platoon was restricted to the base for the weekend. Trapped in that raw, artificial place, in its womanless wooden huts thrown up hastily to house some thousands of frightened boys being converted into sailors of a sort, I spent my mornings bobbing on a whaleboat in the bay, rowing in ragged unison with my freezing mates, and my afternoons ostensibly learning knots and braiding lines but actually lost in an erotic reverie of Teddy—of her slim arms, her tumbling hair, her pulsing lips—gone all wanton and yielding.

By the time we finally met again, I had memorized every line of her, from her slanting cheekbones to her small feet that toed out the least bit—and I could hardly remember what she looked like. We were constrained then, two weeks after the bond rally, not only by what had passed between us but by the heedless souls shoving us away from each other in the 42nd Street entrance to the Times Square subway station. It was the worst possible place for a boy and a girl to meet on a Saturday afternoon, in that blowing surf of old newspapers and candy wrappers, with the hot, rancid smell of nut stands assailing us. We hardly knew what to say to each other.

She smiled at me nervously, and I was emboldened to take her by the hand. "Let's get out of here." Willingly she mounted the stairs with me to the street, but when we came out onto the sidewalk the raw rain had turned to sleet; it cut at our faces like knives. I cursed the world, the war, the weather.

"But if you were stationed at that Merchant Marine camp in St. Petersburg," Teddy pointed out, "we would never have met."

"Oh great," I said. "Now you're going to do the Pollyanna routine."

"I didn't mean it like that," Teddy replied humbly.

"I want to kiss you, that's all. Are we supposed to stand out here in public and freeze to death while I make love to you? Come on, Teddy, let's go down to my friends' apartment. Like civilized people, like folks. What do you say?"

She could tell I wasn't going to push it too hard, so she laughed and tucked her arm in mine. "Come on, Mr. One-Track Mind, let's get out of the sleet."

It was driving down hard, and we had to run into a doorway, which turned out to be the entrance to a second-floor chess-and-checkers parlor. When Teddy laughed, still gasping a little and shaking off wetness like a puppy, and said, "I wonder what it's like up there," I took her by the arm and led her up the stairs. It never ceased to amaze me how a New York girl could know so little.

Teddy hadn't played much chess, only with her brother (their father had taught them), so I showed her a few openings, but she was frankly more interested in sizing up the habitués.

Later, while we were having a drink at an Eighth Avenue hotel bar (I teased Teddy into having a Pink Lady instead of her usual ginger ale), I asked her if she'd ever eaten a real Chinese dinner. She looked a little disappointed. "We have Chinks in the Bronx almost every Saturday. Sometimes we even take it home with us."

"I'm not talking about chop suey, Teddy. I'm talking about the greatest cooking this side of Paris."

As if I'd ever eaten in Paris, much less in Peking! But that made no difference. I knew a real restaurant down on Doyers Street, and when we got there the headwaiter even remembered me. Or at least he claimed to, which was just as good; and when he followed the bird's-nest soup with platters of crisp glazed duck, Teddy gazed at me in awe.

Afterward we walked off the dinner through the dim, narrow streets of Chinatown, echoing with soft, slurring voices, and then took a subway back up to midtown in order to see Noël Coward's *Blithe Spirit*. We were fortunate to get tickets, and made it just after the curtain had gone up, groping our way to our seats.

Teddy poked frantically in her purse and came up at last with a pair of shell-rimmed eyeglasses. She was seeing bright comedy on the stage for the first time; I was seeing her in glasses for the first time. For both of us it was a revelation. She thought the play was brilliant; I thought she was delicious.

When the play let out, we stopped in at Jimmy Ryan's on 52nd Street, ostensibly for a drink, but actually so that Teddy could see how casually I greeted the boys who were playing there—Pee Wee, and George Brunies, and Zutty Singleton—poker-faced at the drums like Joe Louis—and Art Hodes, whose daily jazz program, I told Teddy, I used to follow on WNYC. But since Teddy's musical background was confined to André Kostelanetz and Lily Pons, she was only impressed, and not overwhelmed, by my acquaintance with the great. I took her across the street to hear Billie Holiday.

We stood at the bar, Teddy's back against my chest, and stared through the throat-tearing smoke at Billie, who sang "My Man" and "Strange Fruit" and "Gloomy Sunday."

Teddy's eyes were wet and shining. She raised her head. "You're opening a whole new world for me."

That was precisely what I was trying to do, but it bothered me to have her put it so patly. It reinforced my conviction that she would always be like that, forever, and that there was no point in my even considering that she might ever be otherwise.

She went on, "And I don't know that it's such a good thing. For either of us. Why should we kid ourselves? It's not going to be my world—it never will."

It was a somewhat melancholy note on which to end the evening, but in a way I preferred that. It struck me that it would be almost diabolically patient to let Teddy stew overnight, torn between guilt and gratitude. The next day was to be the climactic one. I forced myself to kiss her more lightly in parting than I wanted to, and we agreed to meet the next day by the lions in front of the Public Library.

For a change the weather was on my side. The wind was brisk, and Teddy had tied her print scarf around her blond hair babushka-style—it accentuated the slope of her cheekbones when she laughed—but the sun was out. We walked all the way up to the Frick Collection and were lucky enough to get in to the Sunday concert. Teddy had never even heard of the institution and made no attempt to conceal her ignorance.

Although she knew no more of chamber music than she did of jazz, Schubert stirred her, and she held tight to my arm throughout "Death and the Maiden," breathing softly and shallowly while she squinted (no glasses in the daytime) at the musicians. When the recital was over, we walked on up to the Metropolitan Museum, which Teddy hadn't visited since she was ten.

I led her directly to El Greco's *View of Toledo*. "This is worth the trip, this and the Courbets inside. Better to see just these than to get a headache from looking at too many."

How insufferable I must have been, lecturing Teddy first on music, then on painting, about which I knew so little! But she smiled at me gratefully, and let me know by the way in which she clung to me that I was both patient and wise.

As we left the Metropolitan and walked south through Central Park, darkness caught up with us and the wind came up too. Our breaths frosting, we hurried on across Central Park South against the traffic, skipping in and out of the dimmed, blurry headlights until we had gained the rococo refuge of Rumpelmayer's.

Warm, snug, soothed, we spooned up the great blobs of whipped cream floating on our hot chocolates and laughed over inconsequential things, and then suddenly, as if by common accord, we both stopped. I stared into Teddy's lavender eyes, so soft and moist that I wanted to kiss them closed, and she opened her mouth but without speaking, as if she dared not utter whatever it was that she wanted to say.

"I must kiss you," I murmured.

She nodded dumbly.

We went outside. In the dimout across the street the aging men who took you on carriage rides through the park and along Fifth Avenue were adjusting the straps on their horses' feedbags and hoisting blankets over their hides to protect them from the chilly evening. I signaled the leader of the line.

Teddy said apprehensively, "This must be terribly expensive."

Without answering, I raised her up into the carriage and climbed in after her. The driver tucked us in with a warm comforter, swung himself aboard behind us, clucked to his horse, and we were off.

Teddy and I turned to each other so precipitately that we bumped foreheads, searching, in the sudden dark of the covered carriage, for each other's lips. We rode on through the lamplit evening, clinging to each other, kissing, until the current that flowed between us warmed not only our lips but our cheeks and our hands, our fingers and the tips of our fingers.

"You have been so nice to me, so nice to me," Teddy whispered.

I responded by kissing her into silence. It was only after a long time that she could protest, trembling in my arms and frowning, "You shouldn't kiss me like that."

"Like what?"

"You know. It's not right, that's all."

"Nobody can see."

"Silly! I mean, I think it's for married people, or anyway for engaged couples, and like that."

We weren't engaged or like that—the very thought was enough to frighten me out of my ardor—but I had every intention of our becoming lovers, and the sooner the better. "There's only one way," I whispered into her ear, "for you to stop me."

"What's that?"

"Kiss me back the way I kiss you."

Before she could express her shock, I had stopped her mouth again. We must have been near 72nd Street on the west side of the park before we drew apart, panting.

"You know where I'm going to take you to dinner?" I asked. "Where?"

"Phil and Charlene's. And I'm going to cook it myself. Wait till you taste my soufflé! On the way down we'll pick up some French pastries, and—"

"They're not there, are they?"

"Who?" As if I didn't know.

"Phil and his wife. Because if they're not there, I'm not going. I don't think you ought to take advantage of the fact that you're so attractive and I'm so weak."

I forced myself to be calm and reasonable. "Teddy, darling, what's so terrible about our being alone together for a while?"

"I don't trust myself. Any more than I trust you." She uttered the words with as much heartfelt emotion as though she had invented them—as though no one before her had ever even expressed such thoughts. And she looked more ravishing, more flowerlike than I had ever seen her before, her lips fuller than usual, a little swollen perhaps, her eyes staring piteously at me, her hair escaping from her scarf in little tendrils that clung to her forehead.

"Is it so awful," I demanded, "for two people who care about each other to be alone together?"

"But what you care about isn't me, it's getting me alone." Teddy paused, as if to give me time for a fervent denial.

I could say nothing. I was not the noblest or the most honorable twenty-three-year-old left in the United States, but I was incapable of promising engagement rings to young girls in return for their favors. And this much at least Teddy understood about me. The damnable truth was that I couldn't even imagine myself falling in love with, much less marrying, a girl who would make a big issue out of protecting her virtue. And on top of it all, I had been keyed up for what was going to be a triumph. I still wanted Teddy very badly, but it was obvious that I had failed completely.

After a long while she said, "I think I'd better go home."

She wanted to be contradicted, as with her other assertion that we had left hanging in the air, but I could no more find it in me to protest this time than before. I was too hurt and too shamed.

But so was Teddy, and when we had been brought back in jolting silence to our starting point, she jumped out and began to walk away toward the Sixth Avenue subway so swiftly that after I paid the driver I had to run for the better part of a block before I caught up with her.

"Please, if you insist on going, let me see you home."

"There's no need. Really. And I don't want you to think I'm angry with you, because I'm not. I had a perfectly lovely time. You'll never know how much I loved it—every minute of it. I'm just angry with myself, that's all. You and I are very different, and it's my fault, not yours. I should have faced it right at the beginning."

Still dumb, I shook her extended hand and watched her hurry off toward the subway and the Bronx.

Three days later I stood by my bunk staring at a letter from Teddy, incongruously pink and girlish on the coarse blue of my

Navy blanket. For a moment I was afraid to touch it. Finally I tore it open.

It was the letter of a pen pal, jolly and comradely. A friend had given her two tickets to the Columbia-Brown game this coming Saturday. (I was learning that when a girl says a friend she means a boy—otherwise she specifies.) Wouldn't I please be her guest, so she could repay me just a little for all the fun I'd shown her?

If I had been older probably I would have said no. But I was desperately lonely in those barracks, graduation time was nearing for my platoon, and I thought, If I say no, she'll think I'm still pouting. And besides, hope revived: If I turned her down, how would I ever know for sure that she hadn't changed her mind and was using the football game as an excuse, a means of saying I'm sorry, I was wrong, you were right, I'll do whatever you want?

So I awaited the weekend as fervently as I had all the others, and to calm myself on the long, long subway ride up to Baker Field I did a crossword puzzle. Teddy met me by the entrance on the Columbia side, as she had said she would—but so much more real, so much more beautiful than my imaginings of her, that I could almost have believed I not only wildly wanted her but wildly loved her too.

It was apparent immediately, though, that we were to be pals. Teddy was dressed for late November, and for this last game of the season, in plaid flannel skirt and a heavy mackinaw and little fuzzy earmuffs. She looked adorable. When she arranged her small lap robe across our knees I reached around her waist and hugged her tightly to me, but all I could feel were layers of wool and bulky insulation.

"It's my brother's mackinaw. Do you recognize it?"

"It looks better on you than on him."

"This stadium must seem pretty tiny to you after those Big Ten games with seventy and eighty thousand people in the stands."

It did, it did. I could hardly take any of it seriously, the scrimmages, the end runs, the quick collisions, the slow roars, the cheerleading. And especially not the athletes, so puny compared to the hulks on football scholarships with whom I had eaten in my Ohio coop. Not when so many other young men my age were burning and drowning, trapped in torpedoed tankers less than a hundred miles from where we sat cheering. But then it was going to be a long war—everyone promised us that —and these boys on the field would get their chance to die, some of them before the next year was out.

As we shoved our way through the crowds onto the street, weaving in and out of the crawling cars, Teddy turned to me, her face glowing. I had never seen her prettier—or happier.

"That was fun, wasn't it?"

"What's next on the program?"

She laughed. "Know anything about bowling?"

"I know what you're up to," I said. "You're trying to wear me out."

We went to an alley she knew of in Washington Heights where a young crowd hung out—refined, she said, not bums or low-class. To me they looked like high-school graduates waiting to be drafted and their kid sisters. No doubt their younger brothers were working as pin boys. We drank two Cokes and bowled two games. Teddy was a little clumsy, but I loved watching her strain forward eagerly, frowning over the progress of her ball down the alley.

If only, I thought, if only. But I couldn't even plead with her, not when she was content to be surrounded by dozens of shouting kids her own age. Why keep pushing her? I asked myself. Why not leave her to her games and her soft drinks and her soldier pen pals in Greenland, North Africa and Australia?

We had steaks—black market, to judge from the price if not the taste—at a restaurant on upper Broadway, and as I chewed I mumbled, "We've had football and we've had bowling; now all we need is swimming to make our day complete."

"The St. George pool has mixed swimming tonight. Let's go!"

"I see enough water all week. We have to jump into the

damned bay with rubber suits on; sometimes they dump out a couple barrels of oil and set them on fire to make it more interesting to swim through."

"I didn't think," she said, crestfallen. "Anyway, it's too cold."

Of course when she spoke like that I had to insist we go. We rode the Seventh Avenue subway all the way down to Brooklyn, got off at Clark Street and went up by elevator straight into the hotel without even setting foot on the street. We parted for the first time all day at the lockers, urging each other to hurry.

I got to the pool first. Teddy came in a moment later, a little shy, tugging at the nether parts of her rented tank suit as she stepped forward on the damp tiles, her pink-tinted toes curling gingerly upward. Her body was slight, paler than mine, and vulnerable. Her embarrassment only increased my own; I turned my eyes away and dived into the water at the deep end. But she slipped in after me and came up alongside me, dripping and cheerful.

"Isn't it great? I'll race you down to the shallow end!"

Actually, although Teddy thrashed bravely, she couldn't swim very well. But she splashed me happily, slipping loose from my grasp when I reached out to paddle her. Laughing and gasping she hauled herself out of the pool and flung herself upon the tiles. She grinned down at me as I hung from the lip of the pool, my legs dangling in the water.

"I'm so glad we came. You were sweet to bring me. Isn't this more fun than all that other stuff? You know what I mean."

"No," I said, "it's not."

Teddy's little bosom was rising and falling regularly; the droplets of water clinging to her bare arms and legs glistened under the lights. I was infinitely touched by the way in which the fine golden down smoothed itself around the soft flesh of her thighs and her forearms. I had never seen her with so little clothing. Her body was not only tender and almost childishly graceful; it was so appealing that it was physically painful for me to survey it without being able to touch it, and I shrank down into the water.

"Why?" she asked. "What's wrong?"

"Everything." I reached up and took hold of her ankle. It was so fine that my thumb and forefinger nearly girdled it, and it seemed to me that I could feel every little interlocking bone as she flexed it in an instinctive frightened withdrawal. "Do you know what I'd be doing now if there was no one in the pool but us?"

Teddy giggled. "There'd still be those people up in the balcony, looking down at us."

"I mean if we had the pool entirely to ourselves . . . I wouldn't even start by kissing you. First I'd peel your suit off."

Her grin faded. She withdrew her foot from my grasp and pulled her knees up tight against her chest, hugging them as if she had taken a sudden chill, or perhaps wanted to hide from me as much of herself as she could.

"I'd pull you down here into the water, both of us naked," I said desperately. "I'd hold you against me so we could feel every inch of each other. I'd run my hands up and down your back, and I'd—"

"Listen," she broke in nervously, "why don't you come up here and sit next to me and we'll talk about something else?"

"Because I'm in such a state I'm ashamed to get out of the water, that's why. Now are you satisfied?"

"I don't know what you're talking about."

"Well, if you don't you're even more childish than I thought."

At that she colored all the way down to the base of her throat. She turned her head swiftly, anxiously, to either side, as if to make sure that the handful of Saturday-night swimmers, mostly older women, could not overhear us.

"Please don't be angry with me," she said. She released her hold on her legs and leaned forward so that she could speak softly, confidentially. The front of her shapeless gray tank suit fell away from her chest, and I found myself gazing raptly into the shadow between her small breasts. She spoke so eagerly that she disregarded my gaze. "If you could get those urges satisfied elsewhere—I mean with some other girls, some other kind of girls—then you and I could just have fun like we did today. Couldn't we?"

"You're joking."

"No, no, I'm not. Not really. I mean, if you wanted it like that—" she sucked in her breath and laughed jaggedly— "maybe I could find a girl who would—you know—do those other things for you. Then you could get off that one track you're always on with me."

I didn't know whether to laugh or to cry. All I could think of to say was, "Here I'm telling you that you're adorable, that it's you I want and not some stranger, but nothing registers. It's obvious that you don't care about me, or you wouldn't say such fantastic things."

"No," Teddy muttered, not looking at me, "it's you who don't care for me. Do you think, if you loved me, that we'd—" She broke off with a quick shudder. The little golden hairs were standing upright on her arms and legs. "See," she said sadly, "I'm all goose pimples. I'm going to take a hot shower. We've done enough for one day, haven't we?"

I remained in the barracks after that, brooding, waiting to ship out into the North Atlantic. I made no effort to get in touch with Teddy. Finally, since I had time on my hands for the first time in months, and access to a typewriter in the Master at Arms' office, where I often stood night watch alone, I wrote a short story.

It was a bitter story, of course, about a young serviceman who, because he is denied physical intimacy by the girl who claims to love him, goes recklessly to his death, a snarl upon his lips.

I made two copies. The first went to *The New Yorker*. After debating with myself for a day or so, I wrote across the face of the carbon copy, *Here is the most I can offer you for Christmas, something I made for you myself, from the bottom of my heart.* I signed my name and mailed it to Teddy.

Within two days the original came back from *The New*

Yorker. I stuck it in a fresh envelope and shipped it off to the *Atlantic Monthly*, where I knew from experience that it would rest long enough for me to go off to sea under the happy illusion that it was being seriously considered.

I heard nothing at all from Teddy. After a few days I could stand it no longer, and one night I rang her up from the pay phone in the rec room. She answered, but from her tone, a little frightened when she recognized my voice, I was sure that her mother was there.

"Teddy," I said, "I've been worried by your silence. Are you all right?"

"Yes, I am. Are you?"

"Yes, of course. Is your mother there with you?"

"I don't see what difference that makes." Then she said what her mother must have been coaching her to say, against the moment when I should phone again. "My mother feels I shouldn't see you any more. And I think she's right."

I was so shocked that I forgot to ask about my story. I stammered, "But all I wanted was to see you one last time before I ship out. Does that seem so unfair? For us just to get together this Saturday afternoon?"

"If you had any respect for my wishes," she said stiffly, "you wouldn't press it any further."

I muttered goodbye and slammed down the receiver. But the next day, after a night spent cursing myself for not having let it rest with my sardonically inscribed story, I received a note from Teddy.

She apologized for the way she had spoken (I was right; her mother had been listening) and went on to add that if I still wanted to say goodbye she'd look for me on Saturday at one o'clock in the waiting room of Penn Station. She would tell her mother she was going shopping at Macy's.

It was Teddy's willingness to deceive her mother that encouraged in me the wild hope that maybe my story had accomplished what my physical presence and my pleading had been unable to do. But when I dashed into Penn Station, Teddy came up to me unexpectedly and offered me only her hand and not her lips.

The hand was gloved, but I had the feeling that her fingers would be cold; her lips were pale and bloodless and she smiled at me tremulously.

"You look well," she said. "I'm sorry I can't stay very long."

People were bumping into us in their anxiety to reach the escalator. The vaulted terminal was bleak, drafty and—to me at that moment—terrifying.

"My God, Teddy," I said, "you can't just shake my hand and walk away." I pointed to the bag hanging from her left hand. "You've done your Macy's shopping already. That ought to satisfy your mother. Can't we get out of here? Please?"

"If we could just be happy one last time—like we were for a little while . . ."

"Come with me." I took her by the hand. "I know a good French restaurant near here. While we eat you can talk and I can sit and admire you."

"You'll have to promise that you won't get personal like that."

"Supposing I get personal not like that?"

By the time we reached the restaurant we were laughing together; you might have thought we were just getting to know each other. But in a matter of minutes the laughter had faded away and we were face to face more nakedly than we had ever been before.

We entered the restaurant and passed through the long, narrow bar where three elderly Frenchmen were having their apéritifs. We seated ourselves in the glassed-in garden dining room in the rear courtyard and ordered our hors d'oeuvres. Suddenly Teddy pouted, as one does when one remembers a forgotten obligation. Then she reached into the red-and-green, holiday-decorated shopping bag and handed me back my story.

I stared at her, my spoonful of pickled beets suspended in air.

"Teddy," I said at last, "that was a present. A Christmas present. You don't give back presents."

"I have to. I just can't accept it."

"But why?"

"It, uh . . ." Teddy swallowed. "It was insulting, that's why. Here, take it, please. Then we won't have to talk about it."

"The hell we won't. Do you know how hard I worked on it? Maybe it's not the greatest story in the world, but it's the best I have in me, and you might at least have acknowledged it, even if you didn't like it."

"But I did. I do." Teddy gazed at me in agony. "It's just that you shouldn't have put down all those intimate details."

"I can't believe that you felt like that when you first read it," I began, and then I stopped. A suspicion formed in my mind. "Wait a minute. Did you show that story to anyone else?"

"Well . . . just to my mother."

"I knew it." I was too sickened to be triumphant. "You might as well give me her literary verdict. I'm sure she had some memorable comment."

"She said it was dirty."

I jumped to my feet and flung down my napkin, knocking a knife and a fork to the floor. My legs seemed to be entangled with my half-tipped-over chair. A French family at the next table looked up in surprise from its *pot au feu*. So did three ladies on the other side of us.

With her knuckles at her lips, Teddy asked, "Where are you going?"

"I'm leaving. What did you expect?"

She began to cry. Ignoring the tears that were welling from her eyes and dropping onto her artichoke hearts, she whispered, "Please, please, please, don't go. Don't leave me like this."

Frightened by her tears and by the enormity of what I was about to do—walk out on a sobbing girl under the disapproving gaze of a roomful of people—I hesitated.

Teddy went on. "I promise not to say anything more to upset you. All I ever wanted was for us to have fun together, without hurting anybody, before you shipped out."

I sat down. Weeping softly, Teddy told me that I had expected too much of her from the start, that she wasn't like all the other, older girls with whom I had been intimate (there had been only two, but Teddy imagined scores).

"I suppose the trouble was," she mused sadly, somewhat more under control, "that it was all just a little too cold-blooded. If I had felt that you cared for me . . . I couldn't lie to my mother about that. Don't you see, maybe she's not so smart, but she's all I've got, she and Stevie, and I have to live the way she expects me to. The way she wants me to."

If before Teddy had made me enraged, now she was making me squirm. Seeing this, she reached across the table to touch me lightly on the arm and added, "Don't ever think I'm not grateful. You can't imagine how much you've done for me."

Mollified, I disclaimed any special virtue, and we left the restaurant almost as calmly as we had entered it. We strolled up to 42nd Street and then east through Times Square to Bryant Park, stopping under the movie marquees to study the stills of the Ritz Brothers and the Three Stooges, of Lynn Bari and Jean Parker.

We sat on a stone bench under a leafless tree in Bryant Park, discussing books and observing the types on their way into the library. We were careful not to talk about ourselves, or about Christmas, or about what the new year would bring; when we bumped knees, we excused ourselves. But then it began to rain again, the fine but mean rain of a Manhattan December, and as we looked hopelessly at each other and then at the forbidding bulk of the library, I remembered the movie houses on 42nd Street.

"Come on," I said. "I'll take you to see *Intermezzo*."

"I really must go home. I'm expected."

"Not yet." I tugged her off the bench. "You yourself told me Ingrid Bergman is the most beautiful girl in the world. You bragged about seeing her in front of Bloomingdale's."

Laughing and protesting, Teddy allowed me to hurry her to the theater. But *Intermezzo* was a mistake. We had to sit through the last hour of an anti-Nazi epic, plus a newsreel of Mrs. Thomas E. Dewey launching a Liberty ship, before we were rewarded with Leslie Howard making love to Ingrid Bergman.

They went off together to celebrate their illicit passion in a sun-kissed Mediterranean villa, knowing—or at least Ingrid knowing—that it could come to no good end and that she would have to tiptoe out of Leslie's life in order to spare him for his art.

I sat with my arm around Teddy's shoulders, but I might as well have clasped a statue. She held herself absolutely rigid and stared fixedly at the screen through the little shell-rimmed glasses she was no longer self-conscious about wearing, her elbows tight against her sides, her fingers locked together in her lap. By the end of the film I was intoxicated all over again with the odor of Teddy's damp blond hair and lightly fragrant perfume, and she was biting her lips, fighting back the tears as Ingrid took leave of her unsuspecting lover. The theme music swelled to a crescendo, and we groped our way out to the street.

It was almost pitch-dark, the dimout was on, and the rain was driving directly into our faces. Luckily I captured a cab and we tumbled gratefully into it, slammed the door behind us and waved the driver on. Then, to my astonishment, Teddy flung her arms around my neck, held me so tightly I could hardly breathe, and proceeded to kiss me as I had taught her to kiss.

My God, I thought, have I won at the last possible moment? And when the driver called back, "Which way, folks?" I whispered to her, "Let's go down to the apartment. Now!"

I have thought since then that if I had been a bit more mature, more masterful, if I had simply directed the driver down to Jane Street, I might have won out. But I doubt it. For Teddy shook her head fiercely, even while she continued to caress me, and muttered, "No, no, no, I'm going home, I'm saying good-bye to you here."

We remained clasped in each other's arms all the way up to the Bronx. In front of her apartment house, while I stood, distraught, counting bills into the cab driver's hand, Teddy ran a comb unsteadily through her hair and apologized for the expense of the long ride.

"I'm the one who should apologize for never taking you home before," I said. "Let's go on up."

In the back of my mind, I suppose, was the final hope that Teddy's mother and brother would be out. The old red brick building was shabby, with peeling hallways; but what was worse, it was a walkup, and Teddy lived on the top floor.

We climbed slowly and awkwardly with our arms around each other's waists and on the fourth floor Teddy told me, blushing, that we still had two more flights to go. "The higher you go, see, the cheaper the rent is."

As we moved dreamlike up the last flights, I thought how often she must have flitted up and down all these steps—no wonder she was so slim!

When we reached the top floor she indicated silently the door which was hers: 6B. But before she could say anything I unbuttoned her coat—my pea jacket was already open—and pulled her close to me. As I began to kiss her she went limp. I was kissing her hair, her ears, her eyelids, her cheeks, but when I pressed her lips to mine she did not respond with the ardor which had so surprised me in the taxi; and even though she opened her mouth under the pressure of my lips, she remained absolutely passive, drooping like a flower deprived of sun, her eyes closed, as I raised her unresisting arms and slipped them around my neck.

For some reason this passivity drove me wild, and I tore at her woolen dress, searching for the zipper and the buttons, until I had worked my hands through. Her underthings slithered to my touch, and in a frenzy I pulled up handfuls of her slip until my fingers reached the smooth flesh of her back and her belly. She remained motionless, neither assisting nor opposing me, as I worked open her brassiere and freed her breasts.

My hands roved frantically, attempting with desperate speed to discover what had been denied them for so long. Her body was more delicately wrought than her wistful, pretty face, and I was stunned to feel the sharp, childish wings of her shoulder blades, the fragile bones of her rib cage behind which her heart was throbbing, the pathetic soft buds of her breasts.

Suddenly I was crying. "Teddy, Teddy, Teddy," I whispered, and I felt her give way in my arms. In another moment we would both have sunk to the cold stone floor; but at that instant the steel door of 6B swung open and Teddy's mother flew into the hall like some great bird of prey.

She could have been no older than I am now, but she seemed a dreadful old bag, a harpy, her hair half crammed into a net, her eyes darting venomously out of a craggy face slimed with cold cream. As I released Teddy, she pulled her coat together to cover her gaping dress, and then, yanked forward in her mother's iron grip, stumbled blindly into the sanctuary of their apartment. Her mother flashed me one scornful glance—part rage and part pure triumph—before she slammed the door.

I stood there dripping rain and sweat, too shocked even to be conscious of frustration. My eye was caught by the Macy's shopping bag, stuffed with gaily wrapped Christmas presents, that had fallen from Teddy's hand to the floor. I bent to pick it up when the door opened again. Teddy's mother snatched the bag from me without a word, and before I could open my mouth she had slammed the door.

No doubt it was the shopping bag, decorated with holly and mistletoe, that reminded me of my story, my gift to Teddy. As I made my way slowly down the long flights of steps, pulling myself together to face what had to be faced in the world beyond Teddy, I discovered that I did not have the manuscript she had returned to me. It must have been kicked under the table at the restaurant, and as I swayed out into the dreary street I thought, Well, I'll never see the restaurant, I'll never see the story, I'll never see her. Never again.

I was right, of course; at least in that limited realization I was right, if in nothing else. But a few weeks ago I had to see an editor about a manuscript, and I drove into New York and pulled into a West Side lot. It was a raw wintry day, with the soundless wind rushing papers about the streets to remind one that beyond the solid brick and stone, nature still strove to do you down. I gave myself one more moment of my car heater's warmth before braving the cold, and while I was checking the contents of my briefcase and putting on my hat to protect my bald skull, I was overcome by the eerie sensation of having been here once before, in some different incarnation, younger, hatless, without a briefcase. But in an empty lot?

The attendant rapped on the car window with his knuckles. "What do you say, Mac? I haven't got all day. Leave the key in the car."

"Wait a minute," I said. "Do you live around here?"

"I was born exactly two blocks down the street." He was an underslung, argumentative Italian, remarkable only for his long nose and for his pride in the place of his birth. "Anything you want to know about the neighborhood, ask."

"What used to be here, before the parking lot?"

"Rooming house, like everyplace else on the block. Restaurant on the first floor."

My eyes began to smart. I closed them for a moment. "A French restaurant?"

"French, Italian, what's the difference? A restaurant."

I got out of the car and shuddered in the chill wind as loose sheets of paper plastered themselves against my shins. They were not likely to be pages of the story I had left behind, a story which had surely turned to ashes with the restaurant, and probably long before. The story was gone; so was the little blonde who had sat just here, weeping as she handed it back to me—and so was I, the would-be writer, pompous but still unsure of his craft and his magic charm.

We have all three died, as surely as if the war had done us in; but did we really die forever? Teddy still lives in my mind as she was then, whether she has gained the chairmanship of her P.T.A. or not. And I, too, live again in my mind as I was then, whether or not I have won my way to what I dearly desired to be. Only that well-meant and ill-written manuscript, that rejected gift, deserved to die forever. It is *this* story—called up by the sudden stinging recollection of two young strangers, the boy and girl at the last table of the garden restaurant, yearning for everything but understanding nothing—that is the real story for Teddy.

SOMETHING
A LITTLE SPECIAL

SITTING AT the Genoese sidewalk café with his bearded
chin cupped in one hand and a glass of cool white wine in the
other, Sam Keller glanced at the bowed blond head of his
pretty wife, bent industriously over the *conto* for the luncheon
of *frittura* and rolls, which she had ordered in a brave and
hardly faltering Italian. If it were not for the camera dangling in
its tan leather case over the wire back of his chair, and the new
open-top Fiat glittering in the spring sunlight at the opposite
curb, with their luggage strapped to its rear, they might have
been old-time residents or expatriates, he thought happily, instead of mere tourists with just two weeks of vacation travel
ahead of them before they turned around and headed back for
San Francisco. For the first time since their honeymoon four
years earlier, abbreviated to accommodate his budding career,
they were utterly free—with the exception of one little obligation. At the thought of it, Sam frowned, and as Ellen looked
up, satisfied with her calculations, her sharply observant eye
caught his uneasiness.

"What's the matter, Sam?"

He concentrated on paying the black-coated waiter, counting
out the tip carefully to familiarize himself with the money. Then

he said, "Not a thing." Knowing what her response would be, he persisted nevertheless. "I just wish that we hadn't promised Nick to look over his property. Couldn't we just go on to Como and Milano? And maybe afterwards—"

"Afterwards! And you're the big planner! The farm is practically on the way to Torino—you know that. Unless we go there now, we might as well forget it. Besides, it'll be fun. An adventure. Sometimes," she added, a bit coldly, "I think that you chose your profession to give you an excuse for regulating everything. Why not take things as they come, and get some pleasure out of doing a little favor?" Then, as if to take the sting out of her words, she squeezed his arm as they approached their auto. "You only child, you."

But it wasn't his being an only child, he knew, that worked on her nerves. It was his insistence on keeping remote from family and family responsibilities; it was his refusal to make up with his father ever since their last shouting match, which Ellen had witnessed as a shaken bystander. Why did his throat get dry every time that scene arose in his mind? He swallowed.

"It's not that I'm being stuffy," he said, knowing that he was being just that. "It's simply that I wanted the two of us to be all on our own. A kind of honeymoon."

"We will be. From tonight on we'll be able to do whatever we feel like."

"You know what I want to do tonight? To celebrate our arrival in Italy? I want to make love to you on foreign soil for the first time."

"You'd better," Ellen threatened. But he was pleased to see that beneath her mock toughness she was actually blushing a little.

Then why, he thought, driving as casually as if he were at home through Genoa's northern industrial suburbs and its beach towns, and then onward to Savona, why did the idea of this little favor fill him not with expectation but with dread? Was it Nick? Or Nick's need for family souvenirs?

Nick's property was above a hill town, high on a mountainside not too far from Cuneo, on the southern slope of the Italian Alps. To get there they would have to drive from Savona up the autostrada—here Ellen consulted the map while he wound the wheel through green, lovely hills not unlike their own in northern California—then, after the end of the autostrada, up successively narrower roads until they came to a monastery not marked on the map because it was abandoned, but known to the nearby villagers. It was ten minutes' walk, Nick had said, from the monastery, where they'd have to leave their car, to his ancestral acres.

Nick diGrasso was somebody the Kellers had met by chance one Sunday afternoon while they were driving around back of Sonoma, looking for a family-owned winery where they might picnic and take home some good table wine. They had stopped in at a small restaurant to inquire on the off chance that the proprietor would know of such a vineyard nearby. The proprietor was Nick.

He had taken them into his hearth, bade them taste the wine that he bought for his own table, given them a note to his vintner, and introduced his wife, Betty, and their four small children, each born within a year or so of its predecessor. Nick was just Sam's age, although he looked younger, clean-shaven and with a mop of curly black hair. Betty and Ellen were of an age also and spoke the same language, even if Ellen's Italian had come from her junior year abroad, while Betty's had come from the family kitchen on Grant Street.

Although Sam and Ellen drove out quite often after that, sometimes with friends, they didn't really have much in common with the diGrassos. Sam had gone to Stanford and done his graduate work at MIT, thanks to his father (who never tired of reminding him of it), while Nick's education had stopped short of the *liceo*, after his widowed father had been ambushed by the Social Republicans, the last-ditch Fascists in northern Italy. Sam had a strong sense of profession; Nick, who had beaten his way to the USA with the aid of a GI after the war, would try almost anything for a buck. He'd apprenticed himself to a pastry cook, taken business management at night at San Francisco State, worked weekends at a crab stand down on Fisherman's Wharf, and saved. When the chance came his way to buy up a small restaurant, he was ready.

But if Sam had done none of those things, not even saved (they'd sold some of Ellen's bonds for this European vacation), he'd read a lot of books and listened to a lot of music which Nick had never heard of. This was perhaps why Nick admired Sam inordinately. He made you feel, Sam often thought, as though he had been waiting impatiently all week for you and your wife to pay him the honor of eating his cooking and passing a few cheerful Sunday-afternoon moments with his lively family.

"I'll tell you something else," Ellen had said when Sam had mentioned this talent of Nick's on their way home from his restaurant one Sunday evening. "He makes me feel as though I'm beautiful."

Unwilling to admit that he was shaken, Sam had replied promptly, "But you are," and peered hopefully at her, curled up in the dark beside him.

"You would say so," she had murmured almost scornfully, and then added, "Besides, I don't mean exactly that. I mean, he makes me feel I'm voluptuous. And don't tell me you think I'm that."

Well, pleasing women was supposed to be an Italian gift. And Nick, who played up to Ellen's love of Italy (as well as to her vanity), was overjoyed when he learned of their vacation plans.

"You're just the ones," he had said excitedly, "to find out for me. Wait till you get up in those mountains above Savona. Man! It won't take you too long, and you're gonna see something different, I promise you, something a little special."

The farm where Nick had lived until he had run off to America had been his since the death of an uncle some years ago. It was tenanted now by a fellow named Ugo Fannini, with whom Nick had played as a boy and who had never left home; Ugo lived there in the diGrasso house with his wife and small boy, his father and mother, and worked somewhere nearby as a mason or roadmender. The question was, Had Ugo kept it up? What was the place worth now? There had been a fine stand of horse-chestnut trees; and no matter what might have happened to the property, the view was really sensational. Sam was a big expert: when he looked it over, he'd be able to say whether the property ought to be sold or converted into something more modern.

"No point in tying up money in the old country, right? It brings me in next to nothing. I could use the cash here in my business."

It was the sort of responsibility Sam hated to take on, the sort that relatives continually asked of you—if things turned out badly, they always blamed you—and if this had been Nick's sole request, he would have sought a way to get out of it, even though Ellen had practically consented as soon as the words were out of Nick's mouth. But Nick had been shrewd enough to realize that he could really commit them by making a more sentimental demand.

"What I'd like is a souvenir of the tribe—you know what I mean?" He had leaned forward confidentially. "Ugo wrote me he's been keeping everything. If you could bring back some pictures of my family—you know, the old folks—especially of my father, *mio caro padre* . . . " And he had lapsed into Italian with Ellen.

Sam was more annoyed than he dared let on at Nick's using Ellen in order to get at him, and at the use of family piety to milk him for a professional opinion on that land. He and Ellen had not had as easy a time of it as people thought who only saw them clam-digging or holding hands at concerts: She had been stunned by the discovery that he and his father could say the things to each other that they had. What was more, she could not understand why he should shrink from her father's generosity ("What do you mean, he's trying to buy you? That's paranoid!"), as if it were simply the converse of his father's meanness. Despite the messed-up lives of her sisters and brothers, she insisted that it had been fun growing up in a large family, and she resented friends' assumptions—assumptions she dared not deny as yet—that she was still childless because she and Sam were not ready to "settle down."

So now, having duly turned off at Savigliano, in quest of a place he was not eager to find, Sam said hesitantly, "Maybe Nick thought he was doing *us* a kindness."

Ellen glanced up from the map, puzzled. Then her brow cleared. "Maybe it'll be a kindness all around. I bet the Fannini family will be glad to have news of Nick."

"If we get there."

For a while it looked as though they wouldn't. Finding Santa Maria dei Fiori was easy enough, yes. At the public washbasin in its unpaved square, women in black balanced baskets atop their heads, old men in berets and felt slippers gazed at them incuriously, a mangy dog yelped as they slowed down, a spavined goat tied with rope to a rickety cart raised its tail to drop its beanlike black excrement onto the dust. Three small boys came running out of a churchyard with books under their arms and heavy wool socks dropping down their calves, chasing one another and crying shrilly until they caught sight of the new Fiat.

"I'll ask them the way to the monastery," Ellen said.

Laughing, the boys nodded as Ellen spoke (even to Sam her Italian sounded harshly Nordic), and they vied with one another to give directions. *A sinistra, a sinistra,* that much he got, but just where to turn left he could not make out. After saying *grazie* three times and punctuating her thanks with candy bars, Ellen turned to Sam happily.

"At the end of the village, a real steep road, not paved, goes straight up to the sky."

"They said all that?"

But at the end of the village the road petered out into a mountainside meadow, with no ascending road in sight. They turned about and still did not find it; they asked an old man, but he had no teeth in his head and seemed to be mumbling, according to Ellen, the opposite of the children's instructions. They tried it his way and found nothing, and by the time they reached the town square yet again, Sam was ready to go on to Torino.

"Once more around," he said glumly, "and the old ladies at the washtubs will think we're out of our minds."

"I'll get out and ask them. They must know."

Ellen came back confidently. "The kids were right. We must have missed it. We have to cross the river."

They had been bemused by the glorious stream, carrying melted snow from the Italian peaks all the thousands of meters down to the Mediterranean, from which they had mounted an hour or two earlier. It leaped like something alive, from boulder to boulder, singing dangerously to distract you from the insignificant road which snaked over it on a trembling wooden bridge and promptly bent out of sight around the mountainside.

So they crawled over the bridge in low gear, and then around and up a stony track so eroded that it should have been strewn with the cracked axles of wrecked carts, abandoned after they had bent and slipped to death part way up the mountainside.

"We're ruining a brand-new car," Sam grumbled, but actually he was happy, with Ellen crying out in delight and clutching his arm as they swung out over seeming emptiness, with the leaping stream now fifty, now a hundred feet below.

"If we keep on going, Ellen, we may wind up in Switzerland."

"Or in heaven."

"Well, where's the monastery?"

"You need faith, Sam, if you want to encounter the house of God."

"Faith in God, or in the car?"

"In yourself. That's all I've ever wanted of you," she said cryptically. "Look, there it is."

The brick-and-plaster monastery stood squarely on a grassy knoll, the one level spot on the mountainside. The only unusual thing about it was that it should be there at all, hulking and bulbous as a Victorian exposition hall, utterly unlikely in this remote corner. It seemed to be quite deserted.

But as Sam swung the car about on the hard-packed dirt in the shade beneath a jutting bay, a strolling couple came into view. A farm woman in a shapeless and all but colorless dress, her arm hooked through a heavy woven market basket, walked beside her husband, a sunburned, knotty-looking man whose collar lay open and whose shirt sleeves were rolled up to expose his white neck and arms and who looked younger than his wife, perhaps because of the proudly careless way in which he bore their little boy high on his shoulders, like a prize he had won at a village fair. They strolled on, too shy to stop and stare frankly at the strangers, alone in the empty square.

Sam pulled up the handbrake. "Let's find out if they know where the Fanninis live."

Ellen had already snapped open the car door and scrambled out to confront the couple, who awaited her in silence. Addressing them eagerly in the dusty piazza, the wind whipping her pink skirt about her thighs and the sun glinting on her lacquered toenails in her Sausalito sandals, she might have been a child of this workworn couple, come back from California with news of a new world. It was startling to think that his wife, talking bravely in her high, clear, unyielding American voice, was probably as old as this couple, who looked as though they might have been cast, centuries before, out of some hard and ruthless material.

Ellen turned to Sam while he was striving to disentangle his long legs from the babylike shell of the little car. "Sammy," she cried, "these are the ones!"

They confronted him now, not cold or inhospitable in the least, but wary, like forewarned children, waiting for proof that he had not come from the bank or the government.

"*Buon giorno*," he said uneasily. The little boy sat still on the man's shoulders, gazing down from that height as unsmiling as his parents and with the same smoldering black eyes. Sam stuck out his hand, although it felt as awkward and artificial at the end of his arm as a divining rod. "*Sono un amico di* Nick. Nick diGrasso." Desperately he turned to Ellen. "Was that right? I wasn't ready to start talking."

But the man was pressing his hand with his own, which felt as though it had been carved from oak. His brown face was wrinkling like a bent leather glove. "*Benvenuto,*" he said, "*benvenuto a* Santa Maria dei Fiori."

I'll be damned, Sam said to himself. It works! "What do you know," he said to his wife. "I can understand. He says 'Welcome.'"

Ellen was already exchanging greetings with the little boy, who dimpled at her as his father swung him down to the ground, and his mother, suddenly worried about appearances, bent to wipe the child's nose. Ellen had learned the boy's name at once and was rummaging in her handbag for more of those candy bars, cooing at the child, "Eh, Gian Paolo, *cioccolata!*" and demanding belatedly if his mother objected to his being stuffed with Hershey bars.

Sam reached quickly into the car for the camera which Ellen's father had given them for a going-away present. At once the family began to primp, as though they had gotten dressed up for a ceremonial family photograph. Sam did not wait, but while Ugo Fannini dug his thick calloused fingers into his tough wiry hair in an effort to pull it into place, and his wife tucked her child's blouse into his shorts and pulled up the dangling folds of his heavy woolen stockings from his clodhoppers, he clicked, wound, clicked. Ellen said angrily, "Has it occurred to you that you're invading their privacy?"

"They don't seem to mind," Sam replied, and then said to the Fanninis, pointing to the camera, "*Per* Nicolò. O.K.?"

Ugo Fannini nodded animatedly and said something Sam could not catch.

Ellen explained, a little tight-lipped, "They'd like us to come up to their house."

Sam extended his hand to the little boy, who was already leading the way, waving them on with his Hershey bars.

They had to climb up one more hillside which a jeep could hardly have mounted. The path proceeded jaggedly through the woods at sharp herringbone angles, unsupported by wall or balustrade. Its flagstones, embedded in dirt and enlaced with wandering roots, were worn hollow, like the pavings of an old church, by generations of plodding feet.

"We're in a different country, at last," he said to his wife. "I can feel it under my feet."

But Ellen was conversing earnestly with Ugo's wife, leaving Sam to tramp along stolidly with Ugo and the skittering little boy. He wanted to ask, but did not know how, if these trees through which they were making their arduous way were the chestnut grove that Nick had asked him to examine. He had looked up the word "chestnut" earlier, in their cabin, when Ellen hadn't been watching, but now it escaped him completely. Still, these must be the trees. They were old, potent, sturdy as the people who chose to remain among them. Greening once again and twinkling in the clear spring light, they rose splendidly through the thin mountainous air toward the blue bowl of the sky.

Then the stone-and-plaster cottage came into view just below the crest of the hillside. At the final few steps Ugo Fannini reached down, as though it were something that was always done, like crossing yourself, and clasped his boy's hand to swing him up these last couple of feet. For a moment Sam was stabbed with a queer pang of irrational envy.

The sound of their coming had roused a silky-haired hunting dog and the older Fanninis too, who came out together from a barn which faced the farmhouse and was tied to it by a rotting, unpainted grape arbor under which stood an uneven work table, a wooden bench and several copper kettles. The old lady (no more than sixty, maybe, but she could have passed for eighty) began to shell peas nervously, more to keep her hands occupied than to finish the task, revealing as she smiled—the wrinkles around her eyes deepening into channels—that it was she and not her husband whom Ugo resembled.

The old man did not smile. He seemed to have grown up out of the ground like the grapevine before which he stood, gnarling, twisting and darkening over the years, his skin seaming with the seasons like the tough bark of a deeply rooted vine. Even his clothing—the shapeless beret wedged between his ears, the blue work shirt bleached almost white, the flannel trousers flapping over the frayed carpet slippers—seemed always to have been a part of him, and added to the sense he gave off, almost like an odor, of stolid permanence. His gaze, fixed and impersonal as he attended, with no sign of interest or comprehension, to his son's rapid introductions, came from but one eye, for the other had been enucleated. In its place he had plugged a colorless twist of cotton wadding, the end protruding villainously from the socket into which it had been stuffed.

The forbidding gaze from his one blue eye was more than patriarchal; it was ferociously piratical. Or maybe, Sam thought, I am romanticizing. But the next instant, as Ugo was saying something about Nicolò, the old man leaped upon Sam.

The dark wrinkles of his face splitting into a smile, old Fannini began to pummel, pinch and shake him, all the while emitting a startling high-pitched wheeze. It was an ardent greeting —it could be nothing else—for the old man slapped Sam's cheek affectionately and even tugged at the point of his short beard, cackling, "Hey, *barba, barba!* Hey, *barbato!*"

Sam wanted desperately to thrust aside the old man, who was no longer just a carving of someone's idea of a father but a live peasant, smelling powerfully of dried sweat, garlic fumes and stale pipe tobacco. But he dared not move. As he submitted passively to the embrace, little Gian Paolo jumped up and down, like his barking dog, which was careering wildly, leaping into the air as if possessed. His grandmother stood expressionlessly by his mother, her wrinkled hands folded before the waistband of her apron. His father, Ugo, was conversing rapidly and jerkily with Ellen.

Sam muttered to her, "Would you please get this old man off my back?"

But Ugo was taking hold, talking loudly to his father and, over his shoulder, more slowly to Ellen.

"Sam," she said, "Grandpa is deaf. He thought his son said you were Nick, when he was only saying that you were from Nick."

The old man released him, his eye gone suddenly blank and guarded again.

Sam put his hand to his face. "What was that business of grabbing my beard?"

"Just teasing. He hadn't seen you since you were eleven—I mean Nick, of course."

Sam could not exactly brush off the old man's lingering imprint, not with everyone looking at him as though in truth he had suddenly been changed into someone else. The grandfather had resumed his original stance, exactly as though he had never done that wild capering, and so completely unembarrassed by it that now, only moments later, Sam could hardly bring himself to believe that he hadn't imagined the entire episode.

"Now that you've had your fun," he said to Ellen, a little more stiffly than he had intended, "would you ask Ugo if he'd mind showing me around?"

Motioning to him to follow, Ugo trudged off, the tawny dog trotting along at the rundown heels of his fiber sandals.

Ugo led him up behind the house on a sloping path through the vegetable garden until they had attained the highest point of the diGrasso land. From this small clearing they had a spectacular view. Had they been giants they could have leaped, it seemed, over the beets, cabbages and beans and landed directly on the roof of the Fannini cottage; and from there one more great bound would have taken them yet farther down, to the dome of the monastery beside which stood, alone on the dusty piazza, his little toy of a car, glittering in the spring sun, and far below that, sharply separated from them by the jagged white lightning of the mountain stream whose torrent they had crossed on the way up, the rooftop tiles of the little village of Santa Maria. What was more, it was easy to discern, with the aid of the defining sweeps of Ugo's arm, the limits of the di-Grasso property, the grove of chestnut trees which Nick had spoken of with such deserved enthusiasm. It was a fine few acres, but it was hardly likely that the property could be put to much better use than that which the Fannini family was making of it now.

With the aid of gestures and a few English words, Ugo explained, stumbling and reddening, that he was frightened by the implications of the Kellers' visit. Was Nick unhappy with the terms under which the Fanninis were living on his property? Did he have something new in mind?

Sam tried to protest that he was not in on Nick's big decisions, that he was simply looking the place over for Nick.

"What you do?" Ugo asked, pointing to Sam's hands. He wanted to know, it appeared, what Sam did for a living. Sam did his best to explain what a city planner was, but he might as well have tried to explain bird watching or polo playing to Ugo, who, Sam feared, understood only that his visitor was some kind of landlord's agent.

Nevertheless Ugo was polite. Sam was truly pleased to be able to explain, even haltingly, how he would tell Nick that his property was in good hands.

Sam was pleased, too, with the knowledge that he was not kidding himself. There was really no more practical use for this mountainside than the maintenance of the Fannini family. The chestnut trees looked healthy, but there weren't enough of them to log, and in any event the hauling would be too hard; it was a glorious site for skiers, but again it was much too far from any place remotely fashionable; and the land itself, although you could keep a kitchen garden or even a subsistence farm of sorts, was too steeply pitched for anything more ambitious than what the Fanninis were doing. Nick's best bet would be to leave things as they were, even if the Fanninis paid him no more than a couple of dollars a month.

Scrambling down the garden path with Ugo, Sam found himself disposed to admire the simple improvements the Fanninis had made in the years since Nick's departure—the freshly plastered walls, the new timber supports for the trellis, the drainage ditches dug behind the old folks' living quarters to protect them from flash floods.

Ellen, on her knees in the dust, had been playing with Gian Paolo, the boy laughing shrilly as he sought insincerely to flee, his mother red with pleasure, the grandparents watching remotely in the shade.

"He's a love! A perfect love!" Ellen cried as the shadows of the two men fell athwart her and the child. "These are nice people, aren't they, Sam? I'm so glad we came. Did you have any trouble making yourself understood?"

Sam shook his head.

"Signora Fannini wants to show us through the house—she's been waiting. Come, let's go." And she nodded to Ugo's wife, who led the way into her cramped parlor.

The ceiling was so low that Sam had to duck. Indeed, there was hardly room for the six of them and the little boy, but as they moved on to the kitchen, with its massive wood-burning stove, and to the one bedroom, dominated by a high narrow bed and a loud chromo of the weeping Christ above Gian Paolo's ancient blackened crib, he could not resist the foretaste of his description of this tour when he returned to his colleagues on Post Street.

Their hosts seemed more dutiful than proud. It was only when Ugo took them across to the other building, which sheltered both his old parents and his cow, that he lost his taciturnity.

Flinging open the split door to display the somnolent beast, which was indoors because it had only recently calved, Ugo said, proudly, "*Nostro migliore possessione.*"

Sam would have liked to see how the old people lived, in the dirt-floored one room separated from the cow by a partition and warmed by the heat of the beast, but Ugo's mother unexpectedly barred the way. Wrenching her veined hands, she shook her head violently and muttered something that Sam could not catch.

"It's not fit, she says," Ellen said.

"What's not fit?"

"Their home. For visitors."

"Then let's say our goodbyes and shove off."

But Ugo was bringing out wine and setting a tray on the table under the arbor. This was the real proof, Sam felt, that they were being regarded not as accomplices of a far-off landlord, but almost as friends. Ugo wiped the dark bottle carefully before drawing the cork, his wife pressed water tumblers on them, and little Gian Paolo helped his grandmother pass a dish of hard speckled cookies. Only the grandfather stood aloof, wine-glass in hand, his blue eye shaded by his beret and by the trellis under which he remained.

"*Salute!*" Sam said boldly, raising his glass. Then he turned to his wife. "How am I doing?"

"This is our chance to ask for that souvenir—the pictures, remember?"

Sam was suddenly touched by a vague sense of alarm. "I wouldn't do that. Nick can get along—"

"Nonsense. Didn't you see all those old pictures by Gian Paolo's crib? They're of the diGrasso family, not of these people."

Before he could ask how she was so sure, Ellen had proceeded with an explanation of Nick's request. Ugo and his wife listened intently. Then Ugo said something to his wife, who hastened back into the house, wiping her hands on her skirt.

"You see? They're probably glad to get rid of the pictures and to send Nick something a little special at the same time."

It was too late to argue. Sam gave Ugo an American cigarette (the old man declined with the merest horizontal gesture), and they were lighting up when Ugo's wife returned, bearing a green embossed box the size of a Whitman's Sampler.

"*Ecco!*" said Ugo Fannini. He opened it for Ellen, saying

something about how glad they were to return these pictures
Nick had left behind. "With our compliments." At these words,
Gian Paolo burst into tears and, as Ugo cried out in mortifica-
tion, pounded his fists against his father's leg.

Astonished, Ellen released her hold on the box, photographs
fluttered through the air like dying moths, and the little boy
scrambled about swiftly, trying to catch the photographs as
they fell, tripping over his dangling laces and bumping into Ellen as she stumbled back in an effort to stand clear.

"I didn't mean . . ." she said helplessly, but stopped, for
everyone was talking at once, the Fanninis apologizing, the old
lady saying something incomprehensible as she grabbed at the
lopsided table against whose legs Gian Paolo was colliding. A
tumbler half full of wine tipped over; the dripping red pool fell
into a sticky puddle at the child's feet.

It was the old man who swooped down, grabbed his grand-
son by the arm, yanked him half erect and cracked him viciously
across the behind.

"Hey!" Sam started in anger as the little boy uttered a
scream. He took a step forward to protest. It brought him face
to face with the glaring old man, separated from him only by
the body of the squirming, squalling Gian Paolo, held by the
middle under his grandfather's arm like a slippery little pig.
Ugo was attempting to explain, but his wife seized her child
and carried him away into the cottage.

The old man now retreated once again, just as he had when
Sam's identity had been made clear to him. Sam turned from
him to expostulate with Ellen, who was helping Ugo to retrieve the photographs.

"I told you we shouldn't have done this." Sam knew that the
reminder would annoy her—she could never stand being told
that she had been forewarned—but he couldn't help himself,
not with the old man's eye still fixed on him.

From her squatting position Ellen said shortly, "It was just
that the child was used to playing with these."

"Then why do we have to take them away?"

"They're not his."

"For God's sake, did we come here to teach the kid property rights?"

"His parents want us to have the pictures. And his grandparents. I don't think we can refuse them now. I offered to take something else of Nick's—they wouldn't hear of it."

"You're ruthless, you know that?"

Ellen rose. She smoothed out her skirt and, accepting the green box from Ugo, said quietly, "Better that than weak."

Sam was infuriated. But then Ugo's wife was back with the child, amazingly fast, with the boy's face washed and wiped, quite composed, and with every trace of jealous hatred gone from those great black eyes. It was fantastic. Why, Sam thought, in wonder at how the memory came unbidden, when my father slapped me for stealing pennies I bit his hand; but here was Gian Paolo, peaceably accepting Ellen's placatory presents. Rummaging through her purse, she brought out ticket stubs, packets of Kleenex and photographs of Sam himself, younger, *sans* beard or wife. Gian Paolo, neither snuffling nor snubbing her, accepted Ellen's random and hurried offerings with a pleased grin.

Everyone was mollified; there were smiles, smiles wherever you looked—except for the old one, who remained grim and motionless, almost as though he were standing in judgment, even when Sam hoisted Gian Paolo up onto his father's shoulders as he had been when they had first met down behind the monastery. Ugo offered to walk down the path with them to the piazza, but Sam demurred. "He climbs the hill often enough," he said to Ellen. "Tell him it'll be more pleasant to remember them all this way."

After she had explained, Ellen said, "Now you can take that family portrait."

The old man, however, either did not understand or refused to budge; in any case, the others had to cluster around him. His wife stood on one side, still somewhat tense, his daughter-in-law on the other; before the three Ugo knelt, with little Gian

Paolo still grinning atop his shoulders. Sam shrugged and focused swiftly, and was startled to see, when he peered through the view finder, that the cow in the barn behind the family had stuck her ruminating head out the upper half of the stable door.

"I have it," he said and snapped the picture. It was only after he put down the camera that Sam became aware of how the old man had stubbornly hung back, hands behind him, chin against his chest, blue eye in shadow, the string sticking out of his empty eye socket like a wick ready to be lit and so to set him afire.

Sam made no effort to shake hands with the old man after he and Ugo had said their farewells. Ellen kissed Gian Paolo, embraced his mother and then took Sam's arm for the precipitous walk down through the chestnut grove, with the family slowly waving farewell.

At the car door she released her hold on his arm and turned to look up, although the trees separated them from the Fanninis. Her face was flushed—whether from the walk or the excitement, he could not be sure—and it struck him, even in his annoyance with her, that she had never looked prettier. He was going to say it, but Ellen jumped into the car without even giving him the chance to hold the door for her, and he saw that she was clutching the little green box very tightly.

"Listen, Ellen," he said as he clambered into the driver's seat and started up the motor, "I'd appreciate it if you'd leave that box behind."

"That'll be the day."

"There's nobody else around. They'll find it here in the piazza."

"I don't doubt that."

"If you won't put the box down here, we'll have to leave it for them in the village. Or mail it back."

"I have no intention of sending it back. It's Nick's."

He released the clutch so swiftly that the car almost stalled as he swung it about. "What's the matter with you?" he demanded hotly. "You saw how much those pictures mean to the kid."

Ellen held herself rigid in the lurching car. "Look who's talking—shooting off that damn camera in their faces as if they were monkeys in a zoo. Everything is a project for you. You had to take pictures to prove to the idiots in your office that you were here."

"And what do you have to prove with that box you're hanging onto so tight? You don't care about those people up there—it's Nick you care about."

"I knew you'd throw him at me sooner or later."

"Why not? It's the truth." Even in second they were descending too fast, and he had to hit the brake while he wrenched at the wheel. "All you want those pictures for is to ingratiate yourself with him. And if Nick doubles the rent on those people, or evicts them, you couldn't care less, could you? What matters is having Nick slobber all over you for bringing those silly pictures of his dead old man in a soldier suit."

Ellen's face was contorted. She shouted at him over the wind and the rising babble of the mountain stream below them. "You're not jealous just of me. You're envious of Nick, because he loves his father, because he's happy with his family. Because he makes babies."

Sam shot out his right hand and twisted Ellen's bare arm so brutally that she dropped the box. "How do you know I can't make babies? How do you know?"

"I've been waiting four years. Betty diGrasso didn't have to wait four years."

"And you're not Betty. How do I know it's not you? You wouldn't go to a doctor, would you?"

"I've got news for you. I don't have to. What do you think of that? Watch the road!" she cried as he bent down to retrieve the box. "Give me back those pictures. You and your noise about the kid's playthings. He doesn't even miss them. I saw how you envied his father. And hated his grandfather. Yes, hated that poor old man! That's when you give yourself away. Just because he made a simple human mistake and tried to put his arms around you!"

"I didn't hate him. He smelled bad, that's all."

"Like your father, I suppose. Is that why you haven't talked to *him* in all these years? The whole human race smells bad to you, and all you can do is lie to yourself."

"You're the honest one, you and your Conversational Italian, swiping a kid's toy just to be able to suck around Nick."

"You lie to yourself. Not just to me. To yourself. You hate happy people like Nick because you're not happy, you hate men like Nick because you're not a man. Beard or no beard, you're a spoiled baby. Talk about little Gian Paolo. Look at you—jealous of your own wife because she speaks Italian!"

"You're not even honest enough to say why. You have the soul of a cheat."

Ellen began to laugh. It was that laugh, defiant, bitter, unyielding, that enraged him past the point of any restraint; it goaded him on to destroy her mocking superiority.

He lifted the green box high to pitch it into the swirling stream swinging into sight below as the car careened on down the swerving road. With a cry Ellen was at him. She managed to deflect the sweep of his arm so that instead of soaring through the air and disappearing into the river, the box sprang open as it flew upward, showering them with pictures.

Half blinded by the fluttering photographs that glinted as they tumbled topsy-turvy about him, and thrown off balance by the sudden weight of his wife's straining body, Sam lost control of the wheel. The car bounded from left to right, once, twice, thrown from rock to rock as though flung by the same hand that sprinkled the glossy, sparkling prints through the air; and as he heard his wife's high wailing scream rising and then declining with their violent thrust through space, he was hurled forward, his head smashing against the glass of the windshield at the impact of the car against the great gray boulder which impaled it so that it hung helpless, its wheels spinning uselessly, above the wild blue-white torrent fifty feet below.

Then, as the blood began to trickle down his forehead, oozing hot and sticky like spilled wine in the afternoon sun, his wife flung herself into his arms, sobbing wildly. Clinging to each other fiercely in the sudden stillness, they sat listening to the pumping of their hearts and to the waters rushing away beneath them.

BOBBY SHAFTER'S
GONE TO SEA

IT WAS on a T-2 tanker, some years ago, that I became a particular friend of the steward. He was a stocky, smooth-spoken young man of about thirty, of mixed Negro and Indian and Irish ancestry. His name was Bobby Shafter, and what happened to the two of us, one steamy night in Panama, I am only now beginning to understand.

We had been knocking around the Caribbean for some months—Aruba, Curaçao, Galveston, La Guaira, Mobile, Paramaribo—but with very little port time in any single place. So we were delighted with the news that we'd be laying up at Balboa to wait for engine-room parts.

Nevertheless, Panama City—and the Zone—soon wore itself out for me. There was an air of malign vacancy about the broad, empty tropical streets that was oppressive and even sinister. There, in all their nakedness, gaped the tourist traps, bulging with Dutch gin, Swiss watches and English woolens that the inhabitants could not afford and had no use for anyway, and the grog shops sprinkled with drunken sailors and pregnant prostitutes. Even sex turned sour after I was accosted at four o'clock in the morning by an adolescent girl at least six months gone.

If there is no revolution afoot, life in these latitudes must imperceptibly degenerate for the visitor into the kind of lethargic vegetating that the existence of the inhabitants seems to him to be. So it was with me.

I did join nighttime crowds, squatting in their white ducks and huaraches and laughing without comprehension at old Marx Brothers movies thrown onto improvised bed sheets in village plazas; I did follow, from a hunger for both music and love, youths strumming guitars and singing romantic Latin ballads through half-deserted back streets—until they saw me and closed their mouths; I did buy a pretty parakeet from a sandaled Indian who knew how to squeeze for an extra balboa; I even tried to enter the lives of some of the whores at the Villa Amor, my closest connection with the republic. But you cannot buy conversation any more than you can buy intimacy or love, and finally, appalled by the utter absence of any strenuous ambition, by the seemingly absolute unawareness of even the possibility of any largeness of social prospect, I found myself lapsing into the torpid colonial mindlessness of those around me—sailors and savages, Yankees and Indians—my days punctuated only by the rains that from one afternoon to the next came pounding at us all with the relentless insistence of death itself.

I was more than ready for anything Bobby had to propose. One afternoon I ran into him in a cantina, impeccable in his gold-braided dress blues and white hat. He shook his head sadly at my loud sport shirt and stained khaki trousers and drew me aside. "I've got a date for Friday with one of the sharpest babes on the Isthmus." He winked. "We're in love."

I congratulated him.

"Nita's a Nicaraguan, and very proper."

"You like them that way."

"True, but it raises problems, pal, problems. For this ball she insists on bringing along her two sisters."

"You'll be a busy man."

"So will you. One of them has a husband; the other'll be your date."

Bobby was already married, to a square chick from a shanty

town outside Nashville; I had seen pictures of her, and I knew that when they had been married, in a formal Catholic ceremony, she had cried for two hours from shame at her own ignorance and fear.

Bobby could joke about his Catholicism to me as he couldn't to anyone else aboard ship: "Man, there was a time when you scored zero on the turf if you didn't belong to the Church. And if you did, you made the society column, dig?" Yet the ceremonial of the Mass touched him deeply. He enjoyed the white man's religion and the white man's church; still, he retained a lively contempt for his fellow Negroes who wore out their mouths trying to suck their way into the white man's world.

Bobby had been born and raised in Florida. His grandfather, a Seminole, had bequeathed to him his copper coloring and his name. His father had worked for the express agency, his mother had taken in washing, his sisters had studied bookkeeping and stenography and had nevertheless wound up as maids. Infuriated, he himself had gotten out while the getting was good, expelled after one year from a Negro agricultural and mechanical college. He was more specific about his early sexual adventures: pleased by my incredulity, he insisted that Southern white girls were allured by Negro men.

"During the ten months I worked as an orderly in the state hospital, there wasn't a week passed that I didn't make out with one of the nurses."

"White nurses?"

Bobby laughed at me. "You think there was any other kind? The first few times I couldn't believe it, but later I got to taking such crazy chances, it makes my hair stand on end now to think back."

"How old were you?"

"I turned seventeen that year. A wild kid. Once we were parked out in some stump-jumper's field, and when he snuck up pointing his flash I had to take off with my pants around my ankles, shaking like a treed raccoon. I left for Harlem the next week."

When he hit 125th Street, he had already been tempered by

his audacious nights with the aggressive nurses, by the money he had earned as a kid selling bootleg corn to and for white men beneath the grandstand of the local ball park, and by the bitter knowledge that his parents and his sisters were grinding their lives away because they were both frightened and resigned.

Because Bobby was neither frightened nor resigned, he threw himself into the labor movement, picketing the cafeterias whose tables he bussed and the docks where later he longshored. The Communists took him up, and for a while he took them up. The idea of a career as a leader of the oppressed—planning, telephoning, haranguing—had its appeal for someone who hated being shoved around as much as he hated work, but Bobby was too shrewd to let himself be exploited as a kept boy. He broke with them, but delicately, without destroying those connections that might later prove useful, and moved on to new fields.

He ran numbers, and then jobbed hot cargoes from his long-shore friends; afterward there were stimulants, from pep pills to goofballs, and then party pictures. At one time he was living with twin sisters, and three really frantic show girls were working for him part-time. All these activities brought him more and more into the odd zones of the white world, from Cancer to Capricorn, so perhaps it was understandable that it was precisely during these years that he joined the Catholic Church—just as it was at the height of his involvement with the party crowd that he bumped into poor little Ceelie Mae, cutting through the Greyhound Bus Terminal on 34th Street. Bumped into her as she was waiting tensely to roll back to Tennessee, conned her into staying, and married her.

"It was a revelation," he murmured, fondling their wedding photograph, "that a girl could be so pure. I mean, she didn't even know what she had it for. And for once I managed to re-strain my appetites. In fact I couldn't imagine touching her un-til we were married."

He and Ceelie Mae lived happily on Sugar Hill. She knew nothing of his activities, whether for human rights or for his bank balances, and had never gotten over her original Cinderella bewilderment at their fine apartment, or the splendid clothing that he chose for her.

Then suddenly he shipped out to sea. It had nothing to do with Ceelie Mae, who was no doubt as bewildered by it as she was by Bobby's other activities and who accepted it (he assured me) as she did everything that he decided to do. I suspect that it was some nastiness connected with either the party pictures or the profits from girls, or both. Within a few years he had worked himself up (probably with the help of well-placed friends) to chief steward on this tanker.

The one great thing that had happened since then was that at last, only some six months before, during Bobby's most recent shore leave, Ceelie Mae had succeeded in becoming pregnant. It was the one fruition that Bobby had always wanted of his marriage but had never been able to admit that he yearned for; and now he was happy.

So we sat in his cabin, more often than we did in mine, because he had a record player, and we talked about all this while we listened to his record collection. Bobby had no use for jazz and didn't care for classical music. He did love operettas, and he adored the little encore pieces of Fritz Kreisler. There was one record called "Kreisleriana." How can I ever forget those evenings with the sentimental Viennese waltzes sobbing away, the moonlight floating through the porthole as our ship knifed through the warm black waters of the Caribbean, and Bobby confiding in me about daisy chains in Central Park West duplexes at dawn, and the lovely twins who spoiled him, bought him delicately engraved gold slave bracelets and white leather driving coats, besides turning over to him half of their earnings. He made it all sound not vile or even sordid, but like something out of André Gide.

Bobby's expenses were heavy, and he turned to unorthodox ways of augmenting his income. He and the Old Man had agreed to split the kickback on the ship's stores which Bobby was responsible for purchasing. It was not a particularly unusual arrangement; what made it so in this instance was that the captain was from Georgia. But as Bobby said, "If you can show a cracker how to make a buck, he can be mighty big about prejudice. The long green is the one color line he won't draw."

Bobby had other ways of making money. He bought cut marijuana in bulk from *campesinos* who grew the weed undisturbed in the fields of their tiny farms on the fringe of Panama City. Occasionally he took it aboard on his person; sometimes he had it carted aboard with the ship's stores. Brisbane (which was where we were headed, sooner or later) jumped with cats who had developed a taste for tea during the Yank invasion of World War II and who would pay a dollar for a box of twenty cigarettes. So every evening after dinner he spent a quiet hour locked in his cabin, whistling between his teeth while he stuffed cigarette tubes with marijuana, clipped the ends and packed them neatly in the more elegant boxes—Benson & Hedges, Sheffield, Melachrino.

After we became friends I kept him company while he rolled his cigarettes, although some obscure, indefinable compunction held me back from helping out. As he worked he chatted about some of the strange things he had done in his time and about his hopes for his unborn son, who was going to be called Bobby Shafter, Jr. His manicured fingers worked nimbly, his soft, deceptively innocent countenance glowed with pleasure as he regarded the ornately framed wedding photograph. And behind us, the *zigeuner* music filling the night air, causing Bobby's liquid eyes to fill with tears for very pleasure at all the beauty that the world contained. What a sentimental man!

On Friday evening he shamed me into wearing my only suit for our date. He found me swiping halfheartedly at my brown-and-white shoes. In mock anger, he reached out and plucked the cloth from my hand.

"For God's sake, man," he drawled, "you so cheap you gotta stoop to shining your own shoes? The liberty boat's alongside. Come on, I'll treat you to a first-class shine."

He did, and after that we clambered into an enormous old Cadillac cab that he had commandeered, slanging a little with the adolescent Negro driver in broken Spanish and island-accented English as we chattered through streets still soaked from the afternoon rains.

Bobby dug me in the ribs with his well-ironed elbow. "Better than riding like a smelly sardine in a chiva, eh?"

He never rode the chivas, those nickel-a-ride buses converted from superannuated Chevy panel trucks into crumbling rust-eaten jalops with two facing benches, each side holding, squeezed tightly, four Indians, Negroes, goats, chickens and their assorted smells; he knew that I did, and he couldn't resist teasing me about my stinginess.

We cut across a part of the city that I had never bothered to explore and rolled to a stop before a modest white stucco cottage set in a row of similar houses, each with a tiny lawn, a cactus and a flowering geranium or two.

I took Bobby by his uniformed arm as he was telling the driver to wait for us. "Did you let these people know that I'm white?"

He flashed me a confident but wary smile. "They'll accept you, just the way your friends would me."

That was equivocal enough—maybe not for the captain, but for me. I followed Bobby up the steps and on inside.

Bobby's almost-fiancée Juanita, a terribly young girl with huge, dark, frightened eyes, was seated on the very edge of a sagging couch with a young woman a few years older, whom I took to be her sister, and a very handsome if severe-looking young man who was surely the brother-in-law. They were an attractive trio, gotten up for an evening out in semiformal dress, a little nervous, their complexions—more Latin than Negro—a trifle strained. Across from them, stiffly upright in a worn barrel chair, sat a mountainous Negro lady. It was hard to guess her age from her impassive black face, but she was at least ten or twelve years older than the others and seemed to have nothing in common with them; even her shapeless dark dress bore no relation to the frocks of the young ladies. A neighbor woman, perhaps? Or an aunt?

Bobby rubbed his hands together. "Hi, everybody, *buenas*

tardes, here's my buddy, Nita, her sister Maria, Maria's husband, Evan Jones, and sister Concepcion."

I gaped. Was *this* my date? I turned to Bobby, appalled. The only thing that got me over the next few terrible minutes was the realization that Juanita and her sister and brother-in-law were almost as ill at ease as I. One or two desperate attempts to communicate with Concepcion exposed the final horror: she knew almost no English. It was no go, despite the fact that Mr. Jones, an extremely well-mannered Jamaican whose Spanish was excellent, did his best to help.

"Have you been living here long?" I asked her. I waited, miserable, while the brother-in-law made this important question clear to the lady.

Old Stone-face nodded once. "*Sí.*" That was that.

I tried again: "I suppose all three of you work?"

"Yes." Nothing more.

I gave up. When we got out on the walk and helped the three sisters into the back of the cab (Bobby and I were to sit on the jump seats and Evan Jones up front, next to the grinning driver), I grabbed Bobby and whispered, "Why the hell didn't you tell me?"

He smiled blandly. "I didn't think you'd be color-conscious."

"It isn't that. She's old enough to be my aunt. And I can't talk Span——"

He waved me into the car with a flourish and said to the driver, "To the Jockey Club, man, and steer like a deer."

The Jockey Club was maybe not the most exclusive supper club in the area, but it wasn't the cheapest either. I had certainly never been there for dinner and dancing under the stars, which was obviously what Bobby had in mind; I was more easily satisfied. What was more, it was certainly Gold and not Silver. The social life of the Canal Zone was built around these two fantastically artificial designations. Gold for the whites and the wishful-whites; Silver for the hopelessly dark Negroes from the islands and the Indians from the backwoods and the jungles. There were Gold rest rooms and Silver rest rooms, Gold commissaries and Silver commissáries, Gold swimming pools and Silver swimming pools. I was no agitator. I used the Gold facilities, but it always left a sour taste in my mouth. And the Jockey Club was about as Gold as you could get.

This was not lost on the women or on Evan Jones, all of whom looked at Bobby with such trepidation that he started to laugh. "What's the matter? This is a big night. Relax."

The unworthy thought had already crossed my mind that Bobby had invited me to join his family as his front man to gain them angry admittance to forbidden ground. But I didn't dare tax him with this, certainly not in front of his guests.

It was only when the big cab pulled up in front of the Jockey Club and a uniformed Negro doorman handed us out that I began to get the picture. For not only was the doorman deferential; so was the scuttling Negro headwaiter; and we were shown to a table that was quite near the Latin American band and well in the clear of the palm trees that fringed the unroofed dance floor. Only then did I really try to see the six of us through the eyes not of one who passed through the Gold doors perhaps wryly yet really unfeelingly, but of one whose every waking moment was colored by the unending dreary decisions to be made every time his hand reached for the Silver door and his eyes lingered on the Gold door.

We could all, save for big, black, stolid Concepcion, have passed for light enough to be acceptable in a world where the line had to be drawn not between white and nonwhite but between approximately light enough and impossibly dark—and by someone not too exigent, someone who would do almost anything to avoid trouble. And that someone would have deftly arranged—as in truth our black waiter did—for Concepcion to be seated at the darkest and most inconspicuous corner of the table, from which she might appear to inquisitive eyes as perhaps a hired chaperone or superior kind of mammy, with our party but not really of it.

The Jockey Club was favored by American naval officers. I counted four junior-officer submariners with their dates, young

civil-service stenos or the adolescent daughters of Zone em-
ployees (in any case, looking as emptily fresh and untroubled as
their cousins in the country clubs back home). There were also
a number of tourist couples and businessmen of the type who
could afford this kind of evening out. They all took their turn
in whispering about our party, in gesturing surreptitiously—and
sometimes not so surreptitiously—at the six of us.

But I detected no obvious animosity, nothing more than curiosity or bewilderment, and after a while I began to enjoy the
new situation. The puzzlement on these well-bred faces, so used
to the easy pegging of their fellow creatures, gave me a kind of
secure pleasure. Who were we? Was Bobby an Indian? A South
American naval attaché out with his wife? The Joneses, he with
his acquiline nose and neat mustache, she with her large-eyed
loveliness and good grooming—maybe consular visitors from
one of the islands? And I, with my precious skin so patently
and painfully fair that I could not expose it to this tropical sun
for so much as half an hour without its shriveling and dying? As
for Concepcion, it would be no more than a poor pun to say
that she was beyond the pale. She was quite simply unthink-
able, and all around us our fellow revelers were peeking in uneasy bafflement.

This was fun. I felt a bit of a celebrity and I enjoyed watching Bobby, his arm casually draped across the back of Nita's
chair, his face wreathed in a genial smile of self-satisfaction.

Evan Jones, I learned, was a bacteriologist from Barbados,
now working at the Gorgas Hospital in Ancon, from which he
and his quiet but very sweet wife had come up for this night on
the town. As yet they had no children, and they shared one
great dream: to get away from the artificially imposed restric-
tions of this colonial outpost, steaming with prejudice and tropical lassitude, and to make a new start either in New York City
or in Rio de Janeiro.

Their chances were very slight indeed. Evan and Maria were
painfully realistic about this—yet still they dreamed. They had
no notion at all of the rank slums and isolated provinciality of

Rio, about which I tried to tell them a little; but maybe they were right in not taking me seriously, for they had both already forgotten more than I could ever learn about such matters, and they were concerned not with those familiar miseries but with escaping the abomination of the color label.

I got through a little better about New York; but even here they opposed me with a stubborn disbelief that I just couldn't understand, until they pointed to the reason for their willful infatuation.

"Harlem, like the upper East Side, is exciting only for the rich," I remarked sententiously. For the first time Concepcion was following me, at least when Maria bent over and whispered rapidly into her ear. "The limitations the whites impose on you are still there, for the few rich Negroes too."

"I can't believe this," Evan replied. "I see the evidence against it."

"Evidence?" I stared at him, uncomprehending. "Where?"

He nodded toward the dance floor, where Bobby and Juanita, the most attractive couple on the floor, were executing a nifty tango.

"*There* is a different kind of Negro." Evan's hands were clasped tautly, dark against the expanse of white tablecloth. "You can't know what that means to us."

Unexpectedly, Maria leaned forward, her face alive with excitement, and placed her delicate fingers on my arm. "You see, none of us is like Bobby. He has self-assurance. He walks in with us where we would never go. He looks not to one side or the other. He has no fear, he does not lower himself. You see?"

To my amazement Concepcion, after listening to a machine-gun burst of translation, slowly turned to me and nodded. Her black face glistened in the dim glow of the torches around us; she was perspiring heavily. Had I been wrong about her also?

"Yes," I said at length, "I think I do."

There was no point in my adding that now I understood too their real hopes, which were not for themselves but for their little sister, who was still young enough and for whom now a golden door had been opened by the bold young American. Even if they did not admire him so, they would have been duty bound to flatter him and to encourage her.

"Well," Evan said, "if you'll excuse us. I want to give Maria a whirl."

We arose and he took her in his arms and twirled her off in the direction of Bobby and Nita. I said to Concepcion, "Would you like to dance? To dance?" and pointed toward the floor, now quite crowded with gliding couples. To my relief, she shook her head slowly and gravely.

So I sat down. With my planter's punch in one hand and my good cigar in the other, I leaned back grandly and surveyed the scene before me. Those who had been staring at our table, at me and Concepcion, lowered their eyes or glanced too quickly in another direction, but I felt no triumph. I felt instead rather sick for Nita.

If I didn't share the Joneses' admiration for Bobby, it wasn't because I was censorious of his past. I could even understand why he enjoyed romancing gullible girls with vague hints of a life together under the shelter of the American flag. But now, having met one of these girls and her family . . . How crushed these gentle people would be!

I determined to take Bobby aside to tell him that I wouldn't be a party to this game any more, even though I knew he'd persuade me not to spoil the fun for the others. But I had no opportunity for even this much conscience-salving; instead I was thrust almost immediately into a posture of solidarity not just with Evan Jones and the three sisters but with Bobby too.

What happened was that after the dance set Bobby and Nita returned to our table, hand in hand and glowing. As Evan and his wife came up too, Bobby, driven either by pity for Concepcion or by a belated readiness to relieve me of my burden, bent gallantly over Concepcion's chair and demanded of her the privilege of the next dance. I was astonished to see Concepcion smile slowly at him, then hoist herself out of her chair by pressing down hard on the arms with her palms, as heavy people will. I stood there for a moment, transfixed.

Partly to cover my confusion, I asked Juanita to dance with me. We all moved off—Nita and I, Evan with Maria, and Concepcion solemn as ever, but flexing her great haunches with surprising grace as she followed the tricky steps executed by Bobby, who grinned shamelessly.

I didn't have a tenth of his deftness, even though I was a little drunk, which is ordinarily helpful. So, although I was anxious to talk with Nita about her sister and Bobby, I didn't open my mouth once during the three numbers we danced together for fear (or so I told myself) of losing count before all the watching eyes.

One thing I was bent on, however, was testing Concepcion. As soon as the dancers had drifted off the floor, I accosted her and Bobby.

"My turn," I said. "How about us switching partners?"

"*Como?*"

Bobby laughed. "The mate wants to navigate with you, baby."

Nita whispered rapidly to her sister, who shook her head and finally smiled broadly, showing me two gold incisors, then, murmuring something, placed the palm of her hand approximately over her heart, on her massive black-draped bosom. Juanita turned back to me. "She says she's tired, she's out of breath."

Bobby took Nita by the hand. "Tell her she'll sleep better. Greatest thing in the world for her." And he clapped me fraternally on the back and sailed off with Nita as the music started once again. Perhaps Concepcion's spirit had toughened. She presented herself to me, and as the tourists and naval officers gaped—she dark, looming and indomitable as an aircraft carrier, I skinny, lost and tense as a sailor on his first encounter with a woman of the streets—we worked our way somehow around the floor, not bumping into the other couples only because they carefully cleared a path for us.

After the first number Concepcion detached herself from me with absolute firmness. Once more her hand went to her bosom; this time, having gained my little victory, I was willing to concede. At our table we were shortly joined by Evan and Maria, too considerate to leave us trapped with each other, and later, when the music had stopped, by Nita and Bobby, who summoned our waiter with an upraised forefinger.

"Repeat for everybody, man."

When the waiter had returned with the drinks, Evan raised his glass. "Ladies and gentlemen," he said, then paused while his wife translated for her older sister, "I should like to propose a toast. To Bobby and to—"

He stopped abruptly. The waiter had been leaning over Bobby's shoulder, whispering urgently. Suddenly Bobby straightened in his chair, took the startled waiter by the lapel of his mess jacket and spoke out in a perfectly audible voice.

"Put that in writing."

The waiter stared at him in dismay. "I can't hardly write."

"Go tell the captain what I said. And if *he* can't write, let him deliver the message in person instead of sending you to do his dirty work."

Evan jerked about to stare at the retreating waiter, then returned his gaze to Bobby. "What is this?"

"Never mind. Drink up."

"Please tell us what it's all about."

Bobby ground out his cigarette in the conch shell ashtray and looked us over almost disdainfully. "They want to put conditions on our staying here."

"Conditions?" Evan placed his hand to his mouth as if to hide his lips, thumb to one corner, index finger to the other. "Of what sort?"

"Let the captain tell you when he comes."

We all drank then, without a toast, in a newly oppressive silence. Evan gave his wife a light; she had to steady his hand with her fingers in order to draw flame to the tip of her cigarette.

After a long moment the headwaiter hove into view, with our waiter tagging wretchedly behind. The headwaiter, who minced as he moved, was a Negro too, but many shades lighter and many years older than our original waiter.

He worked his way around the table, skillfully, so that he could stand between Bobby and me. "If I could see you two gentlemen alone . . ."

"Knock it off, Jack," Bobby replied coldly. "Spit it out loud and clear."

"I only wished to explain the management's wishes in regard to your pleasure. If you gentlemen—" he indicated Bobby and Evan— "wish to dance with the ladies you are escorting, or with this lady, that is fine. And if this gentleman—" he inclined his head in my direction— "wishes to dance with either of your young ladies, there is no objection."

Bobby jabbed his thumb at Concepcion and me. "But you don't want her to dance with him. Right?"

"We would prefer not."

"Why not?"

The headwaiter stared at us miserably. He did not answer.

Bobby repeated the question. "Why not?"

The waiter extended his pink palms pleadingly. It was as if he were demonstrating the evidence of his color. "Maybe if we step into the lobby . . . There is no need to disturb the other patrons."

Evan picked up his wife's wrap. "Bobby, I do not enjoy being where my family is not welcome. Nothing will be gained by making a scene."

"That's what you think." Bobby showed his teeth.

"Wait," I said. "I'm the one whose behavior is questioned."

"I assure the gentleman . . ." the headwaiter muttered.

I stood up. "I'll sit with whom I please and dance with whom I please." At last. I felt virtuous.

"Don't waste your breath on this joker," Bobby said. "We'll talk to the manager. Period."

The headwaiter was trembling. "He will speak to you by the door."

"Never mind that jive. If he can't come here there's only one place I'll meet him, and that's the kitchen." Bobby put both hands on the table and stood erect. "Clear? Now shove off."

Evan Jones shepherded the sisters, stunned by the abruptness of it all, away from our table and toward the kitchen, which opened off the lobby. He touched Bobby's elbow. "None of us will enjoy prolonging this. Can't we leave quietly? Why the kitchen?"

"Just let me do the talking."

Head up, Bobby marched into the kitchen leading all of us, and the two waiters, as smartly as though he had earned his uniform at Annapolis. He paused at the great chopping block and allowed the headwaiter to scuttle before him with his funny crablike gait. There we found the manager, a fat Panamanian with an octagonal diamond that glittered on his little finger, and an eye both sad and greedy.

The manager extended his hand to Bobby and nodded gravely. "I'm afraid we have inconvenienced you."

Bobby ignored the hand. "I bet this is the first time you ever had Gold and Silver dancing together on your floor."

"You understand, to me it makes not a particle of difference."

"Oh sure."

"But we simply cannot afford to disrupt our guests."

"Maybe we educated them a little tonight. But I'm not concerned about them." Bobby raised his voice. "I'm concerned about my own people."

He aimed his finger at Evan, at Maria, at Concepcion, at Juanita—and then at the kitchen help, the cooks, the pearl divers, the busboys, the waiters, the musicians, all dark-faced, all beginning to grin and whisper. Suddenly we had an audience of over a dozen; and it grew every second, as more waiters came through the swinging door and pressed against each other in order to see and hear. Then I knew what Bobby was up to.

"We proved tonight," he said, "that if you are determined, you can do things that were never done before. We proved that you can be a man, if you really want to." He snapped his fingers at our waiter, who stared at him openmouthed. "What do you think about it, man?"

"I guess that's right."

"You *guess*? Don't you want to be a man before it's too late, before you're nothing but bones in a box? Black man can be just as much man as white man."

"That's right!" a voice called out.

"You tell them, Yankee man!" cried a squat black dishwasher in an ankle-length rubber apron, in accents as British as those of Evan Jones.

"All right, I'll tell you," Bobby shouted above every kitchen noise, above splattering faucets, clattering dishes, rattling silverware. He waved aside the enraged manager.

"I'll tell you that I wouldn't work in a place where my black brothers were insulted. I wouldn't work where my black brothers weren't served. I wouldn't work—" he dropped his voice to a virtual whisper, now that he had us— "where I had to be the one to tell a black man or a black woman to sit in a corner.

"I know you've all got mouths to feed. But you can refuse to degrade yourself or your people. Right?"

"Right! Right, man, right!" They pronounced it *mahn, mahn,* but I knew what it meant.

They pressed on him from all sides to shake his hand, to clap him on the back, to touch his gold-ribboned arm, laughing and shouting with pride and delight. I found myself jammed against the great wooden door of the meat locker, with Evan and Maria squashed breathless against me, gasping and shining-eyed.

"You see?" Evan demanded. "You see? He's champion, simply champion!"

I looked down into his little wife's glowing eyes. Yes, I had to see. I looked across, beyond Bobby and his cheering admirers, to Juanita, who stared with silent adoration at her laughing, perspiring hero, and to Concepcion, who, despite the monumental impassivity with which she stood, arms folded across her vast bosom, now exuded an air, almost an aroma, of justification, like a mother who has lived to see her maligned boy vindicated at last. If I had known a little less, I too would have been wholehearted in my admiration for the way in which Bobby—a live symbol of the intoxicating possibilities of freedom—had so swiftly engendered this renewal of faith and self-confidence.

Then the manager, after a tense and voluble consultation

with his headwaiter, came up, his fury reined, and asked us please to consider that we had all been his personal guests. Cheap at that if it would get Bobby out of the kitchen and his help back on the job. But Bobby capped the evening.

"We don't want any free rides. You know what we want? To be treated exactly the same as anyone else. That shouldn't be too hard to understand, should it?" And he draped his arm almost paternally around the manager's pudgy shoulders. "Now if you'll just let us square our bill, we'll be on our way."

Out in the street five minutes later, Evan and the three sisters were still hardly able to believe that they had been a part of Bobby's feat. I whistled up a cab; this time Concepcion insisted on hoisting herself into the front seat, obviously to let Bobby ride in state between Maria and Nita, who held his hand in quiet rapture while Evan and I perched on the jump seats.

Evan could not contain himself. "This has been one of the greatest evenings of my life. How rare to find a man who is personable, charming and brave. One of our own! With fifty, a hundred, a thousand men like that, what couldn't we accomplish?"

At the sidewalk in front of the girls' home, we chatted for a few moments more, in order that Bobby and Nita might have their parting embrace alone in the shadows. It was just getting to be uncomfortable when Bobby came bounding out, dancing a little soft-shoe routine and patting his lips with his handkerchief.

"Let's go man, go," he called to our cab driver; and we took off with a jolt.

Bobby dragged deeply, with a contented exhilaration, on his cigarette as he drummed his fingers rapidly against the window. He turned to me, bright-eyed. "Maybe we ought to dig up a couple chicks to finish off the evening."

"Not tonight. Let's sack in. I stand watch in the morning. Tell me something, Bobby: You set up the whole show tonight, didn't you?"

He looked at me blandly. "Son, I wouldn't know what you're talking about. How could I know they'd kick up such a breeze?"

"You knew damn well Negroes don't go dancing at the Jockey Club."

"Maybe they will now. And maybe the help will be a little more aggressive." He looked me over challengingly. "Is that bad?"

"Not for Evan. But is it good for the sisters?"

"Are you going to turn preacher on me now?"

"I suppose you're going to marry her."

"I could do worse. She's neat and clean, and she loves me. I wouldn't be the first cat to keep two households going. I'm really a family man at heart." He winked at me. "I can't bat around night in and night out like you single guys."

"You know something, Bobby? You stink."

He laughed out loud. "If I thought you meant that, I'd poison your cornflakes. I do want to thank you for coming along tonight. You helped me out of a spot with Concepcion."

"I was the fall guy."

"It didn't hurt, did it?"

"Come on, here's the pier."

As we strolled toward the liberty boat bobbing on its line, Bobby clapped me on the back. "Buck up. Maybe one of these days you'll be my best man!"

But when we got out to our anchorage and climbed aboard, a telegram from Ceelie Mae was waiting for Bobby. He was the father of a baby boy, named Arvel Shafter, born prematurely, weight nine pounds two ounces. Tears of joy sprang to Bobby's dark eyes as he stood in the companionway clutching the telegram.

"I'm a father," he whispered. "I'm a father."

I murmured congratulations, trying to make up for our words of a few moments earlier.

"Come into my suite, man, and let me break out the VSOP. You wouldn't refuse a nightcap with a new papa at a time like this."

So we started to drink all over again. It must have been something like four o'clock in the morning.

"The situation calls for my Fritz Kreisler favorites."

"It's your party, Dad."

Bobby laughed. "I like that: Dad! You know I was just kidding about that little Juanita, don't you?"

"Sure."

"I mean to say, at bottom I'm the kind of square john that needs romancing even more than he does a roll in the hay." He raised his glass. "Mud in your eye, baby."

As I listened to the tremolo of the sentimental violin for the hundredth time, quite drunk and very sleepy now, something made me say, "That's a mighty big baby, Dad."

He smiled proudly. Then his face clouded. "Say, how would you know?"

"I'm an uncle twice over. Average babies run six, seven pounds."

"Maybe, but I've been building up that little chick with buttermilk and chocolate shakes."

I looked at him. "Two months premature, wasn't it?"

"So she says." Suddenly his hand shot out blindly, like a snake's tongue, and fastened itself in a painful clamp on my wrist. "Do *you* think it's possible? Do you?"

"Let go."

He stood over me, glaring down at me. "Do you?"

"I don't know. I guess not."

"The stupid little chippy. Not even enough sense to lie about the weight."

"Wait. Don't jump too fast."

"What kind of a sucker do you take me for? She named him after her old man, not me. You know why? Because nine months ago I wasn't home. I was five thousand miles away on a goddamned tanker. So she moves up the date to when I *was* home —for three weeks—seven months ago."

"Bobby, it doesn't sound like the girl you described to me."

"Weren't you giving me the same bit about Nita? Do you think she'd be any different? They all smell the same between the legs. If anybody ought to know, I should."

"The least you can do is give her a chance to explain."

"Explain!" Bobby hurled his glass to the deck in a rage. As it broke, a thin pool of Scotch trickled along the fiber rug between us. "Listen, baby-face: When I paid off after the last voyage, I found her in the apartment with a sailor, a homely little jerk. Cousin Willie from Nashville, she said. Five foot four, black as the ace of spades, never finished grade school, eighteen years old. Would you think that a girl I picked up in a bus station, and put a silver-blue mink in one closet and seventeen pair of shoes in another, would shack up with an ugly, undersized, seasick teen-ager? Why, the poor shnook threw up every time his DE passed Ambrose Light. He asked me for a recipe for seasickness."

"Maybe Ceelie Mae wasn't used to being alone. You told me how dependent she was on you."

"I had to ship out. That's one thing I don't discuss."

The record had finished. The needle was swinging wildly across its smooth core—*ticketa, tocketa, ticketa, tocketa.* I caged the arm.

"You were very happy about this baby," I said, "until it got born. You told me you'd been trying for years."

Bobby glared at me wildly.

"Maybe Ceelie Mae wanted a baby even worse than you did. And maybe she knew how much it would please you to have a son, even if it had to be from a kid—"

Bobby was already shoving me to the door. "Go on, get out of here. Take off, get lost." He gave me a push that sent me stumbling over the coaming. "You're just as superior as all the rest." He slammed his door.

The next day we sailed for Australia. Bobby's supplies were swung aboard early, so there was no need for him to go ashore again, or even to turn up on deck.

In any case he did not, not for three days thereafter. We were worried about him in the saloon, but the purser assured us that he had spoken to him through the door. The captain would have been just as pleased if Bobby had died in his cabin, so nothing was done.

One day at sunset I stood at the fantail, idly watching our wake and thinking about Evan Jones and the sisters, when I felt Bobby at my side. I turned to find him rather drawn and bloodless, but composed.

"Can I apologize?" he asked.

"Forget it."

"It's that last crack I made. I was upset. I really don't feel that way."

I shrugged in some embarrassment. "What are you going to do, Bobby?"

"I could kill her—that's one possibility. Or I could pretend to believe the whole silly story and play Daddy. Or I could go back to Panama and marry Nita, at least long enough for her to do the same thing to me."

"Oh, come on."

"You know something? No matter what I come up with, I can't win."

The one thing he did not say was that I had pushed our friendship too far, that I had presumed on an acquaintance that was, in the nature of the situation, unbalanced. It was just too easy for me to be superior; in fact, he understood it all better and more bitterly than I ever could.

We passed some quiet hours after that, he and I, on the long voyage to Australia and then on through Suez; but there were no more long sessions in his cabin, with the record player spinning sentimental music and Bobby snowing me about his conquests, and I asked him no more about his wife than I did about how he disposed of his cigarette boxes. When at last we tied up at the slummy nethermost reaches of Staten Island, supposedly home but in reality as far from our dreams of home as Tierra del Fuego, we paid off in the saloon and parted with a handshake, leaving unspoken the common realization that it was only now, in our own city and on our own soil, that we had to part.

"So long, kid," he said, reaching out to straighten my carelessly knotted tie. "Don't rush into agitating—or marrying."

In fact I did marry two months later and gave up the sea. And with it gave up the possibility—or so I begin to feel now, after all that has been happening in a world beyond my reach and my personal involvement—of ever again being as close to another troubled wanderer as I once was to Bobby Shafter.

WHERE DOES YOUR
MUSIC COME FROM?

WHEN I WAS sixteen and a junior in high school, my whole life changed. Until then I had led a very ordinary existence, growing up in the postwar years with my younger sister on an elm-lined street in the house in which my mother had been born. I had a Rudge bicycle, a chemistry set and a crew-cut, and the only thing that marked me out from the rest of the kids on the block, apart from my height, was that I really liked my piano lessons and shone at the annual recitals of Miss Wakefield's students. Indeed, I used to daydream of going to New York City and playing the Grieg Piano Concerto under the stars at Lewisohn Stadium, with thousands cheering me as they did Artur Rubinstein.

My father, an uneasy real-estate broker, regretted an enthusiasm fostered mainly by my mother, and tried to steer me from music toward medicine, starting with the chemistry set and later taking me on long Sunday-morning walks in the course of which he tried to convince me, man to man, that there was nothing like being your own boss. He ran his business from a wooden cottage attached to the back of our house, so he was home a lot, between phone calls, and he probably exercised more of an influence on me than most of the fathers on the block did on their kids.

It was only after I finished junior high and began to flounder around with swarms of strangers in Franklin Pierce High that I discovered how many different worlds lay beyond the placid, comfortable one of Buchanan Street. There were boys who smoked marijuana and girls who got pregnant; longhairs who did math problems in the caf while the others fiddled with their jalopies and hot rods; Negroes who disappeared after school as though they had been swallowed up; jocks who stayed until it got dark, playing soccer or jogging around the track as if they had no homes to go to and no pianos to practice. I didn't settle into any of the cliques, because I wasn't ready to limit myself. Belonging to almost any of them would only have confirmed me as being what I already was on Buchanan Street, and I was getting a little tired of that.

So, with the seamless illogic of the sixteen-year-old, I limited myself almost exclusively to one boy's company for so long that people used to kid us about going steady, as if we had been of different sexes, or about being twins, as if we had been brothers.

In fact Yuri was a twin himself, and he walked to school every day with his sister Yeti (born Yetta), the ballet dancer. Yeti's beauty was so immediate that it was frightening. She had long, straight, shimmering blond hair that hung uninterruptedly down her back to her waist, eyes the color of delphiniums in July, set shallow and slantwise above her Slavic cheekbones, and skin smooth as eggshell. She walked with the characteristic half mince, half prance of her craft, toeing out as she advanced, she was as slim and flat-chested as a boy, and because of her self-absorption she was—besides being my best friend's sister and therefore inviolable—as close to being absolutely uninteresting as any girl I had ever known.

Yuri was something else. He was bowlegged, his tough and kinky brown hair barely grew above my shoulder (after a while they called us Mutt and Jeff), and his thick, passionate lips were usually twisted in a cynical grin. He played the fiddle—which he carried with him nonchalantly in its weathered case wherever he went, even into the john—with dazzling fervor and dexterity.

He had been the concertmaster of our school orchestra since his freshman year, but I hesitated to approach him not only because he was so good but because of that grin. The other members of the string section said he was decent enough, if somewhat condescending, like a big kid playing for an afternoon with little ones. They said too that his mother awoke him at dawn so he could practice for two hours every morning before school—later I found that this was true.

One day after ninth period I was in the music room practicing on the Mozart A-Major Concerto, the K. 414, the first movement of which the conductor, Mr. Fiorino, had promised me I could play with the orchestra for the spring festival, when Yuri Cvetic sauntered in and leaned his elbows on the tail of the piano.

He listened for a while, his fiddle case wedged between his torn sneakers, that grin showing the spaces between his front teeth. Finally he said, "Ever do any accompanying? I got a Brahms thing here we could try."

Within days we had exchanged confidences never before revealed to anyone else. Everyone took it for granted that we two would eat together in the cafeteria; and when, because of homework or music lessons, we couldn't see each other after school, we would talk on the phone, more quietly than our sisters but just as lengthily.

Yuri never came to my house more than once or twice. My father complained that he couldn't bear the squeal of Yuri's fiddle being tuned up to the piano. It was no more legitimate than his shouting, after we were in tune, "I can't hear myself talk on the telephone when you guys are playing." I knew I was losing respect for my father when he came out and said that he mistrusted Yuri not only because he encouraged me to have musical ambitions but because he came from the other side of Pierce High, from Cotter Street, a noisy neighborhood of teenagers tuning up go-karts, women arguing loudly in foreign tongues and drunks too shameless to go on indoors.

Yuri shrugged it off with the grin that I suspect bothered my father more than anything else, for it bespoke that wise invulnerability that can unsettle an adult more than any adolescent surliness. After that we hung out together at the park in fair weather, at his house in foul. His family never objected; they were always delighted to see me whenever I turned up at their second-floor flat.

In addition to his twin sister, who, when she was around, was usually polite enough, in her self-centered way, there was a younger sister, Helen, a freshman when I first met her. Not only had her parents used up their inventiveness on the twins' names, but they also seemed to have taken one look at their last-born and decided that a ballerina and a violinist would be enough and that this time they would settle simply for a daughter. Helen was a nice enough girl, with a sweet, even smile and dark, gentle eyes unlike Yuri's and Yeti's in that they were always shadowed, as if she didn't get enough sleep, but she had no interest in music or dance and she never opened a book. She appeared content just to get by in school and to keep the household going while her parents were off working and the twins were off practicing. And besides, she was buxom; she gave you the feeling that if she didn't watch herself, she'd wind up looking like her mother.

I think that was what put Mrs. Cvetic off her youngest and convinced her that it would be profitless to push Helen into the arts as she had done with the twins. Mrs. Cvetic, a practical nurse, was a heavy-breasted, shapeless woman who breathed through her open mouth and waddled so alarmingly that you could practically feel the friction of her thighs. She always wore a wrinkled and stained uniform, not quite white, its pockets bulging with Pall Malls, wooden kitchen matches and professional samples of Anacin and Bufferin, which she chewed as other people do gum or candy.

"Hiya, boy," she would greet me on those occasions when she happened to be home of an afternoon. "You gonna play some music with Yuri today? Okay, stay for supper."

If I declined, she would wave aside my hesitations, the long cigarette bobbing from her lips, ashes sprinkling the bosom of her uniform, while she growled at Helen, "Move away the goddam ironing board so the boys can practice. And let's see how much goulash we got for supper."

The ironing board had no legs. Sometimes Helen would balance one end of it on a kitchen step stool, the other on the edge of the upright piano, and press away at her mother's uniforms (I never could understand why, since Helen was always ironing them, the uniforms were never clean). When I wanted to lift the keyboard lid, she would take the ironing board and lay it on the round oak dining-room table. When she had to set the table for dinner for the six of us, she'd set the plank against the wall. But Mr. Cvetic had bolted a full-length mirror and a long section of three-inch galvanized pipe to the wall for Yeti, and when Yeti hung onto the pipe with one hand, doing her ballet exercises, Helen had to drag the plank, heavy as a painter's scaffold, out to the front hall, where it teetered at the head of the stairs, announcing to you as you mounted the worn rubber runners to the Cvetic flat that Helen must be busy doing something else.

Often it was the meals which, while her mother tended the afflicted and her sister flexed her back, Helen prepared by herself and served as well, eating off in a corner like a European mama, only after she had made certain that the rest of us were taken care of. More than once Mr. Cvetic, having worked overtime, came in when we were already on our dessert and had to be served separately. But Helen never lost her composure, even if her father complained that the meat balls were no longer piping hot. It confused me that a girl so downtrodden should look so contented.

In our house the dinner-table conversation was predictable. If mother had the floor, it would be cultural, with quotations from the day's speaker at her club, John Mason Brown perhaps, or Gilbert Highet. If father was in a talkative mood, and nothing of note had happened in his business during the day, he would inform my sister and me of George Sokolsky's opinion

in the afternoon paper, or of what Galen Drake had philoso-
phized about on the auto radio.

At the Cvetics, you never knew. They ate noisily and greed-
ily, as though each meal was to be their last, and they talked
fast and loud—all except Helen, who rarely spoke—about
whatever popped into their heads. Slender Yeti put away enormous quantities of everything—three slabs of seven-layer cake
were nothing for that girl, whose bare arms, when she reached
for more, were like match sticks—and she rattled on, in a voice
as thin as her arms, about Madame Tatiana's yelling fight with
the accompanist at ballet school. Yuri, chewing fiercely, mocked
Mr. Fiorino's efforts to conduct Von Suppe ("You'd never
catch me doing that, teaching fifth-raters to play fourth-rate
music"), and simultaneously, in counterpoint, his mother gave
us free professional samples of the folk wisdom she had picked
up from her years of nursing chores.

"Gertie blew up like a balloon, poor thing," she would say,
spooning up her soup with a loud trill, "and when the doctor
stuck the drain in her belly the smell was like the stockyards.
But sometimes you got to do that, you got to let out the poison.
Helen, bring in the rest of the cauliflower."

Her husband was small, wiry, wizened, and good-humored.
I never saw him (but once) in anything other than working
clothes—a brown leather jacket over khaki shirt and trousers—
just as I never saw Mrs. Cvetic (but once) in anything but that
wrinkled white uniform, size forty-six. Mr. Cvetic worked as a
journeyman plumber—actually as a plumber's helper, I think—
on the new housing projects that were going up; he drove a
clanking old Ford with a busted muffler, and you wouldn't have
thought that he would be mad for theosophy.

I hadn't been in his company more than ten minutes when
he asked me what I knew about Rudolf Steiner, and when I
said, Wasn't he the man who wrote the operettas? I was in for
it. Yuri groaned rudely and Yeti wandered off to do her bar exercises before the mirror, but Mr. Cvetic ignored the twins and
plunged ahead into a basic description of the anthroposophical

lifeview. It was all very confusing—it seemed to take in everything from organic farming to better kindergartens—but after a while I took some comfort in observing that it was confusing to the rest of the family too and that even Mr. Cvetic himself grew hazy when it came to details.

"But I learn," he would say to me, snapping the calloused fingers of one hand while he picked his teeth with the other. "That's the big thing, to learn from the great minds of the ages. You'll see some day how beauty comes from unity."

"From unity?"

"And unity comes from variety. The flower comes from the seed, the seed comes from the flower. Where does your music come from?"

"I don't know. From the composer?"

"The mind comes from the body, the body comes from the mind. You get me?"

Mr. Cvetic took magazines I had never heard of. In our house we got *Reader's Digest* (my father would still be reading the February issue when the March one arrived) and *Harper's* and *Book of the Month Club News*. But Mr. Cvetic read *Tomorrow* and *Manas* and a magazine the name of which escapes me, published in some town in Pennsylvania and dealing with compost gardening, even though he didn't have so much as a potted plant. He liked to read, moving his lips as he did, about subjects that he didn't agree with or even understand, which startled me, and what was more he was always grinning with happiness over the wonderful variety of material for argument. He stayed up late making notes (for what purpose I never found out), while his wife shuffled about in house slippers the heels of which had long since been crushed to death under her bulk, dropping ashes on the bare floors and opening windows so the kids wouldn't have tired blood and sluggish bowels.

Yuri was fed up with all this, just as I was growing tired of the atmosphere in my house, but at least his folks didn't quarrel with what he was doing; they were proud of it and encouraged him in fulfilling their jumbled-up expectations. Besides, they accepted me practically as a member of the family and were frankly proud that Yuri's best friend was from Buchanan Street and a musician to boot.

"Man, when the day comes," Yuri said to me one afternoon in his quick slurred way, running the words together between tongue and full lips much as his father did, "I'm going to have an apartment with Oriental rugs so thick you can drop a golf ball on them and never find it again. I'm *sick* of bare floors just because they're supposed to be closer to nature or better for Yeti's posture."

I tried to sympathize, when actually I envied him. But what did he mean about when the day came? We both had our dreams of glory and were bound together by the discovery that our separate daydreams could interlock so beautifully, but I didn't really see how our exchange of confidences and intimacies had anything to do with money or Oriental rugs.

In Yuri's eyes I was, I began to realize, like a boy who fantasies great success with girls—rescuing them from drowning or halting their runaway horses, causing them to fall madly and pliantly in love with him—but dares not visualize a consequence consisting of marriage, children and passionless slippered evenings yawning at TV over a can of beer. If for me our music was going to make us famous, that fame would serve only to make us more desired and more famous—and so on, into Carnegie Hall and Lewisohn Stadium, in tails and smiles. But for Yuri the fame was going to bring him Oriental rugs.

It was disconcerting to learn that he was so practical, but I started with the recognition that he was the better musician and that he was the soloist too. What was more, he took the initiative with my mother, who was a little awed by him, in getting us invitations to perform Schubert, Brahms and Bartok for her clubs and her friends' clubs, for the Soroptimists, the AAUW and the Matinee Musicale Society, some of which got us excused from school, others of which actually paid us. We were big shots in a small way, and I wasn't the only one to realize that I owed it to Yuri. Even my father had to admit that Yuri wasn't doing me any harm, if I didn't get a swelled head from the recitals, which wasn't likely to happen as long as I was merely the accompanist.

One unusually hot June afternoon we were ambling along Cotter Street after a final exam in Spanish, licking at Dairy Queens and sizing up the strolling girls in their thin summer dresses. We came into Yuri's front hallway and looked up to see Helen's broad, soft behind undulating gently at the head of the stairs; she was on her hands and knees, scrubbing the steps. At the sound of our entrance she turned, raising her dripping hand to brush away the dark hair from her forehead, and regarded us with a still childish gravity.

"Hi, Helen," I said.

Then she smiled down at us. "I was trying to do the steps before anybody got home. Where's Yeti?"

Yuri shrugged. "Probably downtown, seeing *Red Shoes* for the fourth time." He stepped over her pail and waved me onward, calling back over his shoulder, "Make us something cold to drink, will you, Helen?"

The rooms were half bare, as usual, the floors strewn with a knocked-over heap of Mr. Cvetic's magazines. Usually I loved entering that apartment, but now it struck me for the first time as somewhat bleak and airless, smelling still of Mrs. Cvetic's cigarette butts. We went on out to the front porch and flopped onto the glider.

I said, "Why do you give Helen such a hard time?"

"You don't mean me, you mean all of us."

I was embarrassed. "I mean, we could have gotten our own drinks from the icebox."

Yuri shrugged again, drawing back his full lips over his teeth. "Division of labor. My old man works for the rent and the groceries. My mother works for the music and the ballet lessons. Yeti dances and can't spoil her feet, I fiddle and can't spoil my hands, and Helen takes care of the house. What's wrong with that?"

I wasn't quite sure. Maybe, I thought, everything was taken for granted just a little too readily. But Yuri waved away my discomfort.

"Never mind that stuff. You know something? There's room in this town for another kind of music besides rock-and-roll and Schubert. What future is there in Schubert? Fifty bucks a night, two nights a month? All we need is four, five more fiddles, bass, percussion, couple horns, and we're in business. Then, with a booking agent and some stylish arrangements—"

"What kind of music are you talking about?"

Yuri blinked rapidly, as though he were signaling me. "Strauss waltzes, gypsy fiddle music, things people can dance to without being acrobats and hum without being self-conscious. I could be like a strolling violinist, and you could conduct from the piano."

Helen was standing in the doorway with a pitcher of lemonade. She spoke before I did, in a tone that I had never heard her use. "Is that what everybody's been knocking themselves out for?"

Yuri turned on her swiftly. "Who asked you to listen? What do you know? You're fifteen years old, you still think I can go off to Europe and win one of those international prizes and live happily ever after. I'm trying to be practical."

He was, too. At seventeen we weren't ready to organize the kind of society orchestra he had in mind—but in a few years we would be. And in the meantime he knew, better than I, that we simply weren't up to the cut-throat concert world. Given his teaching, his instrument and his practicing, Yuri would at best qualify one day for a first-desk job with the city symphony. In order to supplement his income he would either have to teach ("What a drag! Look at Fiorino!") or play hotel music, which at least had some of the glamour that he thought we had been talking about all these months.

Unlike me, Yuri was daydreaming, I began to see, not about impossibilities but about reality. It troubled me as much as it did Helen, maybe because Yuri was beating me to the cold compromises involved in growing up. And I could not put out of my mind the way the lemonade pitcher trembled in Helen's hands before she set it down by the glider and hurried away.

Yuri spoke no more of the dance orchestra that day or for a long time thereafter. I got a summer job as a camp counselor, and Yuri, who had wanted to go to Tanglewood or Marboro, had to take a paying job with the Civic Pops Orchestra, which did a summer season in the municipal park.

When we came together again as seniors in the autumn, we were both anxious to make up for lost time. We resumed our duets at once. I had almost forgotten the intensity of the pleasure you could derive from making such music with a friend.

But then, starting as an undiscussed eventuality and looming larger as the year rushed by, there was the prospect of my going away to college. My father, who had managed only a year of college before the depression caught up with him, worked at convincing me that in a Big Ten school "You'll make contacts that will be invaluable to you in later life."

When I made the mistake of repeating that to Yuri, it broke him up. But his mocking laughter jarred me, and I began to think not about how square my father was but about what it might be like, really getting away from Buchanan Street once and for all.

Yuri was bright, school was easy for him, but he couldn't have cared less about going to college. And it wasn't simply sour grapes. I knew his parents would do without necessities to send him to a conservatory, but they hadn't brought him up to face the prospect of being one more poor fish in a great big pond.

"I'm not kidding myself," he said when I raised the subject. "The best I could do after Juilliard, or one of those trade schools, would be an audition for a job with a big orchestra. What's so big about that? I can do better right here with help from people like your mother and without getting gray waiting for a break."

I stared at him. I said, "Are you satisfied to stay here forever? Don't you even want to try to make it in the big time?" I was on the point of adding, What else have we been dreaming about all these months? but something in his face stopped me.

He extended his hands. "Why throw away a sure thing for a mirage?"

He was pleading for more than understanding; he wanted me to tie my future to his. As my best friend, he was hoping against hope that I would turn my back on my father's ambitions for me. It wasn't just that Yuri wanted my moral support and my physical presence. What he wanted even more, it struck me with ferocious suddenness, was the kind of real help from my mother and her friends that would depend on my sticking with him.

I was hurt at Yuri's readiness to use me in this way; I would rather he had come out and said what he wanted from my mother. But that would have involved different admissions on his part, so I held my tongue, and we went on more or less as we had.

More or less, except that even while we were reading duets and rehearsing for recitals, I was studying for my finals and trying to decide among various Big Ten schools. When I finally made up my mind, and then was accepted by several, I didn't run to tell Yuri or his family, as I might have a year earlier. Nor did he bring up the matter with me again.

Yeti too was itching to be out of school. She had been running with a show-business crowd, or the nearest approximation that our town could boast (little-theater actors, modern dancers, and a part-time beatnik group just coming into its own), and after a number of auditions, including one breathless trip to New York, she caught on with the road company of a Broadway musical. She was to join it directly after graduation, and she was trembling with the first real excitement I had ever seen her display.

If Yuri was not particularly impressed, and Helen, smiling very enigmatically for a sixteen-year-old, said nothing, at least their parents seemed pleased. The twins, they decided, were entitled to a big graduation party.

"Listen, boy," Mrs. Cvetic said to me, "you come next Friday night for sure. We're gonna have one hell of a big blowout."

"You couldn't keep me away," I said. "You know that."

"Okay, but this time bring a girl."

I was a little disconcerted. The few girls I could take to movies or concerts wouldn't have known what to make of the Cvetics. So I mumbled something about seeing whether I could dig up a date.

I didn't even try, but on the evening of the party I took the steps up to the Cvetic flat two at a time. In the hallway the noises of many voices talking at once sounded reassuringly familiar; the odors of Mrs. Cvetic's and Helen's cooking smelled familiar too—stuffed cabbage, eggplant salad, savory pudding.

But when I walked in I felt that I had entered a strange house. The noise wasn't coming just from the family but from a throng clustered here and there all through the apartment, which had been decorated like a dance hall with twisted streamers of crepe paper, Chinese lanterns, and life-size pencil drawings of Yeti in her tutu and Yuri with his fiddle.

I recognized some kids from the school orchestra and the glee club. In addition there were a number of middle-aged strangers, friends of Mr. and Mrs. Cvetic, I guessed, and a gaggle of bony girls and slim-hipped boys from Yeti's ballet school.

It was fairly early, but the air was already exhausted, fogged with smoke, and as I blinked my way through the mob, peering around for Yuri, somebody cracked open a can of beer under my nose and swung it about, lashing a circle of suds onto the bare floor. Girls shrieked, but Mr. Cvetic, ignoring everything, had a classmate of mine pinned to the wall and was exhorting him, as near as I could make out, to eat eggshells for their mineral value. When he caught sight of me he waved, his hand clutching a stuffed cabbage transfixed with a skewer to a slab of rye bread.

"Hey, go by the dining-room table," he called out amiably. "Helen and the missus have got food there for an army."

He wasn't kidding, but I wasn't hungry. I took a beer and went on to the piano, where I found Yuri, with a new haircut and a new sport shirt, surrounded by a crowd of kids from school. They were egging him on to do an imitation of me accompanying the glee club.

Yuri mussed his hair to approximate mine, and, flinging his hands over the keyboard to make them appear long and scrawny like mine, pounded out the Rudolf Friml medley from *The Vagabond King*. Everybody was laughing. I had to myself, in order not to look like a stuffed shirt, although I didn't think it was all that funny. When Yuri caught sight of me he stopped and held up his hand.

"Here, you do it," he said, making room on the bench. "This is your instrument, not mine."

I was stuck for quite a while after that. The gang pressed more beer on me so that I would give them the cocktail-hour classics that they wanted, but finally it palled and I begged off. I shoved through the knots of dancers and talkers and found myself pushed smack up against Mrs. Cvetic, who was fishing stuffed cabbage out of a Pyrex bowl. She thrust a steaming plate at me.

"Whatsamatta, boy," she asked, squinting to fend off the smoke from her dangling cigarette, "you on a hunger strike or something?"

I made a pass at eating and congratulated her on the party.

"The kids deserve it, they didn't let me down, they worked hard all this time. Besides, you only graduate once, right?" She dug me in the ribs. "So have a good time, the party is for you too."

I wandered on through the apartment, very confused. Mrs. Cvetic was more unselfishly hospitable than my own parents. But was she really doing the twins a favor, making such a big deal about high-school graduation?

At the end of the long hallway I entered the kitchen, intending to leave my plate on the counter and maybe leave the party, since I felt out of place. But as I put down the plate I heard a step behind me, and I turned to face Yuri, who was standing in the doorway, grinning his grin.

"Looking for something?"

"Helen is the only one I haven't said hello to. This is where she punches the clock, isn't it?"

"Stick around, she'll turn up. Can I get you anything in the meantime?"

"Not a thing. Great party." I could see that he expected more, so I added, "I was accepted by two colleges this week."

Instead of asking why I hadn't told him before, he said negligently, "Make up your mind yet?"

"I'm waiting to hear from one more before I decide for sure."

"In any case you're going away. That's it."

"That's it."

I hadn't meant to be flip about what was terribly important for both of us, but Yuri seemed to want it that way. Scratching at the fiddler's rash on the underside of his left jawbone, he said, almost as if it were an afterthought, "I didn't hurt your feelings before, did I? I mean, imitating you at the piano."

"Don't be silly."

"Okay then. Let's split a beer."

I was going to protest that I was full, but something in his face stopped me. I held out a glass, and Yuri poured half a can into it. We drank in silence, not looking at each other.

"Well, I've got to circulate. Anything you don't see, just ask for it." And he swiveled about and walked out of the kitchen.

I should have left then. But it was true, I told myself, that I still hadn't seen Helen, and she was one person whose feelings I didn't want to hurt. So I wandered through that crowded apartment one last time.

By now the guests had progressed from talking to shouting —about the Korean fighting, which had just broken out, about homosexuals in the ballet and the State Department, about compost heaps and wheat germ—and from dancing to banging beer cans together in rhythmic accompaniment of a monotonous folk singer. Helen was not in sight.

I made my way on through the dining room and the living room to the front porch. The awning was rolled down and the living-room blinds were drawn, and it took my eyes a moment to grow accustomed to the darkness. Then I saw that several couples were embracing against the railing at either end of the porch. I was about to retreat and leave them to their business when I realized that a girl was sitting motionless on the glider, hands folded in her lap. It was Helen.

When she heard me she looked up and smiled and motioned to me to sit beside her. I was a bit uneasy, but she insisted, mouthing the words, "It's all right. They won't care."

I glanced to my right. I was a little shaken to see that the blonde digging her fingers into the hair of the boy pressing her against the railing as though he was trying to shove her over the falls, his leg between hers, was Yeti.

"She won't care either?" I whispered, gesturing at Yeti.

Helen shook her head mildly. "It's just her boy friend."

"But what are you doing here? Don't tell me you're the chaperone."

"It's the only quiet place. I worked pretty hard getting the food ready."

"I bet you did." I had to bring my head closer to hers in order to keep my voice low. "I've been looking for you all evening."

That wasn't strictly true, but it was becoming true as I looked at her. Perhaps because of the heat or the long hours in the kitchen, she had put up her thick dark hair; her face was more mature now, calm, self-assured. She smiled at me again, her cheeks rounding, and she was no longer just Helen; she was someone strange and beautiful.

"I don't think you'll be seeing much more of us," she said, "after this summer."

"What do you mean?" I asked stupidly.

"You'll be going off to college. And then . . . people grow away from each other."

"Not good friends. Good friends stick together." Something made me add, "Besides, I'm not a hundred per cent sure I'll go away. Why can't I go to college here? Right now I'd rather be here with you than any place else in the whole world."

"You mustn't talk like that," she said agitatedly. "Not when you've got the chance to go. Anyway, you'll see. You'll see, when you make new friends you won't need the old ones so much."

Her insistence, stubborn as a child's, was charming; and yet I was touched by a sudden premonition that Helen, unlike Yuri, knew more than I—and always would.

Suddenly her dark eyes filled, and I was in terror lest she begin to weep. "Yuri loves you," she said, "you know that? I hoped you would influence him to be idealistic like you, to use his talent for the best. If it turned out the opposite, and he was the one to influence you . . . it would be better for you if you never saw us again."

"I promise you one thing," I said. "No matter what, I'll never forget the Cvetics. You've been nicer to me than my own family."

"We just like you, that's all."

Encouraged, I added what would never have entered my mind five minutes earlier but now seemed profoundly true and important. "You know something? You're not only the nicest one in the family—" I pressed forward, whispering so that Yeti should not be able to hear—"you're the best-looking."

Helen shivered, as if taken with a sudden chill, and grasped her bare upper arms defensively.

"What's wrong?" I asked. "Are you cold? Here, let me rub you."

I touched her smooth flesh with my fingertips and discovered that it was not cold but blood-warm, not goose-pimpled but satiny. Helen released her grip on herself and raised her eyes to mine.

As we sat there staring at each other, with my palms on her soft arms, we could hear the shuddering sighs of the embracing couples on either side of us, and the rich wet sound of lips and tongues meeting, sticking, parting. Helen drooped toward me, I slid my hands around her back, she raised her hands from her lap and began to caress my temples. When her fingers reached the back of my neck I pulled her to me, overcome as much by the unexpectedness of what was happening as by the beauty of the moment.

Just as our lips swelled and touched, each to the other's, in that instant of exquisite revelation, the porch door swung outward. I opened my eyes to the startling beam of light and raised them to meet those of Yuri, who was standing in silence, his fists clenched, staring at us.

How can I ever forget the look on his face? His glare was compounded of rage, disgust, contempt—and a strange, frightening kind of envy. And in the next instant there glinted in his eyes, I could have sworn, a scheming flicker, a swift calculation of the possible advantage to him of what he saw before him.

Helen sat motionless, not from fear or shock but as if time had come to a stop for her and she did not wish it to start again. Her arms hung free, no longer clasping me; her face was pale but quite composed. It was impossible for me, though, to remain impaled under Yuri's stare. I arose awkwardly, mumbled something, and shouldered past Yuri and on out of the apartment.

Helen had been right, of course, about me and her family. After I was settled in college I sent her a picture postcard of the bell tower, saying that she would like the quiet, regular, pealing music that it made; but even though I printed my return address, she did not reply. The only acknowledgment I got was a postscript at the bottom of one of Yuri's letters: "Helen asks to be remembered to you."

I wrote Yuri in some detail, but without undue enthusiasm, about my new life. Yuri's occasional letters, on the other hand, struck me as not only provincial (anecdotes about classmates I had hardly known) but increasingly desperate, as if now that I was gone he was discovering, in the blind, lonely thrashing that he preferred to conceal behind a mask of amused contemptuousness, that the times were wrong for what he wanted out of life. I began to think that maybe I had never really understood Yuri.

Then came a last letter in which he told me cryptically that he had joined the Marines. All I could think of at first was that he was trying to beat the draft and in a typically sardonic fashion, fiddling his way through the Halls of Montezuma. But he put it to me in a lower key, in terms of his maybe taking advantage of a new GI Bill for Korean veterans to study conducting "when I come marching home." Maybe he was just saying what he thought might please me or renew my confidence in him. I have no way of really knowing, because after that we lost touch with each other.

It was my father who sent me, many months later, the clipping from the afternoon paper which announced, not without pride, that the gifted young violinist, Yuri Cvetic, who had gone straight from Parris Island to Pusan, had been captured by the Chinese Reds. The best I could do, when I came home in June, was to talk to Yeti and her mother on the phone, for my father's business had turned sour and I had to leave town almost at once for a resort job as pianist with a dance band.

More than once, at the silly hotel by the lake, I reflected on the irony of the fate that found me making a necessary buck out of my music while Yuri was involved in the miserable consequences of a larger decision. I wrote him about this—why not? —through the International Red Cross, because I thought that it just might bring back to his face—even at my expense—that mocking grin.

But he did not reply, and in truth he may never have gotten my letter, for not long after, word came of his death in a prisoner-of-war camp; and I found myself crying, alone in my room, at the idea of his permanent silence. Where had our music gone to?

The papers of that time were full of angry words about the betrayal of the heroic Marines, and in our town the tragic fate of Yuri was coupled with the implication that he must have died a hero's death. I don't know that this was ever substantiated, any more than was the stronger rumor to the contrary when his body was finally shipped home for burial: that Yuri had simply turned his face to the wall and died, as if his capture itself had been a symbolic yielding up of life, which he would not want to have undone any more than he would have wanted to go on living if the joints of his fingering hand had been frostbitten and amputated.

His interment took place on a rare and lovely April afternoon. Yuri was entitled to burial in a military cemetery, but his parents preferred to have him in their own family plot, painfully bought (like his musical education) with their own sacrificial payments. I had just arrived home for Easter vacation, and in fact was not in time for the services; but I borrowed my father's car and hurried on out to the suburbs.

It took me a while to find the cemetery. I got to the graveside just as an honor guard was lowering the flag-draped coffin into the ground. All I could think, as I stood off to one side, away from the family and the faithful friends, inhaling the ineffable fragrance of fresh-turned earth, was that if through some miracle of this heavenly day the dead could draw just one breath, they would burst open their coffins and climb, happily reborn, from their tombs.

I turned to walk away, convincing myself in the usual cowardly fashion that it would be better if I called on the Cvetics later, when they had had the chance to compose themselves. But Helen, walking with a strange doughy-faced young man, caught sight of me, and I could only wait for her to approach. She smiled at me sadly, very white-faced in her mourning costume, and extended her hand with no word of greeting. Her sadness seemed to encompass not just the wasteful death of a young man but, I thought, the tragic quality of life itself for those compelled to go on.

"I'd like you to meet my fiancé," she said to me.

I shook the hand of the young man, who was not only embarrassed but restlessly anxious to get back to his salesman's route before he lost any more commissions.

There was nothing for it then but to await the others, who

had not as yet seen me. Mrs. Cvetic, quite bowed over by grief, was being half led, half dragged away from the graveside by her husband and Yeti, whose veiled hat had been knocked somewhat askew by the exertion. As they neared me on the flagstone walk, their figures dappled with the spring sunlight filtering through the river willows, I could hear Mr. Cvetic panting shallowly under his burden and his wife sobbing jaggedly, like a wounded animal, with each step. They stopped to take breath, and suddenly Mrs. Cvetic, in black instead of white, for the first time, raised her head and caught sight of me.

She broke free from the restraining arms and lurched toward me. Before I could move or even think of what to do or say, she had hurled her heavy, sagging body at me, gasping and sobbing.

"My God, my God, my God!" she cried.

I tried to put my arms around her, but she was shaking and crying and pounding at me with her fists. It struck me with a thrill of horror that she was greeting me not with affection but with hatred.

"His best friend!" she screamed. "You were his best friend!"

Clumsily, I strained to pat her heaving back, but she cried loudly, "Best friend, why didn't you stop him? You didn't even try, you didn't go yourself, why didn't you try to stop him? Who's going to play duets with you now?"

Even if I had been able to think of something to say to her, I would not have had the time. Yeti, her head averted, and Mr. Cvetic, shrunken into an unaccustomed Sunday suit and mumbling something either incoherent or in a foreign tongue, took up their burden again, pulling and dragging her by the elbows. Her wails floated back over her shoulder in the spring sunshine of the silent cemetery, and Helen, nodding an apologetic farewell, hastened after her family, her ankles flashing in their black nylons, her escort hurrying along at her side until they had all disappeared from my view.

From my view, but not from my mind. For years I wondered, Was Mrs. Cvetic right? Should I have tried to stop Yuri from going to his death? Yet I must admit that when I think now of the family that changed my life, my feeling for Helen and her fate affect me just as strongly as my feeling for Yuri and his fate. As for the music, it is enough that I hear it in my mind. Where it has gone, along with my youth, I think I know; but where it came from, during those passionate months of performance with Yuri, I doubt that I shall ever know.

A HOT DAY
IN NUEVO LAREDO

Louise Ridley's main reason for driving rather than flying to Mexico—or at least the reason she had given to those
who asked—was that she wanted to be able to show Dickie
more of Mexico than just Monterey. So, two days after he had
finished fourth grade at the day school, she had packed her only
child and their valises into the aging station wagon and they
had set off for their first trip abroad and—thanks to his father's
cooperation—a Mexican divorce.

Actually she had wanted to be alone with her son on this lei-
surely trip so that he might gradually accustom himself to something even she could hardly comprehend—that from now on
they would be alone together. Alone, with no Roger to call
out, "I knocked off work. Who's for caulking the boat?" or "It
was too hot in the office. Who's for a swim?"

But it had been too hot in the car, after the initial exhilaration of getting away. It had been too hot in Carolina and too
hot in Georgia, and long before they had gotten to the Alamo,
deep in the heart of downtown San Antonio, Louise and Dickie
had lapsed into the sullen rather than companionable silence
that tends to surround immobilized travelers squeezed together
too long. They were bored with the South and with the somnolent heat, and so they grew bored with each other. Since Dickie

was not romantically patriotic, the Alamo—except for the old firearms in its little museum—had proved a disappointment to him, and as they strolled along the banks of the river that meandered sweetly through the heart of the city he had solaced himself with greedy descriptions of what he would be able to buy once they were in Mexico.

A fielder's mitt was what he wanted, specifically a second-baseman's glove, because that was what his father recommended. Roger, who in his time had been a great fan of Charley Gehringer, had adjured him in parting—as if he couldn't think of anything more important to say to his son—that leather and silver were the things to buy in Texas and Mexico. "Ask your mother to pick out a second-baseman's mitt, Dickie, and I'll get you a real major-league baseball to go with it."

The idea of the mitt had kept him busy, or at least animated, most of the dull way down from San Antonio to Laredo. Staring out the windshield at the dusty sun-baked countryside, with no cowboys in sight, no cattle, no nothing, not even oil wells, Dickie would mumble ruminatively, in the nasal, rich-boy's drawl that was all too reminiscent of his father, "It's not the padding in a fielder's mitt, it's the flex-i-bil-i-ty. You've got to have soft leather for that."

And if, gazing fixedly at the flat strip of highway enclosed by her gloved hands and the white arc of steering wheel between them, she neglected to express agreement or even interest, she succeeded only in calling down on herself a nagging reminder: "Mommy, you promised. Don't forget, you promised me the mitt. Are you listening?"

At last Louise decided that it was her job to make a more sustained effort than she had felt up to so far to tell Dickie what lay in store for him. For them, in fact.

"Dickie," she said patiently, "I'll get you that glove. A promise is a promise. But you're big enough now to realize that once we're living together, just the two of us, things will be different than they used to. I'm not going to be able to buy you anything that comes into your head."

Dickie twisted about to face her, shocked. "I know that. Don't you think I know that? But the glove—"

"We'll look for one in Mexico. I just want to make sure that you understand. Nagging for things won't do you any good—it'll only make us angry with each other. There's no point in running after a glove the minute we cross the border, because you wouldn't be able to use it there anyway. We'll probably pick it up on our way back, so we won't have to carry it around with us."

The boy's face had closed.

"Dickie," she said sharply, "are you listening?"

"Yes," he said in a tone that disclosed nothing. "I'm listening."

"You know, when we cross the border, you're going to see things you never saw before."

"I know."

"I wish you wouldn't be quite so sure of yourself. It's one thing to look at film strips, or even to listen to Mrs. Weinberg in social studies, but it's quite another to see things with your own eyes. I could tell you from now to doomsday about the less developed countries. Like the reasons why they're poor and we're rich. But it wouldn't mean anything compared to what you're going to see for yourself. That's one reason," she concluded, sick of her own sensible voice, "that I decided it would be better for us to go to Mexico than to Nevada. For the divorce, I mean."

"Whatever the reason was, I'm glad."

That was somewhat reassuring. They cruised into Laredo at dinnertime and pulled up in the main square before the biggest hotel in town. At that it was nothing fancy, but it promised a better night's sleep than anything they could get on the other side. Or so she explained to Dickie, when he asked why they couldn't keep right on going and spend the night in a foreign country.

"I'm tired from the driving, honey," she said as they ascended in the elevator to the top floor. "Right after breakfast we'll cross over the bridge into Nuevo Laredo. And we can walk around there before we drive on towards Monterey. Look out the window," she said as they entered the room. "That's Mexico, Dickie."

Ignoring the bellhop, Dickie ran to the window. "Man! You mean that little thing is the Rio Grande? It doesn't look so grandy to me."

She tweaked his ear. "Let's get washed up for dinner."

Seated across from her innocently amiable son in the hotel dining room and picking at a plate of cold chicken salad, Louise found herself wondering once again why she hadn't just flown off with him and gotten the divorce over with, instead of wandering through strange towns that she had no desire to visit and that seemed to bring Dickie no visible benefits. Obviously she was putting the thing off; even now she was delaying their entrance into his foreign land on the excuse that she wanted a night's sleep—when sleep never came any more without aspirins and tranquilizers.

It wasn't that she didn't want the divorce. If anything, she should have broken the marriage off years ago, when she had first had to make excuses to Dickie for Daddy's repeated absences. Clinging to that feckless man had done her boy no good that she could see; it had gotten to the point that now, nearing thirty-two and with a long-legged boy who all too soon would be taller than she, she could not even remember why she had married his father or what there had been about Roger that had ever made her think she loved him.

To conceal the trembling of her hands, Louise fussed with her bag, digging about in her change purse for the tip. "You want to pay the check?" she asked. "Then finish your milk."

As soon as they were out on the sidewalk he said, "Can we go to a movie?" but with no real hope in his voice, and when she replied, "No, but you can stay up in the room until eight-thirty," he did not protest, but fell into step with her as she strolled, without aim, from one lighted shop window to the next. The Fanny Farmer candy boxes in the drugstore windows and the Early American driveway signs (The Smiths Live Here) in the hardware-shop windows were no different from those in Montclair, and if that was all there was to see they might just as well have never left home—except that at home you couldn't buy divorces.

The men's furnishings stores, though, of which there were an unusual number, were flamboyantly Texan and aggressively masculine. Hats and boots, hats and boots—who would have thought that the putty-colored men in this scrubby border town could drift into such stores and slap down seventy-five dollars for a pair of hand-tooled boots, or one hundred and twenty-five dollars for a Stetson? Suddenly she caught sight of her reflection and her son's in a mirror behind these overpriced peacock displays.

She looked tall and pale, pale and sexless, sexless and unloved —a lanky and uninteresting woman in a wrinkled linen dress and soiled cotton driving gloves. Beside her stood the boy who resembled her so strongly that she felt sorry for him. Long-armed, long-legged, short-waisted and broad-shouldered as she was, he stood staring at the cowboy boots as she did, with his hand pressing down hair as straight and mouse-brown as her own. Even his expression in repose, now that he was not pleading for something or frowning over a book, bore that deprived look which she hated in herself. At least I earned it, she thought angrily, my father didn't leave my mother and me to chase blondes, he died on us and left us broke; what has happened to Dickie, except maybe me, to make him look so hangdog, as though something vital had been withheld from him?

In truth, however, his face reminded her as much of Roger as it did of herself: those large jug-handle ears, that classically carved but bridgeless nose that grew straight from his short forehead. And those nervous athlete's hands . . .

Louise sighed. "Enough, Dickie," she said. "Let's head back." And she was dismayed to see how amiably he obeyed her, how eager he was to please in the small things—just like his father.

Back in their room he propped up the pillows behind him and disappeared into one of his endless collection of Hardy

Boys books while Louise washed her hair and rinsed out their underthings in the bathroom. At least, she thought, he did not seem lonesome or shaken up—not yet. But that would come later, no doubt, when the vacation and the sightseeing were over and he had to face up to a fatherless routine.

"Time's up," she called out. "Turn off your light."

"I'm writing a letter. As soon as I finish."

When she had draped shorts, panties and nylons over the shower curtain rod, she stepped back into the bedroom, prepared to bawl Dickie out for not listening to her. As she opened her mouth, however, she saw that he had fallen asleep over his letter, with the light on. His book, the sheet of hotel stationery and his ballpoint lay on the quilt by his outstretched hand.

She switched off his bedlamp, smoothed out the covers and took the letter over to the bathroom doorway to see what he had written.

Dear Daddy, she read, *We got to the border. We can see Mexico from our room. Tommorrow we will ride over the Bridge and we will be in Mexico. Mommy says they are poor there. Everything is cheap. So I will get my mitt there instead of in Texas the lether is just as good, mommy says. It is stiffling here just like in Georgea. It is going to be a hot day in Nuevo Laredo. love Dickie*

Louise placed the letter on the bureau and scrounged through her purse for her pills. If only, she thought, someone or something could reassure her that all this would come to an end; if only she would not have to be reminded so brutally of Roger every time her son struck a pose, caught a ball, wrote a letter. Even his poor spelling came from his father. When there was no longer any necessity for the letters, there would be phone calls, visits, weekends together. Then why the divorce? Only because it would free Rog from the obligation to make those eternal excuses and apologies, and it would free her from having to ask herself why she remained tied to someone who was not merely unfaithful but shallow and foolish to boot.

It was not that she hated Rog or even disliked him any more.

It was rather that he made her dislike herself, made her wonder if she really loved her only child. Was she deluding herself now about Dickie as she must have been about Rog, when he had conned her into giving up her hard-won Cornell scholarship for marriage, with only one year left for her degree? What could have possessed her? She had not been impressed with his looks —on their first date she had thought him funny-looking—or with his money—she had known boys with more. He had been persistent, that was all, and so blandly convinced, that young man who had always gotten everything he wanted, from cat-boats to tennis cups, that he had wound up by convincing her too.

Was that all? Was there nothing about him that had charmed her, seduced her, bowled her over? If so, the very memory of it was gone now. Instead she recalled with shame those evidences of his true nature that had been manifest even in the earliest days of their courtship—his turning to appraise other girls' legs when they were out walking together, his grinning mockery of her attachment to those large ideals from which he had gradually won her away. But then she couldn't even say that she had loved him for his weaknesses, as other women had so obviously married because their men were drunkards or mother's boys begging for redemption. Roger hadn't dissimulated—he was what he was—while she . . . Louise touched her fingertips to her eyelids and lay quietly, awaiting the sleep that would carry her away from all the questions.

Finally it came, but it was soon over. Dickie was up at dawn, eager for his new country. Once she was fully awake, in fresh clothing, and with the sun not yet too high, Louise too began to share his anticipation. They packed swiftly, checked out, ate a more rapid breakfast than she would ordinarily have countenanced, and drove onto the international bridge with Dickie clutching their birth certificates bravely.

"Well, we made it," she said after their car had been stickered and they were saluted ahead. "Does it feel different?"

"It sure does. Doesn't it to you?"

Louise laughed. "I'll let you know in Monterey. I'm going to run into the tourist office to ask a few questions and get a map. Will you come in with me, or would you rather wait in the car?"

"I don't want to go in any old office. It's more fun out here. You won't take long, will you?"

"I'm sure I won't."

But when she emerged onto that dusty street, that poor, cheap flyblown imitation of the American streets across the river, the sun was already blindingly high overhead and Dickie was no longer in the station wagon. Taken aback, Louise slipped on her sunglasses and peered anxiously up and down the block.

She was relieved to see Dickie's unmistakable figure framed in the blank daylight at the end of the street, and she hastened toward the shop before which he stood, his nose virtually pressed to its dirty window. The sidewalk was crowded with tobacco-colored women carrying bundles and babies, bony dogs already listless in the baking sun, and barefoot, mud-stained children, none as pale or long-legged as her boy, who turned at the sharp clear sound of her heels and gestured eagerly.

"Hey, Mommy, look here!"

As she approached him, slowing her pace, so did the street urchins, beggars and vendors bearing boxes of junk jewelry and chewing gum. If she did not remonstrate, they would continue to cluster around her and Dickie as thickly as the insects that buzzed about them all.

"V*ayase!*" she said sharply, waving them away, and then, to Dickie: "You mustn't give them anything, or they won't leave us alone."

"Mommy," he demanded, pointing, "look at the leather stuff here. Look at those neat holsters! And that saddle! That's all they've got here is leather, nothing but leather. I bet we can find a mitt inside."

"Well, we're not going to look."

"Just for a minute? It'll only take a minute."

"I told you yesterday, there's no sense in carting a baseball glove all over Mexico."

"But, Mommy, we've got a great big station wagon. I can

tuck a mitt away so you won't even notice it. Please, Mommy, can't we just look?"

Louise did not honestly know whether it was his logic or his whining that annoyed her more. "I said I'd get you one on the way home. Not now. It's a matter of principle."

"Please?"

"And I told you not to nag." She was beginning to perspire. "When you're ready to behave like a ten-year-old instead of a five-year-old, you can come along with me for a walk. Until then, wait in the car. Here are the keys."

And she strode off without looking back, determined not to yield, but sweating with the guilt that breaks out when the inflicting of punishment affords unforeseen satisfaction. Never mind, she thought, I'd rather accuse myself of harshness and unfairness than of overindulgence; one Roger is enough.

It was hellishly hot. She had to force herself to go on past the seedy arcades, dabbing at her face and neck and glancing into the gloomy grogshops, the side-alley groceries and one-man barbershops without customers, the nameless stores with no signs saying what they sold. And the last-chance bargains stacked up as they were all over the world in every last-hope town at the end of the line—watch charms and wineglasses, bracelets and bookends, ashtrays and earrings, scarves and serapes, baskets and belts, monkeys woven from wicker, pillows embroidered "Souvenir of Mexico."

Her head ached, flies rose droning from the horseballs in the gutter, importuning voices whistled Señora, Señora in her ear, a Spanish lover sang tinnily in the cavernous cantina, clouds of dust blew like powder, carrying the wail of a baby, the hoarse quarreling of two men, the last-ditch pleas of the sidewalk merchants. The medley of noises that filled the ramshackle streets, not just unfamiliar but frankly foreign in its steady persistence, deafened her for a moment to the wail she should otherwise have recognized at once.

She whirled about. Dickie stood where she had left him, but his hands were gripping his gut, and he swayed as though he had been shot on this preposterous Southwest movie set. His face was contorted; his usually pale features flamed hotly.

"Dickie!" she cried, her voice quavering. "Dickie, what's wrong?"

As she ran unsteadily toward her son, cursing herself, the half-circle of Mexican children that had formed around him wavered and broke.

"Dickie, are you all right?"

Before he could answer, a bold little boy with flat Indian features thrust a box at her and cried in English, "Chiclets, lady? Jus' one peso?"

She turned from him to her son, but a girl who came only to Dickie's shoulder loosened the greasy black rebozo which she wore like a parcel, pulled back its edges, and revealed a baby whose face was covered with sores. Louise recoiled and drew Dickie to her.

"Have you got cramps?" she demanded.

Dickie shook his head wordlessly. Tears were coursing down his cheeks. The Mexican children looked on interestedly, offering suggestions, making comments she could not catch. The boy with the box of chewing gum wore sandals made from truck tires; the others stood barefoot in the dust.

Louise cradled Dickie's head in her arm and pressed his abdomen with her fingertips. "Let's make sure it's not appendicitis," she said, the words sounding ridiculous even as she uttered them. "You might have a touch of food poisoning."

"I'm not sick," he muttered, shuddering. "I'm not sick."

"Then what is it?"

"I can't stand it," Dickie buried his boiling face in her blouse. "They're so poor."

Louise felt her legs give way. As she slipped to the curb, pulling him down with her, she heard him say, "I gave them twenty-seven cents. It was all I had. I divided it up. What else could I do?"

"Of course," she murmured. She could not remember when she had last cried like this, helpless and broken by the loss of innocence. But no, that was not true; the twanging spasms of her boy's sobs were her own. They revived in her now the stifled memory of the undead past. Her father, fallen out of life without warning, like a precious coin flung carelessly into a fountain, and she weeping in Roger's arms. That fraternity boy, who laughed uncomprehendingly at her infatuation with the distant poor, proved to her how instinctively, without guidance or instruction, he understood the terror of deprivation when it shook and retched within the circle of his arms. And because he proved it, she believed gratefully that he had proven himself, and she fell in love with him.

"It's hard to explain, Dickie," she said to her son. "I tried to, but it was a bum try. Particularly since I didn't realize whom I was talking to. You'll have to forgive me. Here, blow your nose and we'll go look for a mitt."

"I don't want it! I don't want it any more! Don't you understand?"

Louise gazed at him pensively. If she did now, she had not before—that was sure. And it struck her that it was not Roger's early compassion but its perpetuation in his son that was his best gift to her. Now that she was grateful again, maybe it would serve her better.

"I'll try to," she said to Dickie, "if you'll give me another chance. And it looks as though you'll have to, because you're stuck with me." As she arose, drawing her son up with her, she added, "For the time being, anyway. Come on, Dickie, let's head for Monterey."

CLAUDINE'S BOOK

Nₒᴛ so long ago, in the town of Phoenix, a shopping center for upstate New York and western Vermont farmers since the days of the American Revolution, there lived a very bright young girl named Claudine.

Claudine's father, Fred Crouse, was a widower. He had brought his unmarried sister Lily over from Loudonville to cook and keep house for them, which she did very well, except that she was high-strung and got to feeling that she was wasting her life away in an old eleven-room house with no closets but a cupola big enough for a fancy-dress party. As soon as Claudine was old enough for school Lily got a part-time job, working at the local library four afternoons a week. It kept Lily in touch with the higher things and made her feel more worthwhile, but it meant that Claudine was left alone a lot.

Claudine didn't mind. She liked best hanging around her father's Mobilgas station on the state highway, but he didn't want her making all those crossings between school and the station; besides, the language of the truckers was apt to be kind of vulgar for a little girl's ears. Claudine didn't bother to tell her father, who worked thirteen hours a day and was harried with many worries, that she knew all those expressions already. Nothing ever happened in Phoenix was the main trouble. In fact, nothing ever had, not since Joseph Walker, whose widowed mother drank and took in sewing, got drafted and was captured in Korea and then wouldn't come back when the war was over. A turncoat, Aunt Lily called him, and said that when it was in *Life* Magazine about his refusing to come home from China, two New York reporters had interviewed his mother, his school friends and the librarian. But all that was before Claudine was born. Nothing else had happened since Joseph Walker had come back, which he finally did one day, to dig footings for contractors when he felt like working, and looking like the most ordinary man in the world.

But then Claudine looked like the most ordinary girl in the world. At least, you wouldn't have guessed from her appearance that extraordinary things were going to happen to her. Lily always said that Claudine's eyes were her best feature, which is what you always say about a girl who isn't pretty. She was long-legged and short-waisted, so that she seemed always to be groping up through the tops of her jumpers, like a giraffe reaching out over the fence; her nose was long, with widespread nostrils, like her father's, and had a tendency to run with the first frost. What was more, her short upper lip (Aunt Lily said that she had been a thumb-sucker) made her teeth seem unusually long, like Bugs Bunny's. Over all, she looked woebegone —although she rarely felt that way.

Claudine had only one friend. The other children at the consolidated school thought she was stuck-up, or funny-looking, or even dumb. When they caught her making faces at herself in the mirror of the girls' room—even though they did it sometimes themselves—they decided that Claudine was queer and left her to herself.

There was Robin Wales, though. He found none of these aspects of Claudine annoying, maybe because he had his own problems. First of all there was his name: it did him no good to bring up Robin Hood or even the great pitcher, Robin Roberts, because he didn't even try to hide from his tormentors the fact that he despised baseball. "It's boring and stupid," he said, and that finished him off in Phoenix, which prided itself on fielding a good Little League team.

Besides, Robin had no use for people who tried to push him around or play rough. "I'm not afraid of those guys, Eddie and Walter and the others," he told Claudine, and she knew that this was true, that he simply preferred going his own way, doing what she liked to do too.

In addition to his being more intelligent than any other sixth-grader, Claudine thought that Robin was quite handsome, despite his ears, which looked like the handles of a cream pitcher, and his mouth, in which there glittered a fat silver brace. The only thing about Robin that really bothered her—aside from his constantly trying to boss her, simply because he was a boy—was his transistor radio, which he wore suspended from his braided Indian belt that had his name spelled out defiantly and which he never turned off. All his allowance went for batteries, because he loved to surround himself with sound (just as Claudine, when she was not playing with him, loved to surround herself with silence).

"Weather in a word," he would shout when they met after school, "sultry!" But at least he knew what the word meant, and what the pollen count was, and underground testing, and Cambodia, as well as every rock-and-roll hit on the Top Ten from week to week and the Bargain of the Day at Giveaway Gordie's Used Carnival.

Much more important than his ordering her around when no one else even tried to, or constantly banging things in time to the noise that came from his beltline, was his ingenuity in figuring out new places to build huts. Neither could remember when they had started, for it seemed to them that they had been building huts forever. It was Robin's scheme to make a tree-house in the fork of the old hickory above the roof of the Crouses' barn and to make a lookout lodge out of Claudine's cupola where nobody ever went, not even Aunt Lily to store winter stuff. And to build a hut in the back of the abandoned diner off Main Street, using some of the things that Robin's Uncle Burgie, who sold secondhand stoves, sinks, iceboxes, sump pumps and hockey skates, couldn't get rid of, after they'd been standing outdoors for a season or two.

Like many married couples, Claudine and Robin derived separate benefits from their joint household arrangements. What was unusual was that Robin's pleasures were those you would commonly associate with a wife (although there was nothing sissyish about him), while Claudine's were of the kind ordinarily thought of as a husband's (although again she was no tomboy but an almost fragile girl, with those large, wondering, rather bulbous blue eyes). That is, what Robin enjoyed was the planning involved in making each place livable: finding scraps of carpeting, making pictures to hang on the walls, gluing up chairs out of abandoned camp stools, even rigging up hammocks for their sleeping bags, and then decorating with the boat paints and lacquers he grubbed from his father's garage.

But Claudine, although she cooperated willingly enough, was at bottom attached to the huts as sanctuaries. Just as a man will come home from a hard day in the world of affairs in search not of distractions but of a quiet zone for reflection and refreshment, so Claudine looked forward to her hours alone, when she had no obligations at home and Robin was busy feeding his hamsters or taking his accordion lessons.

It was from Robin's Uncle Burgie that Claudine got the big stack of old business diaries. They had some whitish mold on the binding part, and they dated back to 1926, but as Claudine pointed out to Robin, the inside pages were absolutely clean even if the days of the week didn't correspond, and lots of them were personalized with initials and enhanced with fascinating facts, like: Bleriot Crossed the Channel This Day, or Hebrew Feast of Pentecost Begins This Day. Robin wasn't interested in these facts, however, or even in doing much with the diaries.

"Don't you want to find out who Bleriot was? Or what the Hebrew Pentecost is? If you came to Feb twenty-two and it said G. Washington Born This Day and you were a foreigner, wouldn't it arouse your curiosity?"

"Everybody knows Washington. Even foreigners. Besides, I'm not a foreigner. The reason I got the diaries, they'll look good on the shelf."

"What shelf?"

"I know where to get the shelving. If you help me cover it, I'll put it up for you."

In return for her cooperating, Robin turned the diaries over to her. Standing there in rows, they posed a challenge beyond looking up Charles G. Dawes and Gertrude Ederle: all those blank pages cried out to be filled, while she was alone, quiet and sheltered, in one of the huts through which they had scattered the shelving and the diaries like so many branch libraries.

At first Claudine simply copied into them things that she liked. Sometimes it would be a special story out of the newspaper, like the one about the eleven-year-old girl who got up every morning at five o'clock to practice figure skating for two and a half hours before school so she could try out for the Olympics. Then, increasingly, it would be a poem or a stanza from a poem in one of the books that Aunt Lily was always bringing back from the library: live ones like Richard Eberhart and Horace Gregory, dead ones like Mallarmé (because his name sounded like marmalade) and Keats (because his mask was cool and his poems were not). She liked to copy down parts she didn't understand, because often they sounded the best. Sometimes she would look up the words in the dictionary; so she got to know not only Bleriot and Dawes but "sacrosanct" and "hyperbolic."

It took a good three or four months, and a couple of diaries all filled, before Claudine got up the nerve to put her own stuff in them. She started with what she called Wondering. "I wonder," she wrote, "why that girl Nanette got up every morning at five o'clock to go ice skating. Did she set the alarm herself? Did she make her own breakfast? Did she want to show her father she could be the greatest skater in the world? Why didn't the newspaper article tell all the things you would want to know?" Or: "I wonder what made Horace Gregory write that poem about the girl sitting at the piano. Was it just because he saw her once, in his own house? Maybe he made it all up. If I knew where to write to him, would he tell me, or would he think I was crazy?"

When she saw that Robin was really not interested in using the diaries, or even in looking at them, Claudine began to make up things out of her head for them.

"Sayings All My Own" was what she called them at first, and they fitted nicely into the one-day space of one diary, if she didn't write too small. If she was feeling businesslike, she would note that "The weather this day continues brillig and fine for Father's business. It makes people restless, so they get out on the road." Or, if she was moody and somewhat ingrown from having been left alone by her father, Aunt Lily and Robin Wales, she would allow herself to become abstract and general: "Grownups believe that grownup is a babyish word. They prefer to call themselves adults. They don't think of children at all. They worry about them and they yell at them, but they don't think of them. It's more like putting them out of their minds. PS: Where does the expression come from, putting somebody out of his misery? Ask Robin."

But then when Robin asked her one day, "Say, Claudie, are you using those diaries?" she was almost ashamed to reply, "Yes, I put sayings into them."

Robin didn't seem to think there was anything odd about that, though. Claudine became all the more eager to fill the diaries, for now that they had become hers alone, she felt a funny responsibility to fill those hundreds of empty pages with her own words. Copying or pasting would be cheating.

She decided to make up a story with all kinds of things in it, descriptions of herself and her daily life, Robin and his radio, their mutual enemies, so that when she got to the end the diaries would have everything in them, like a good long novel.

"Today begins my life story," she wrote on New Year's Day. "My father was a very brave soldier, wounded during the Battle of the Bulge. Now he is the prop. of a very big service station, the biggest Mobilgas station within a radius of 30 mi. He is 53, the oldest father I know of. My mother was a beautiful

French girl named Adrienne who came to live in Phoenix with my father but could not have any children until I was born after 9 yrs of married life. She named me Claudine after her dead sister and then died herself before leaving the hospital. It was a tragedy of life for my father. I never knew her but Aunt Lily has lived with us ever since and is like a mother to me. Everyone says so. She is 48. Cont. tomorrow."

Next day, alone up in the cupola, Claudine curled her feet beneath her and began to write. "What do I look like? I am four foot nine inches tall and weigh 87 lbs. Aunt Lily says that if I hold up my chin and straighten my shoulders some day I will be a distinguished looking woman. But right now I am homely, and I bet anything I am always going to be homely."

She paused to reach for a hand mirror that Robin had gotten from his Uncle Burgie. It had a fancy curved plastic handle, but the back had fallen off and a piece of the silver foil had peeled loose, so that when you looked at yourself in it there was a little hole smack in the middle of your forehead. You could squint through the hole clear to the tree outside the window, so that instead of seeing the skin on your forehead there would be a chickadee sitting freezing on the bare branch. "It goes to show," she wrote, "that once you can see not only the outside but the inside of your head, what you will find is a bird sitting on a branch where your brains are supposed to be." And while she was at it, she made up a poem about the mirror with the hole in it that showed you the world as well as your face.

Not long after this, Claudine brought a newspaper clipping up to the cupola and stuck it in the diary with LePage's paste. It read: MODERN KIDS KNOW TOO MUCH, STATE PROF CLAIMS. Underneath the headline she wrote, "Why is he so sure. If he went to my school he'd claim just the opposite. Those kids don't know anything except the Top Ten." She hesitated, and then crossed out the last four words out of loyalty to Robin. "The real trouble is, they see more and more on TV, but they know less and less. They act wise but they think stupid."

When there was nothing special in the newspapers, Claudine

wrote about her teachers ("Miss Bidwell wears stretch support stockings but she makes fun of other people"), her father ("I wish he didn't have to work such long hours, but what would he do at home? He never knows what to talk about to me or Aunt Lily"), and how she was changing so much every day it made her dizzy, even though when she looked in the mirror there she was, with the same popeyes and the same hole in the middle of her forehead. The only person she didn't describe, for reasons that weren't quite clear to her, was her Aunt Lily, who had to be in there when she wanted to write about food or clothes or books.

In about six months the diaries in the cupola were all written in. Claudine had to bring in the ones from the hut behind the diner and those Robin had wrapped in a poncho for her in the treehouse hut, and before she knew it they were filled up. Spring had come, and Claudine had been keenly aware of it, deserting the diaries for days on end to go fence walking and bike riding with Robin; but always she returned, when she was alone, to the diaries. It was almost as if without them she would have no excuse for being alone—or even for being.

And indeed it was strange that, once she had finished writing in the last of the diaries and brought her story up to date, putting on paper practically everything she had ever wanted to say, Claudine fell ill.

It was a tremendous worry to Mr. Crouse, who couldn't cope with sickness, especially when the doctor wouldn't put an exact name to it. Despite everything his sister did, from making broths and compresses to reading to Claudine by the hour, her fever did not abate and at last she had to be taken to the hospital. There her weakened condition and lassitude were labeled as probable infectious mononucleosis, a very popular disease with children, but nobody would commit himself for sure. All they knew was that it seemed likely to be a long, slow business.

For Lily Crouse the house was now unbearably quiet, even though Claudine usually kept to herself when she was home. Just the idea that Claudine was up there in the cupola, doing

Lord knew what with the Wales boy or even all by herself, had been comforting; but to come home from the library to that huge, ugly house and find it absolutely empty was almost more than Lily could stand. She would even have welcomed Robin's noisy presence, his piercing whistle and jangling transistor, but he never came by now—she was more likely to bump into him in the corridors of the hospital, where he came regularly to bring Claudine the gossip about Eddie, Walter, Miss Bidwell and others.

One day, driven by uneasiness and loneliness, although she tried to tell herself that it was simply a desire to track down a lost library book (Gavin Maxwell's book on otters, actually, which Claudine had loved), Lily climbed the steep steps to the cupola. She had never once gone there during all the time that Claudine and Robin had been using it as a hideaway. Maybe Claudine had actually asked her not to, and she had promised —she couldn't quite remember. In any case the funny room looked absolutely unfamiliar; the kids had festooned the place with political posters and crepe paper left over from old birthday parties. A tatty, grease-stained straw mat lay on the floor and, against the wall, a lopsided bookcase was propped at one corner with broken ends of brick. In the bookcase were three rows of old diary volumes. Lily pulled one out and began to riffle its pages idly.

Several hours later, Lily crept down the stairs, her legs aching from having squatted for so long in one position. She went directly to her room and sat down at the desk where she kept the household accounts and mailed out statements to Fred's customers. Now she addressed an envelope to Josephine Schaefer, a classmate who had been working in New York for some years as a secretary in a large and aggressively successful publishing house.

Dear Jo, she wrote, *Under separate cover I am mailing you a carton of diaries which I have just found. As you will see, they are numbered in consecutive order with little pieces of adhesive tape. They are the work of Claudie, who has apparently been doing this writing on the sly for quite some time. I don't exactly know what to make of them—which is why I am taking the liberty of imposing on you. Is there someone in your office whom you could show them to?*

Lily gnawed at the corner of her mouth, and then added: *The thing is, Claudie has been in the hospital for some time (that's why I haven't been able to get down to the city) with an undiagnosed illness from which she is recuperating very slowly. I have a feeling now that it is all mixed up with what she's been writing, but anyway I don't want her to know I've been reading her private diaries—much less that I shipped them out of the house for anyone else's eyes. I'm sure you understand. Forgive me for not writing sooner, but as you can imagine things have been difficult here, what with Fred having to have a quick dinner and then scoot off to the hospital. Say hello to Janie—yours ever—Lily*

It seemed to her only days later that the phone was ringing, wildly and demandingly, as Lily entered the empty echoing house. She hastened anxiously to the telephone, reaching out for it as she ran.

"Lily, it's me—Jo. Mr. Knowles says he sat up half the night with Claudine's diaries, and he wants to talk to you about them. All right?"

"Why, yes," she said uncertainly, "I suppose so."

In a moment a man's voice was saying, "Miss Crouse, I am grateful to you for sending us your niece's diaries. I would like very much to publish them, exactly as they are, and I think the firm will agree with me. They're a find. They're brilliant, they're unspoiled, there isn't a false note. Still, I have to ask you something."

Lily wanted very much to speak, but no words would come out. She moistened her lips, but it was no good.

Fortunately Mr. Knowles did not seem to expect a formal reply. "Miss Schaefer tells me that you're a librarian, Miss Crouse, and that Claudine is a small-town child, never been to New York more than once or twice, to Radio City Music Hall and the Metropolitan Museum. Can you assure me that you haven't had anything to do with her manuscript—I mean in the way of suggesting things to her to include or to leave out, or to change in any way?"

"Mr. Knowles," Lily said heatedly, "I never even knew those diaries existed until a few days ago. I never changed one word before I mailed them in to Jo. And if you don't believe me—"

"Your word is more than enough. I would like to take a run up to visit you, though, if I may. And Claudine, of course. When would it be most convenient, Miss Crouse?"

All she could think of to say was "Claudie is a very sick girl."

"Then we'll be in touch. Perhaps when she's well enough to travel, you can both come down here, as guests of the firm?"

That was the way it stood when Lily made her next visit to the hospital—she tried to space her visits between those of Fred and of Robin Wales. Claudine was propped up on two of those long, flat, slablike institutional pillows, her head so small and unsubstantial that it looked like some doll's carelessly placed in the middle of the bed. The pallor of her lengthy confinement accentuated the glitter of those pale prominent eyes, grown even more bulbous during the illness. Her forehead, too, jutted more sharply than ever (I'll have to make her bangs, Lily thought; surely that will help), while her body seemed scarcely to exist beneath the hospital blanket. She had been reading *A Tale of Two Cities*, which lay beside her on the coverlet.

"I like this," she said, pointing to it but scarcely opening her eyes. "Can you bring me some more Dickens books?"

"Listen, Claudie," Lily said determinedly, "I found your diaries."

Claudine gazed at her blankly. "They weren't lost."

"I mean, I read them." More unnerved by Claudine's silence than she had been by Mr. Knowles's talk, Lily added lamely, "It wasn't that I meant to pry. I was looking for a library book, and I just wondered what was in those old diaries, and then when I did open them . . ."

Claudine stared at her, expressionless. She did not protest, or indicate that she had any intention of interrupting. Finally Lily added, "Well, I thought they were just fascinating. Claudie, I do hope you're not angry."

"Why should I care?" Claudine gazed at her in puzzlement. "Listen, no fooling, can you bring me some more Dickens books? Like *Nicholas Nickleby?* I hear that's real good."

Lily stood helplessly at the bedside. It would be better to have Fred there, she guessed, before trying to explain about the publisher; and the doctor too—maybe she oughtn't to reveal anything more without consulting him. "Of course," she said. "I would have brought them with me now, except that I was a little, well, flustered."

Claudine could not have said why, but this announcement of Lily's, which only a month or two ago would have made her so angry that she would have been tempted to throw a babyish tantrum, now gave her a comfortable and comforting sense of relief. Is it like a secret that you don't want to tell but are sick of keeping and are glad when someone else finds it out and relieves you of the responsibility? It was almost better, she thought sleepily, snuggling down into the blankets, than the pills that the nurse gave her to swallow every evening and that made her drift off to sleep as though someone were paddling her off into the darkness on a Venetian gondola. As she heard Aunt Lily's footsteps fading away down the corridor, Claudine found herself thinking dreamily, It's over, it's over, and I'll get well now.

As soon as she awoke, refreshed and clear-headed, Claudine remembered those drowsy speculations. She had been right—it was all over—and she was restlessly eager to get out of the hospital. But the funny thing was, she observed in the next few days as she became more aware of others around her, that now Aunt Lily seemed to be suffering from the same symptoms that had afflicted her.

"I hope Aunt Lily didn't catch that bug from me," she said to her father when they were alone at home together, with Lily off to the library once again.

"Tootsie, what are you talking about?" Mr. Crouse demanded. "She's not sick or feverish. In fact she's back at work."

"Yes, but she's acting far away, like I was when it was first coming on. In fact . . . so are you."

And her father refused to look her in the eye. What was it, then? He was stubborn, like all adults, and there was no point in pressing him any further.

But Claudine knew she was right, and her suspicions were confirmed that Friday when she found her aunt furiously cleaning the house, as it had never been cleaned for as long as she could remember. What was more, Aunt Lily had made her a new corduroy jumper and bought her a blouse to go with it. Both had to be worn on Saturday morning, when Aunt Lily herself came out of her room with a brand-new outfit and two bright red spots on her cheekbones that might have been rouge but more likely were just plain excitement.

"What is this, the Fourth of July?" Claudine asked and was immediately sorry, for her aunt looked stricken.

"You know my friend Jo," Aunt Lily said, all in a rush. "Well, she is going to stop by for a bite of lunch with her boss, Mr. Knowles. He looks forward to meeting you."

"Me?" The whole thing sounded fishy. But it wasn't; it was all just as Aunt Lily had said. When it was over with, when Jo and Mr. Knowles had driven off in his little white sports car, Claudine couldn't even wait to wave goodbye to them before she was off to explain everything to Robin, who had been forbidden access to the house, much less to the cupola, for the entire day.

"He's a great big stoop-shouldered man with the most beautiful shoes you ever saw," she explained to Robin when she found him at last, up in the treehouse. "They look like they're hand-made out of that cloth they use to put over loud-speakers —you know, with the little nubs in it."

"What's so great about that?"

"He wants to publish my book."

"What book?"

Claudine had to tell him the whole business of the diaries,

which in fact she had almost forgotten about until Mr. Knowles brought up the subject.

"Wait a minute," Robin said wisely. "Wait a minute. You mean that guy came all the way up here from New York City just to see those old books I gave you? Just because you wrote some stuff in them?"

"He read it already. He wants to call it *Claudine's Book*. He says it's one of the best books he's read in a long time, and anyway I'm the youngest person he ever heard of to write a whole book."

"Are you going to get money for it?"

"I don't know. We didn't talk about that. Anyway my father would keep it for me, like he does my birthday money. Mr. Knowles was more interested in how I wrote the book, and where I wrote it, and all that. He made me take him up to the cupola and show him just how it was."

Robin was eying her somewhat suspiciously. "Did you tell him all about our huts?"

"Only what I had to. I mean, about your giving me the diaries and things like that. He didn't care about the huts, he just wanted to make sure I wrote it all myself."

"Who did he think wrote it? Me?"

Claudine shrugged. "What's the difference? I told him you were my very best friend, and that was why you gave me the diaries, and he said if I wanted to I could dedicate the book to you, instead of to Daddy or Aunt Lily."

But Robin had already lost interest, which was all right as far as Claudine was concerned, because in her heart she was even more surprised than he that anyone else, particularly a grownup, should be all that interested in what they had been doing. Robin had a pretty grandiose plan for a dam that would convert the little creek behind the Wales house into a fish hatchery.

They put a good part of the summer into the dam, with very few arguments except when Robin insisted on being insufferably bossy, and Claudine felt no great need to be off by herself, clipping newspapers and writing thoughts down—the way it was last winter, she reflected, when I was younger. They never did exactly finish the hatchery, because school started before they had collected all the stuff for the dam. And then, a couple of months after school had begun, Claudine's book arrived.

On the front of it was a great big picture of her with a dopey expression and her hair pulled back with a ribbon, and underneath in big letters, *Today begins my life story* . . .

"Gee, I look awful," she said to her aunt.

Lily stared at her, astonished. "Aren't you excited? Aren't you proud?"

"I guess."

"Wait till the other children see the book. And your teachers! Then you won't be such a cool one."

It was true: the fuss was really something when the books turned up all over Phoenix. Kids that had ignored her for years wanted her to sit with them in the cafeteria. She was elected vice-president of her home room and made playground monitor. And Miss Bidwell—the old faker!—acted like she and Claudine had always been dear friends, and even asked her to sign her autograph on the title page of the book.

"But you know something?" she said to Robin as they pushed through the piles of heaped-up leaves on Genesee Street on their way home. "I think the whole thing is a pain in the neck."

"This is only the beginning, folks!" Robin shouted at her. "You ain't seen nothin' yet!"

"I'd rather be left alone."

"Then you shouldn't have written all that. Who forced you to do it? Nobody twisted your arm. When you make your bed you have to lie in it."

"That's a cliché. You don't even know what a cliché *is*."

But it did make her uneasy in the days that followed, being stopped at her father's service station or in front of Dohrmeyer's Meat Market by total strangers who wanted her to pose with them for pictures, or sign things, or tell them what she would be when she grew up: was it really all her fault for writing in Robin's diaries? Claudine became more irritable as the demands on her got worse, and finally she took it out on Robin, mainly because instead of sympathizing he kept giving her more clichés.

"If it hadn't been for you and your Uncle Burgie and all those old diaries, I never would have gotten into all this trouble."

Robin was very hurt. He said she was ungrateful and bratty, and he wasn't going to play with her any more. In fact he wasn't even going to talk to her. She could hang out with her new fair-weather friends instead.

In the middle of all this a group of strangers checked in the Al-Rae Motel up the street from Mr. Crouse's Mobil station and fanned out from there like a bunch of G-Men after a kidnaper —as if everyone in Phoenix didn't know what they were up to even before they had unpacked their bags. There were four of them, three men and a young woman researcher. They were all employed by a big picture magazine—the bearded Hungarian, weighted down with leather tote bags, was a photographer, the cynical young man with pockmarks was a writer, and the man who spoke in a whisper (as though, Claudine thought, he was ashamed of his own voice) was a consulting child psychologist.

The girl researcher, who was pretty, with a big wide mouth and an Irish grin, turned up everyplace you could think of, the photographer trotting along after, muttering in Hungarian and measuring the air with his light meter. They walked right into the school as if they owned it—you could see them through the seventh-grade window—and took millions of pictures. Then they went off in their rented Ford to the F. Crouse Mobil station, and the next day, which was Saturday, they were prowling around Robin's huts, even trying to climb into his treehouse. Claudine was afraid that Robin would think she had tipped them off (actually, they must have studied up on the huts in her book) and would get twice as sore. But he was keeping to his promise not to talk to her.

The other two, the pock-marked writer always grinning skeptically, as though he didn't even believe that the world was round, and the whispering psychologist, were much less in evidence. For a while Claudine didn't even know where they were, and it wasn't until they came to her house and sat down in the parlor with Aunt Lily that she got wind of what they were up to.

Aunt Lily thought Claudine had gone to the movies with Robin to see a Charlton Heston movie about God, so it was easy to sneak in through the kitchen pantry and listen. The child psychologist was doing most of the talking, in his tiny baby voice, and Aunt Lily, all dolled up with coral earrings and toilet water and her silk scarf, was sitting on the edge of her chair ready to fall off, listening so hard her earrings were practically standing on end.

"Surely it is obvious to a woman of your intelligence, Miss Crouse," the child psychologist was whispering, "that you have been responsible for the upbringing of one of the most remarkable children of modern times. That is, assuming that Claudine did all of the writing of the book herself."

"Why did you add that?"

From her vantage post Claudine could not see the psychologist, but she was in line with Aunt Lily's bust, rising and falling very fast, and with the pock-marked writer, grinning like an absolute fiend.

"Because in all of my years of experience, both in the clinic and in the field, I have never encountered such a combination of insight and steadfastness in one so young."

"You have to remember, Dr. Fibbage (that was what the name sounded like to Claudine), she has been very ingrown. She's had only one real friend, and no one but me to turn to for books and ideas."

The writer broke in, "Miss Crouse, I must say that it is your ideas and your sensitivity that I find in *Claudine's Book.*"

Claudine was fascinated by the expression that stole over her aunt's face. It was exactly like that of Aunt Lily's fat friend Marie Klemfuss when someone tried to tempt her off her crash diet with a slice of angel-food cake—a mixture of fear, greed and calculation.

"Well," her aunt said slowly, "if Mr. Knowles believed me when he first decided to publish it, I don't see why I should have to explain any further."

"Mr. Knowles couldn't have known you as we do."

Aunt Lily turned red, and the writer, Mr. Craft, added hastily, "I'm not suggesting that you would ever deceive anyone. But in addition to being an intellectual, you are a very modest person. Obviously you would be reluctant to confirm the extent of your influence on little Claudine."

Little Claudine! All of a sudden she felt like throwing up. She tiptoed backward, pulled open the screen door soundlessly, and bolted off down the street. When she got to the Waleses she went right on into the kitchen without knocking and almost bumped into Robin, who was running his thumb around the inside edge of a jar of Skippy peanut butter.

"Don't tell me you're not going to speak to me," Claudine said breathlessly, taking advantage of the fact that Robin's mouth was stuck with peanut butter. "If you heard what I just did, you'd want advice too."

He listened quite impassively to her description of Aunt Lily and the two visitors, and even turned down the volume of his transistor. But when she reached the part where Aunt Lily got the hungry look in her eye, Robin held up his hand.

"Just a sec." He twisted the dial to a roar. "And now the one you've asked for, the Madmen singing the number-one hit of the week, 'Weeping and Wailing.' "

Robin turned off the radio and said, very practically, "It's all clear to me. Those people are out to make trouble for you. They'll hound you worse than the Beatles."

"Don't you think I know that?"

"They're just zeroing in on you now—I heard all about the technique on Long John's program. First they interview your friends, then your enemies, and then your family. By the time they get to you, they know all about you and you feel like they've been reading your mail or listening to you talk in your sleep. Well, that's the way the ball bounces, Claudie."

"You and your expressions. They'll be after you too, watch and see."

"They were already. Where do you think they came before they got to your house?"

Claudine stared. "What did you tell them?"

"Nothing special." Robin was very casual. "I told them I got the diaries from Uncle Burgie for decoration for the huts. I told them I never knew what you did with them. I told them you had a good imagination, almost as good as mine."

"Thanks."

"They asked me about your aunt. I said she was the smartest lady in Phoenix, smarter than all our teachers put together, starting with Miss Bidwell."

"That wouldn't take much." Claudine thought for a moment. "Got any crackers?"

"Just Ritz."

"I like them." She dug deep into the box he offered her. "I can tell you've got an idea."

Robin nodded. "As long as everybody thinks you did the book all by yourself, they'll be after you. People like that Mr. Fibbage—"

"Dr. Fibbage."

"What's the diff? He'll hang around studying you like you were in a bottle. And they'll keep on pointing at you wherever you go. When you get to high school all the teachers will say, Well, Miss Crouse, I should think anyone who could write a whole book could do better than eighty-two on a simple test. And if you want to go to college—"

Claudine shuddered. "I could change my name, though."

"They're on to you. You think Jackie Kennedy could change her name?"

Claudine listened intently. Robin had a crazy imagination, but he was very smart when it came to practical matters. Smarter, in fact, than her own father, the only other person in the world with whom she might have consulted about this thing. Her father would be of no help at all. He meant well, when he was around, but he had never been able to bring himself to say anything to her about the book (as if it was dirty), so this was a decision she would have to make by herself. Ever since the business about the book had come out, Mr. Crouse had taken to looking at his daughter peculiarly; and now that it had gotten out of hand, he seemed positively frightened of her, as though he had fathered a witch.

Claudine walked home slowly. By the time she got there, the pock-marked writer and Dr. Fibbage were standing on the porch saying goodbye to Aunt Lily, who was clenching her hands tightly together, as if she held something between them, like a little bird, that she was afraid would fly away.

"Well, well, well," whispered Dr. Fibbage, "and here is Claudine. Just the very person I'd like to see."

"Would you like to see *us*, Claudine?" asked Mr. Craft, grinning at her as if he were about to eat her. The way he put it, she would be chicken if she said no. "I'll buy you a soda downtown if it's all right with your aunt."

"If Claudine would like to go . . ." Aunt Lily said faintly.

"Sure I would." Before anyone could say another word, she was leading the way to their shiny rented car. "I'll be back soon, Aunt Lily."

"We won't keep her long."

"A very unusual woman, your aunt," the psychologist whispered to her from the back seat, and peered at her intently.

"That's for sure," Claudine said.

"You're not so very usual yourself," Mr. Craft remarked as he headed the car down to Main Street. "Muscling in on my racket like that. I got enough trouble with the competition without having to fend off eleven-year-old kids."

"I'm almost twelve."

"Big deal."

"Say, Mr. Craft," she asked, "do you like writing?"

"It beats working, I'll tell you that. But then I'm not famous. Just well known. How about you?"

"Oh, I got bored with it by the time I finished up the diaries. I don't think I'll do any more."

"What makes you say that?" the doctor demanded eagerly.

"I just told you. It's boring. Besides, I got sick of my aunt nagging at me to fill up all those diaries."

"You what?" All of a sudden Dr. Fibbage was panting like a dog in the summer sun. "You mean your aunt knew about the book while you were writing it?"

"Hey," Claudine said to Mr. Craft, "stop here, at O'Molony's Pharmacy. They've got the best ice cream, with the little chunks in it, not the Softi-Freeze stuff."

"Wait a minute," Dr. Fibbage whispered at the top of his lungs as they stood in front of the drugstore. "You haven't answered my question yet."

"Can I have my sundae? Then we can talk some more."

In the booth, after she had ordered a Phoenix Monster Sundae, Claudine said to Dr. Fibbage, "Why did you get so shook up when I told you my aunt knew about the book?"

"Because it was supposed to have been as much of a surprise to her as it was to the rest of us, later on."

"Oh, she's just modest. You said yourself she's very unusual. The fact is, she thought up the whole thing, practically. Mr. Craft, be careful, you're spilling coffee on your tie."

"My hands are shaky. That's what too much writing does," the writer said to her. "I thought I heard you say the book was your aunt's and not yours. Isn't that silly of me?"

"Well, if you'll promise not to tell anybody . . . I mean, I promised my aunt I wouldn't tell anybody. But I don't think it's fair for me to keep getting all the credit and have people buying me sundaes and taking my picture and everything, when actually most of the good stuff in the book is Aunt Lily's. She loves to make believe. It was her idea right from the start, except she was afraid people would make fun of her, so she decided to put everything in my name."

She looked across the table at the child psychologist. "Dr. Fibbage," she said, "you look like you just saw a ghost. Did I say something wrong?"

He reached out uneasily to pat her hand. "I'm unused to such honesty from someone so young."

"Claudine is a red-blooded American girl, that's why," Mr. Craft said heartily. "Here you thought you could watch Emily Dickinson grow up under your microscope, Fibbage, and instead you found yourself buying Monster Sundaes for a healthy, normal seventh-grader. Am I right or wrong, Claudine?"

"You couldn't be more right, Mr. Craft," Claudine replied after she had licked off her spoon. "You know something? You talk very sensibly, for a writer. I told my friend Robin Wales that writers could be as sensible as architects—that's what he's going to be. I'm beginning to think maybe some day I'll be a writer after all—I mean a real one, not an imitation. Well," she said, rising, "goodbye now, and thanks a lot for the sundae. I promised Robin I'd play with him if all the reporters and photographers would leave us alone. And I guess now they will, won't they?"

At the front of the drugstore, Claudine turned to look back at the two men who stood at the cashier's counter, their feet nailed to the floor, staring after her. She waved farewell to them and, whistling the "Marseillaise," ran off down the street in search of Robin.

TEASE

For many years I have told a story on myself, the point of which was, I supposed, that as a young man I was a good-natured fool. Now, however, if I regard what happened not as a joke on me but as a revelation of what we are all capable of, I remember something very different. It is as though my young protagonist were no longer the self I cherish with such wry and amused fondness, but had become instead a stranger—a wild and predatory stranger. But here is the story as I used to tell it:

When I was twenty-one a college classmate and I got temporary jobs in the Panama Canal Zone, jobs that seemed glamorous beforehand but turned out to be drab and routine. Only the after-hours night life was fun, and even that palled after a few weeks.

One night we decided to change our luck by crossing the Isthmus and spending the night, and our money, in Colón instead of in Panama City. Not that the program there would be any different. Rum-and-Cokes while we watched the jugglers, the tango teams and the imported strippers, and tried without real hope to make the B-girls, hired to separate tourists, sailors and other fools from their wallets without yielding up anything more than a smile or a dance. It made no more sense than going, say, from Brooklyn to Newark in search of novelty. But at least the décor, the faces and the bodies would be different.

So we went off on the Toonerville railroad that joggled us across the thin strip of jungle separating one ocean from another. We bought round-trip tickets, to make sure that we'd get back, but for the rest of it we decided to leave things to chance.

"Let's make a pact," I proposed to Tommy. He was the kind who could appear calmly sober all evening, and then amaze people who didn't know him by passing out with his face on the table top, or slipping slowly to the floor. "We'll take along twenty bucks apiece and go as far as we can on it. Agreed?"

He understood me. We were already weary of those cold-blooded whorehouses—the Villa Amor, Las Tres Palmas and the rest—where, although you could drink at your leisure and dance with the girls beforehand, you were rousted unceremoniously from their cubicles in order that they might hurry down and hustle up the next customer. We were tired too of the streetwalkers. It was true that they were not supervised and hence were more human: They led you languidly, even at dawn, into the rabbit warrens where they lived and fornicated, down endless ramshackle open corridors teetering above the littered courtyards alive with scrawny squawking chickens, past room after doorless room, one with an Indian mother vacantly suckling an infant, another with a pipe-smoking toothless grandfather opening a mango with fingers gnarled like roots, a third and fourth with a nude couple snoring as they slept or scratching themselves as they quarreled above a wailing phonograph, until finally you reached the girl's own room, her very own because she earned it by flinging herself down on her back on the pallet, yanking her print dress up over her naked belly and giggling as she beckoned to you with her brown hand. Yes, they were all too human, but if they complimented you on your manliness, they could give you no faith in your personal charm.

For that we had turned to the B-girls. The Americans resident in the Zone had promptly discovered, as such people always know such things, that Tommy and I were not even candidate members of the colony but were only transients, and therefore they protected their daughters from us, with perfect justification, as if they knew that our motives were the worst. Those waxen-looking girls living lonesomely in the tropics—of whom we were told by a bartender (citing no authority) that they were pale because they menstruated twice a month—were as unappealing to us adventurers as, say, pygmy women to explorers on safari. They were safer than they knew.

And so we had taken up the game of trying to conquer Latin night-club hostesses who, although they were hired to please, had no slightest intention of allowing themselves to be con-quered, no matter how much money, energy and charm you in-vested in them. Practiced in capturing your interest on the dance floor or at the little tables across which they leaned to display their shadowed charms, they sensed precisely how many drinks of colored water they could con you into buying them, at a dollar a shot, before your patience or your funds ran out, or before the last floor show faded away late in the night. These professional persuaders were more firmly determined to avoid genuine intimacy, we had learned at some cost, than the most carefully nurtured Yankee maidens. But the more we—unlike the tourist suckers—knew of their determination, the more we were tempted to overcome it, not by buying them but by winning them. That was why Tommy understood at once what rules I was proposing for the old game we had tacitly agreed to play in new surroundings.

When the train pulled in, we strolled about and had a lei-surely dinner. Before it was fairly dark we were pub-crawling.

I cannot recall anything about the first places we went to. One drink at each sufficed to convince us that they were no different from those of Panama City. The one we finally settled at, though, remains fixed in my mind, because it was there that I encountered Isabel.

When we drifted in the band was just finishing "Begin the Be-guine," behind a horribly grinning, lacquered male singer. As we pushed through to a ringside table they went into a fanfare, not for us but for an American stripper introduced by the singer as Pepper Mint, or something of the sort. The lights went down and the girl came out bathed in a green spot, and began to glide sinously before us, the horizontal bands of cigarette smoke shifting in the poor light as she disturbed them with her weaving arms, hips and legs.

She was extraordinarily good, gifted at what she was being paid to convey. In a few moments she had wriggled down to nakedness, or to very little more than high-heeled pumps. Her body was magnificent, and it was most disturbing to have that greenish torso twisting and flexing before us within arm's reach. Tommy was breathing so hard as she skidded offstage, her dimpled buttocks winking farewell, that he could not find his voice to dismiss the two B-girls who sidled up and slid into the empty chairs at our table.

"You like to buy us a drink, yes?"

I shrugged. "One round. We're not rich tourists."

The blond one, who had seated herself at my side, laughed unaffectedly. "Was too much for you, the dancer?"

"Not for me," I protested, and sat up to examine her. She was a grinning, self-confident woman in her late twenties. Her dyed hair went well with a creamy skin the color of light coffee. She had slim, quick fingers that flicked and snapped like her eyes when she spoke, and teeth that showed irregular but very white when she smiled her oddly reckless smile.

"Isabel. I call you Toby, you look like a cat with those fat cheeks, okay?"

She had me. She was an impudent one, and maybe it was because of that that I was challenged into making her see me, and admire me, not just as a source of revenue but as a man.

Once the floor show was over we started to talk. My Spanish was impossible; her English was like a movie Mexican's, good for a million laughs. Between laughs, and drinks, I learned that she was in fact a Mexican, or so she said, from some hopeless village near Veracruz, where she had waited on table and earned just enough, entertaining sailors in waterfront bars, to keep from prostitution. She had beaten her way down to Panama for reasons as vaguely stated as mine, but her safari must have involved a nerve that I wasn't even sure I possessed. Now she was selling not exactly her body but her sensuality and her whimsical appeal.

In fact, in precise proportion to the degree that she charmed me, I wanted to charm her, to impress her, to make her like me. Tommy, stimulated no doubt by the luscious memory of the stripper, was more concerned simply with making out with Luisa, a chunky and matter-of-fact woman who could be gay, as she was paid to be, only by some effort of will.

The catch, though, was that in order for Tommy to make out, he had to be charming; and in order for me to be sure that I was really a charmer, I had to make out.

So Tommy allowed Luisa to make admiring sounds as she felt his biceps, and bought her more drinks. And I, good old Toby, bought Isabel more drinks too. The more we drank, the later it got, the more Tommy and I had invested in our endeavor. Isabel and I did not dance even once, although we had the opportunity all evening long on that crowded dance floor to press the lengths of our bodies against each other.

Why didn't we? I didn't want anything so easy, I didn't want to be paid in installments, and as I looked over Isabel's shoulder, sliding so warm and brown within her semitransparent white blouse in time to the band's rhythm, and watched Tommy grappling doggedly with hefty Luisa, dragging her like a sack of maize across the floor already cluttered with sailors and their B-girls, I knew, as though it were written out for me like the printed prophecy that pops out at you from a penny scale, that Tommy would get nowhere, while I—well, I had a chance.

"It's getting late," I said to Isabel. Then, smiling with all my heart: "Let's be serious. You know what I want. I want to go home with you tonight."

"Toby, you sweet, you can't do that." She shook her head solemnly, but softened the refusal by showing me her white, white teeth.

"Don't read me the rules." I reached out for her forearm and took it tightly in my hand. It was almost the first time I'd touched her; I felt a shock of pleasure and was warmed to see her face turn grave. She knew that she could not just put me off. Gripping her arm until I could feel her pulse, I said, "I'm not buying any more fake drinks unless you tell me yes. I don't want to buy you, I like you too much, you savvy? I want you to like me that way."

"I do." Her tone was absolutely unfeigned. Even the fact that she didn't look at me, but sat with lowered lids, gazing thoughtfully at my fingers on her arm, convinced me. Then, as if coming to a decision, she glanced around, checking on the waiter, who was busy at another table, checking on the *patron*, who was bawling out a bartender at the register, and finally fixed her brilliant liquid eyes on me. "You can't go with me—but maybe I can go with you."

"Don't say maybe. Say for sure."

"All right, I say sure, if you buy us a room. But don't tell your friend."

I was happy to promise. I even bought the next round, although it was Tommy's turn. We were both close to being drunk, and closer to being broke, and we arose with exaggerated politeness as the girls went off together to the john. It was late, the crowd had thinned out, and the drummer saluted our gallantry with a ruffle and a spinning of one of his sticks high in the air, grinning and showing us his gold teeth as he caught it.

"*Salud!*" Tommy called out, raising his drink. But to me he said, "The women are fixing to dump us."

"How do you know?"

"Luisa's got a bicycle parked out back. She and Isabel come to work on it, with Isabel sitting on the back fender."

"So?"

"They got to go home the same way."

I had to laugh. "Listen, pal," I said, "if I get Isabel out the front door, you think you can cope with Luisa and her two-wheeler? You think you can cope?"

"I'll tell you one thing," Tommy replied with dignity. "I'm going to give it the old college try."

The girls were already on their way back to the table. I said hastily, "Here's luck. And check your wallet for the train ticket—it's a long walk back."

We made it very clear to the waiter that our spending was over. The *patron* had no cause for complaint; he looked up from counting dollars and balboas and even mustered a greasy good-night smile as his girls checked out. A couple of cabs were drowsing at the curb, and I hustled Isabel into the nearest one before she could change her mind. Laughing and squirming, she twisted about so that she could blow a farewell kiss to Luisa through the back window.

I had my hand on the bony shoulder of the sleepy Negro hackie, but I hesitated before pressing him on, in order that I might get one last glimpse of Tommy and Luisa. I was rewarded. While we craned our necks, Luisa emerged from the shadows of the alleyway next to the night club, whose neon sign had just been cut off. As she pushed her bike to the sidewalk, she was evidently arguing with Tommy, whose head was shrinking down like a bull's to protect him from the rain, which was starting to patter, then to bounce off the ground. She thrust her chunky body forward, climbed aboard and began to pedal off, with Tommy trotting along beside her.

Isabel was laughing, softly at first, and then wildly, her head back against the upholstery, her breasts shaking as she clapped her hands. "*La lluvia*," she gasped, "the rain!"

"What about it?"

"The more it rain, the faster she go. The faster she go, the harder he run. You know something, Toby? He never gonna catch her."

"I never thought he would." I was torn between guilt and gloating. "Never mind them. Where should we—"

Isabel gazed at me sweetly. "I know nice hotel. Brand-new."

"I can hardly wait."

"But we got to stop first. Not too far. I got a girl friend—"

"Another one?"

"You silly! I meet her sometime after work. Poor. No money. In the rain . . ." She looked at me pleadingly.

"You're breaking my heart." There was nothing I could do. Besides, I was curious. "What are we going to do with her?"

"Maybe we get a sanvich."

"It can't be anything more than that. I blew all my dough on your phony drinks."

"No-no, you'll see." She leaned forward and shot a stream of Spanish at the driver, who nodded drowsily, threw the car into gear, and released the clutch with a jerk.

We were pitched against each other. At last. Breathing in her fragrance, a mixture of some cheap lilac perfume and the friendly odor of her warm body, I pressed her to me. She smiled luxuriously and murmured something I did not catch.

"You do like me?" I asked. "Really like me?"

For answer she raised her hand and ran her fingers through my hair. She was a little weary, not so eager as I, and five or six years older, maybe more; but her answer was yes, of that I was convinced. Reassured, I bent to kiss her lips.

But the taxi stopped joltingly. I looked up, annoyed. From the shadows of a darkened store front there stepped forward a big sullen-faced girl with wet hair half plastered to her skull, a terrible complexion and a man's zipper jacket flung carelessly over her shoulders. She opened the door of the cab without being invited, as though she had been expecting us.

Isabel introduced her to me as Gertrudis or something equally ugly—any name would have seemed ugly—but it made no difference, since her lack of interest in me bordered on the absolute. Wedging her wet bulk firmly into the back seat, she launched at once into a lengthy speech none of which I could understand, partly because of that Central American way of speaking as though Spanish consisted of nothing but a run-together series of liquid vowels. Although she salivated as she spoke, and gesticulated broadly with her mannish, reddened hands, she did not betray any genuine animation in speech or gesture. All that mattered anyway was that Isabel was far more excited by her than by me.

We had gone no more than a dozen blocks when the driver brought us to a halt before an all-night milk bar. The girls scrambled out and hurried on inside, their heads bent against the raindrops, leaving me to deal with the cab driver, who had already slumped over into a foetal position, chin against his chest and hands pressed between his upraised thighs.

"*Cuánto cobra usted*—" I began, but the driver interrupted without even troubling to open his eyes.

"I wait."

I glanced through the dripping window at the milk bar. Isabel, laughing and chattering, was urging her friend to eat. It was becoming painfully clear that the whole scene had taken place before. Well, I was damned if I was going to give up now. I clenched my teeth and went on in.

Isabel patted the leatherette stool at her left. "Toby, you better eat too. Is late."

"You're telling me?"

I had a soft drink while I waited and watched. Isabel was sipping at a milkshake in this oasis of light in a darkened city and hanging on her friend's words—uttered between huge gulps of bread and cheese—as though each one was precious. Gertrudis was a big eater—a second sandwich soon went the way of the first—but she seemed to derive no more satisfaction from this than from her talking, which made Isabel's eyes sparkle and from time to time doubled her up with laughter. I might just as well not have been there. At least, not until it was time to pay the *cuenta*.

Isabel looked away with a new-found delicacy as I fumbled through my pockets. The bill was less than I had expected, though, and I managed a smile as she thanked me. Her friend, the boillike blemishes standing out garishly on her sullen countenance in the lavender light of the fluorescent tubes, did not bother to acknowledge me, but simply shrugged the zipper jacket over her meaty shoulders. Before she slouched on out to the taxi, she threw a farewell remark at the counterman, who mumbled something casual around his dry, dangling cigarette butt as he cleared away our little debris. Apparently they were all buddies.

When I re-entered the cab, though, grimly ready to outlast

my new antagonist, Isabel snuggled into the crook of my arm
and pressed tightly against me as we drove off.

"Now we go to hotel."

"I don't want to rush you," I said. "It's only four A.M."

"You funny." She murmured to Gertrudis, *"Está burlesco."*

Her friend didn't crack a smile. It had been clear enough since
she had come into my cab from out of the rain that she didn't
like men. I released myself from Isabel.

"The rain has stopped," I said. "Isn't it about time that we
dropped off your friend?"

"We get out first," she replied equably. "Then her."

While I was thinking this over, I had a chance to survey the
slick, silent streets, which seemed to be getting a little familiar.

"How does this guy know where to go," I asked Isabel after a
while, "if nobody tells him?"

"He knows," she said simply. "I already tol' him."

"Well," I said, "you better tell him to go the old-fashioned
way. We've already passed this plaza twice. Once more and I'll
own the cab."

She leaned forward and spoke sharply to the hackie, who gave
no indication of discomfiture, but continued to drive us se-
dately through the night while the blotchy-faced girl droned on
in her unpleasant way. Even though Isabel was leaning against
me as she listened, I was growing sleepy.

At last we pulled up before a squat, freshly stuccoed building
which, save for its vertical neon HOTEL SUPERBA, might have
been a veterinary clinic. Blithe as if we were off to a Sunday picnic, Isabel hopped out, leaving me for the moment with Gertrudis, who was smoking a little brown cigarette and spitting
tobacco shreds onto the floor mat.

"I go in first," Isabel called to me. "You pay him, yes?"

I paid him, all right, after a miserable effort to argue. When
I put back my wallet it was practically empty, but it was worth
all of it, I thought, to see the last of that rude and sulky
young woman, who said nothing as I hastened eagerly after
Isabel.

I found her in the lobby, shaking the night clerk, who was trying obstinately to stay asleep in his tilted chair, with the immutable stubbornness of the stoically enduring. He had no protection, and no equipment beyond a freshly sawed table desk sitting on opaque glass blocks. Behind his nodding head hung a raw, unfinished rack for depositing mail and room keys. The dark cubbyholes gaped emptily. It was like staring into the vacant sockets of a jaw from which every tooth has been extracted. Isabel and I, it was plain, were alone with the desperately sleeping Indian in a building that might have been put up just for this one night.

I yanked his chair upright by its left leg.

"*Numero once,*" he groaned, scratching his bare brown belly with one hand—his embroidered white shirt hung unbuttoned to the navel—and with the other extending a key hooked to a hard rubber ball so huge that you couldn't stuff it into a pocket even if you wanted to. Someone had painted the number 11 on it in white.

"Hold on." I was very conscious of exactly how much I had left in my wallet. "*Cuánto?*"

He spread the fat fingers of one hand and displayed them. "*Cinco.*"

I looked at Isabel. She had helped a lot of people to my money: not only her boss but also the cabbie, her peculiar girl friend, the counterman at the milk bar, and now the hotel clerk. From each, from all, no doubt, she took her cut.

But then, she had earned it. And I had stuck it out. What mattered, after all, was that she really and truly liked me. At least that was what she seemed to be saying to me as she stood blinking a little in the bare light, her fine legs apart and her bare arms akimbo, daring me not to like her, not to admire her for her dash and her nerve, not to pay. I drew a deep breath and, turning back to the clerk, exchanged money for key.

"*Por dónde?*" I demanded, my voice echoing through the empty hall.

He pointed his dirt-caked thumb dead ahead and then let the

arm fall back against his belly, the fingers working their way into the folds of his flesh, like piglets searching for the teats of their recumbent mother.

"Come, Isabel," I said, leading her down the bleak uncarpeted corridor which, relieved only by grilled doors at regular intervals, had the clanking monotony of a cell block. Six, eight, seven, nine—we had the last room on the floor. I unlocked it and let her in.

With incomparable grace, Isabel held out her arms to me in the quiet of our ultimate sanctuary. A familiar gesture, but she endowed it with a rich and wonderful mystery. Our bodies close, we whispered, not because we had to but because it did not seem right to rupture the before-dawn silence. At last, I thought, at last, I've won! And I kissed her slowly, savoringly, deeply.

Isabel pushed at my arms, and as I lowered them my jacket fell to the chair at the side of the bed. She tugged gently at my loosened tie until she had it in her hand, then unbuttoned my wrinkled shirt and slipped it off too. I stood naked to the waist. As I stepped out of my loafers to more nearly equalize our heights, I began to fumble with the buttons of Isabel's white blouse.

She laughed a little, helping me. "You got big fingers. *Sin arte.*"

"That's because I'm nervous," I muttered. By the subdued light of the bed lamp I stared at her newly exposed throat and soft upper bosom, bronze-gold above the lace of her slip. "I'm dazzled. Isabel, Isabel, Isabel."

"Toby, you nice boy," she chuckled. "You do me one more favor."

I drew back in order to look at her, but did not answer.

"We get a room for my friend. She have no place to stay."

"Now you ask me? Why now?"

"I promise to. Gertrudis can't ask you herself. *Tímida.*"

"She looks it."

"What you say?" Isabel demanded, with just a touch of impatience. "I got to tell her, she's waiting with the taxi driver."

"She'd better stick with him—he's got the last of my dough."

Isabel was gazing at me sorrowfully. I unbuttoned my hip pocket, pulled out my wallet and spread it apart with my fingers. "You're looking at my train ticket and my last dollar bill. If you sandbagged me you wouldn't find anything more."

Even as I spoke, Isabel was buttoning her blouse. She tied the little bow at her throat and picked up her purse. "I go tell her," she said.

"You do that."

"You lie down, you look tired. Okay, Toby?"

"Okay."

After she had slipped out I lay down dizzily and waited, staring up at the frieze of cobwebbed cracks running along the upper wall of the plastered cell, hardly finished but already falling into disrepair. I might have been lying in the bare bedroom of a bleak new garden apartment in Bayside, Long Island. But not alone. Not all alone.

The time passed very slowly. I said to myself, She knew I didn't like that girl. Who would? The fact that I had no money left, for her or for anyone else, was more than just fate. It was her responsibility as much as mine.

But I could not go on talking to myself. I got up in my stockinged feet and padded out into the hallway. It was empty. I could see clear down to the sleeping clerk with no obstruction, human or otherwise. I started to run.

Without pausing at the clerk's desk I went right on to the door, which I struck with my shoulder, skidding to a halt on the slippery sidewalk beyond it. I peered first this way, then that. For as far as I could see, the length of the street in both directions was absolutely bare, and drying out here and there where it was touched by the first flush of dawn.

I walked back slowly into the Hotel Superba, my socks soaked through and plastered to the soles of my feet. I took hold of the snoring clerk and shook him awake ruthlessly.

"Did my girl friend go out?" I demanded. "Did she go away in the taxi?"

"No home," he mumbled. "No home."

I released my hold on his shirt. He fell back to sleep at once and I proceeded on down the blank corridor to its end, my wet socks leaving footprints on the unwashed plaster dust of the still unfinished tile flooring. Inside my room I stripped off the socks and, drawing the blind against the early dawn that was already seeping through the window, I threw myself down on the bed once more. Unslaked, my lust turned—like a glass of milk left undrunk—to a sour, hateful curd. I lay for a long while, burning and seething, frustrated, shamed, humiliated. It was only after seemingly endless hours that exhaustion overcame me, and I fell asleep.

But when I awoke, bewildered for an instant, alone in the strange room, I was finally able to laugh at myself.

That, in essence, is the story I have told others not once but many times in the years that have passed since it—or something like it—first happened to me. Presumably I tell it on myself when I want to show what a sucker, what a fool, a young man can be.

And when people press me—as some do—about what happened afterward, I tell them truthfully that I ate a cheap and greasy breakfast, caught the lurching train back to Panama City, and confessed laughingly to Tommy, once he had admitted that Luisa had outraced him on her bicycle, that I had wound up not with Isabel but with the morning paper.

But observe, as I do now, what a charming self-portrait I have succeeded in painting, what a wholesome person emerges from this "true" recital: good-natured, sporting, able to laugh at himself, and above all charitable. The only thing I have suppressed is the brief epilogue which I must now relate.

Some days after that fruitless evening, Tommy was ordered to the other end of the Isthmus, to Cristobal, for several days' work. The minute that I heard this, I began to think of Isabel, whose very name I had put out of my mind. All of my shame and resentment at being victimized came rushing back, and I was taken by a rage for revenge.

With great casualness I said to Tommy, "I want you to look up Isabel in Colón. You remember, the tease."

"If I get the chance," he said. "But you know, I can't afford that stuff."

"Who can? That's why I want to scare her out of pulling the same trick on anyone else. Tell her I'm good and angry. *Furioso. Frenético.* Wait!" I swiveled about in my chair and jammed a letterhead sheet into my typewriter. Rapidly I typed out, in Spanish: "Señorita: I have not forgotten. You shall pay for your treason." Then I yanked it out and scrawled an indecipherable signature beneath.

"There, that looks official. Tell her I'm negotiating with the proper parties to have her taken care of. Physically."

"My Spanish isn't that good."

"Hers is. You won't have to draw a picture."

Tommy was a good fellow, if a little dull, but I couldn't predict whether he would go through with it. So it wasn't until his return the following week that I learned what had happened. Part of it I could see on his face as he pushed through the swinging doors of the Pacifico, where I was having the usual, Myers rum and Coke, before dinner. He wore a dubious expression, as if he weren't quite sure what to say to me (as if, I thought before casting the notion aside, he were reluctant even to greet me); and the freckles on his forehead had darkened and grown blotchy.

"How did it go?" I asked him.

"Same as here." He waited until the bartender had brought him his drink before adding, "I saw your friend."

"You gave her the message."

"Oh yes. She smiled at first. Either she didn't understand or she figured I was joking. So I took out your note. She stared at it and stared at it. First I thought maybe she was illiterate, but no, she began to jabber a mile a minute. In order to stop her I told her what you said, about hiring the Mafia to knock her around. Well, she started to tremble, you know, and her eyes filled with tears. She was pale, and biting on the letter as though—"

"Biting on what letter?"

"On your letter. The note you typed. Then she turned around

and ran out of the bar like a deer, by the side exit, at the corner of the bandstand. I thought I'd better go after her—I didn't want to carry it too far—but when I asked the bartenders where she lived, they made out like they didn't know what I was talking about. I said to them, When she comes back tell her I was only kidding. But I don't know that she ever came back. If you ask me, by now she's on her way to Tampico, or wherever it was she came from."

I couldn't think of anything much to say. Tommy gulped down his drink a little more swiftly than usual and wound up, looking at his glass instead of at me, "I can't stick around tonight. Fact is, I've got a dinner date. I'll see you."

Why did I do it? None of the excuses that I can muster up even approaches adequacy. Just because she had humiliated me, did that give me warrant to terrorize her? I had accepted the rules of the game. I knew when I started that her livelihood, her very life, depended on her countering aggressive men with all the cunning she could conjure up.

No doubt it was to Gertrudis that she had turned, in miserable panic, for help in fleeing from those bandy-legged little Indian soldiers, strapped into their Sam Browne belts and serving both their provincial masters and whatever rich gringo could afford their services for a job of pistol-whipping. Isabel and Gertrudis knew in their bones what I understood without ever being honest enough to make explicit to myself: that the cards were stacked in favor of the Tommys and the Tobys, the rich, careless Yankees who, if they were outwitted in the skirmishes, could always win the wars simply by whistling up the apparatus of terror and repression that had been invented precisely to crush the victimized and the rebellious.

Well, if Isabel could only know it, this is one time she won. For, despite all my efforts to bring back just that one night when she charmed me and I tried so hard to charm her, to win her not by her rules but by mine, not with money or force but with the assertion of my simple manhood, I cannot really call her up in her mature and weary beauty. All I have, instead, is what I have earned for myself: the woman whom I never saw, but who remains nevertheless indelibly imprinted in my mind's eye, pale, trembling, fearing me, hating me and cursing me, now and forevermore.

THE HACK

Sooner or later everyone who writes, and publishes, is bound to be approached by a supplicant who writes but does not publish. "Would you read this? And be honest with me: Have I really got it?"

Such a plea for reassurance goes straight to the heart, for it is one that every writer has uttered, once upon a time, if only to himself. What could be more natural, in a trade without diplomas, licenses, or name plates? Sometimes there comes a more extreme demand, the most painful of all, and the most painful to answer: "Should I go on?"

A negative answer is implicit in the very uttering of the question. If you do not believe in yourself, even beyond the boundaries of sanity, no one else will. But the cruelty of replying with absolute frankness is easy only when you are young, desperate to assert yourself, and so prove your own gifts, if necessary at the expense of others.

Just before I came of age, I met a man in Ann Arbor named Harold Bangs who threw these questions into relief and so, I gradually came to see, altered my conception of myself. The funny thing is that, far from being unsure of himself, he was fanatically certain—like many eccentrics—that he held an exclusive option on a certain corner of the truth.

After my sophomore year at college I had gotten a summer job as lifeguard at a Michigan beach resort; but instead of spending my evenings making out with the girls at the casino, I had sat up late, night after night, in a kind of fever, writing stories about the people around me, the busboys, the waiters, the lonely wives, the weary worried husbands. By the time fall came around I knew that this was what I wanted to do, more than anything in the world, and I was convinced, in the way that you can be only when you are very young, that I was greatly gifted. Anyway, I had to find a single room, off in some quiet place, so I could write all night, if I wanted to, without disturbing anyone. That was how I met Harold Bangs.

Mrs. Bangs was the one who answered the doorbell of the unprepossessing, run-down house in a courtyard only a few blocks from the Michigan Union, and led me on up to the attic room. Thin, shy and puckered at the lips as if she had just bitten into something bitter, she stood in the doorway of the narrow room and rubbed her hands up and down her flanks.

"I know it's not very big," she said, blinking rapidly in what I later realized was a tic, "but you did say you wanted a real quiet place."

Mrs. Bangs must have had a first name, but I never learned it, nor could I ever have thought of her as anything but Mrs. Bangs, not young, not old, not interesting, just an overworked rooming-house keeper whom I never saw in anything but a J. C. Penney house dress, ankle socks and white open-toed buckle-strap Enna Jetticks, and who always smelled of ammonia and Bab-O while she scrubbed the endless steps to my room and the toilet next to it.

Even the mail, which for her consisted principally of utility bills, catalogues and a weekly letter from a Mrs. J. C. Hurd of Ishpeming, Michigan, was invariably addressed to Mrs. Harold Bangs, that drooping-breasted, down-dropping woman who never relaxed, seldom smiled, and ran the house alone, as if she were a widow woman.

In fact it was the mail that first brought Harold and me together. There were eleven of us roomers in that dark, cool and faintly moldy old house, not counting Mr. and Mrs. Bangs, and it was customary for the one who first spotted the postman stuffing the box to bring in the mail and lay it out in piles on the oak hall table, under a hand-lettered poem, a souvenir of the Chicago Fair, entitled "That's Where the West Begins." That was how I knew about Mrs. Bangs's mail; and that was how Harold came to know about me.

The building, so I was told by two forestry students who'd roomed there the year before as well, had been willed to Harold Bangs by his mother. What was more, he got a monthly pension (I saw that, too, in the front hall) for almost total disability—he had been gassed in the war. Apparently Harold figured that the house and the check for his lungs were sufficient contribution on his part, and that if his wife wanted to eat regularly it was up to her to put in a fifteen-hour day in the rooming house. But I hardly set eyes on the man, who was as indifferent to my existence as he was to the ten other roomers barracked over his head—until the day early in October that two of my literary efforts came back from *Story* Magazine in the very same mail.

All the winey fragrance of the autumn afternoon leaked away as I dropped my load of library books to the oak table and stared miserably at the creased manila envelopes that bore my name and address in my own handwriting. There was no need to open them. I knew their message by heart: *Dear Contributor, This alas is a rejection slip. And heaven knows the editors have had their share* . . . You're no good, you're no good, the two envelopes shouted at me. Yes, you are, yes, you are, screamed the defiant starlings, black, bold and unrepentant in the courtyard elm that grew all the way up past my attic window.

I closed the front door behind me and picked up my books and rejected stories, clenching for the long climb up the dark rubber-treaded stairs to my solitary room. Suddenly a voice called out to me from Mrs. Bangs's quarters.

"Hey, Tommy."

Mrs. Bangs never addressed me by anything other than my

last name—after all, it was I who paid her once a week, and I whose room she dusted and swept. But this was a man's voice, thin and twangy, coming from beyond the end of the hallway, where I had never ventured, from the dining room, whose sliding doors stood somewhat ajar.

"Come on in."

Harold Bangs was sitting in a pool of light at the far end of the round mahogany dining-room table, before an old L. C. Smith office typewriter with a metal circle of keys, the kind of machine that you used to see in pawnshop windows wedged between banjos and golf clubs. He was a long-limbed, lank-jawed man in his middle years, with protruding shoulder blades that pushed out the back of his shirt like hidden wings, and swollen knuckles that he must have cracked a million times, sitting humped over the typewriter. He wore black garters above the elbows to hike up his shirt sleeves past wrists that looked as though they connected his hands to his arms not with bones but with twisted cotter pins. The shirt itself had no collar—I thought they'd stopped making them years before. His skinny shanks were crossed, exposing bare skin, hairless and white as bird droppings. He wore no socks under his plaid carpet slippers.

Although it was bright daylight, the bile-green shades on the dining-room windows were drawn down so far that their wooden spring rollers were revealed. As I approached, he squinted at me across the goose-neck lamp with shrewd frankness. Or at least frankness was the impression he seemed to want to convey; actually, I thought, he looked fanatically self-assured, like an evangelist, although of course I had no way of knowing why or to what end.

"So you scribble too," he said, sizing me up with his ice-blue myopic eyes.

My temper shifted at once from depression to fury. I detested that word; besides, who did he think he was to couple us like that? But, since I could not think how to express any of this without sounding impossibly snobbish, I said nothing, but tried unsuccessfully to glare as I advanced into the circle of light cast by the student lamp, exactly like those with which all the other rooms in the house were furnished. It was now that I observed that his face and neck were covered with a week's growth of graying stubble which further hollowed his already cadaverous cheeks and made him look toothless, when in fact he was equipped with a garish set of store teeth that intensified the fixed insincerity of his welcoming smile. It was only later that I learned that the teeth were a gift from the Veterans Administration, just as I was to learn, from continuous observation, that Harold was one of those rare birds, like Gabby Hayes, the old cowpoke in the Hopalong Cassidy movies, who was never clean-shaven and never bearded but somehow managed to maintain a continuous seedy stubble.

"This is where I work," he said. "Right now I'm knocking out an adventure yarn about two prospectors in the Andes. Going to try it on the *Post* and then on the men's mags."

Still I could find nothing to say. Around the typewriter the dining-room table was piled high with copy paper, manuscripts, carbons, envelopes, and back numbers of the *Writer's Guide* and the *Information Please Almanac*. Over everything hung the foul odor of dead cigarette butts, thousands of them, heaped in dime-store glass ashtrays which had surely not been emptied since his last shave; obviously Mrs. Bangs, always moving through the upper floors with dust mop and toilet brush, was not allowed in this sanctum.

"Tell me straight," Harold demanded. "How does *Story* treat you?"

"I don't know what you mean."

"Do they give you a prompt reading? I haven't tried to crack that market yet." He laughed hollowly, coughed, and spat out a crumb of tobacco. "Not that I've got anything against them. It's just that, according to the *Yearbook* payment scale, they're pretty far down on the old totem pole."

"I wouldn't know. I haven't had anything from them but rejections. Form rejections. They return my stories pretty fast, but that's no help."

"Sure it is." Harold cracked open a carton of Wings, pulled out a fresh pack, and offered me a cigarette. "You should keep a tally of your submissions, like I do." Between us lay an open notebook whose pages were ruled off in columns headed TITLE, DATE SENT, POSTAGE SPENT.

My head was spinning. "I haven't thought much about anything that systematic."

"But you should! Aren't you a serious writer?"

"I think I am," I said. I thought I was the most serious writer in Ann Arbor. "That is, I'm trying to write about serious things."

"Who isn't? I had a feeling, even before I saw your manuscripts in today's mail. When I heard you pounding your machine up in the attic night after night, I knew you weren't just doing term papers. It's too early in the semester," he added, shifting the wet cigarette with his tongue, "for that much schoolwork. I been running a rooming house long enough to know that."

I could feel my face reddening. "I hope the noise hasn't bothered you or Mrs. Bangs."

"The missus turns in early, right after Lowell Thomas and 'The Shadow.' Me, I put in a long day. Fourteen, fifteen hours at the machine is nothing for me. Nobody knows what's involved except another writer, right? Working out plots and outlines, making copies, studying your markets—there's no easy road to riches for us guys. It's a very time-consuming business."

By now I had edged back to the sliding doors. "If you'll excuse me," I said, "I'd better get back up there and start scratching away again, Mr.—"

"Call me Harold, Tommy. That's the spirit. Don't let those rejections get you down—I've got drawers full. And, say," he called after me, "any time you want me to read over some of your stuff, don't hesitate."

I fled.

But that was to be only the first of many such encounters, although I never took him up on his offer. Harold got to know my class schedule, and approximately when I would be returning to the house to drop off books, or change clothes, or do some writing; and all too often at those times he would leave the dining-room doors ajar in order to entrap me.

Just as Mrs. Bangs seemed always to want to wish herself out of my way, blushing when she collided with me as I shuffled out of the toilet in the morning and shrinking against the wall when I clattered down the stairs in the evening, Harold, seemingly nailed to his squealing swivel chair before the L. C. Smith, sought out excuses to lure me into his den. I never saw the two of them together—it was like those mystery movies where you discover that the real reason is because they are both one and the same person, a master at disguise and a master at crime. Except that Harold and Mrs. Bangs loomed larger in my life than did Lon Chaney or Boris Karloff.

Harold, I found out, wasn't all that eager to read my stuff. What he did want was for me to read his, and more than that to reassure him by my camaraderie that we were both members of a very special fraternity.

"I invested a lot of time on fillers," he informed me one day. "Fillers, jokes and funny coincidences. Matter of fact, I even hit 'Keeping Posted' one time. Not bad, hey? That's the top of the market, you got millions of readers going for you there. But you're dead unless you can concentrate on that exclusively. It doesn't pay, Tommy, take my word for it."

He lit one cigarette from the end of another, and dropped the short one in the butt cemetery without bothering to stub it out. No wonder the room stank.

"Besides, I think my forte is in yarns. I've got a tale of the sea here, about two brothers, Alaska salmon fishermen, with a powerful story line and strong romantic interest. So far I've had fourteen turn-downs, all printed, not one personal note. It beats me. Want to take a look at it and tell me your honest opinion?"

I put it off as long as possible, and finally came back with some miserable half-assed corrections of his typing and spelling (even when I am an old man I will remember with sour satisfaction that Harold Bangs wrote "wearwithal" and "mediveal" and "irregardless"), but I could not bring myself to discuss his plot, which was incredible even if you accepted its premise—that a New York society girl would go to Ketchikan in search of adventure. Or its characters, high-flown on one page and mealymouthed on the next.

All I did say was "Harold, when were you in Alaska?"

"Never. But I got it down pretty good, didn't I?"

"Why don't you write about something you know, like the world war?"

Harold cracked his knuckles. "Tommy, I knocked out fifteen Flying Aces yarns—they're all in that corner." He gestured with a blackened fingernail. "Dogfights between Spads and Fokkers, Jennys and Messerschmidts, I wrote them all and never hit once."

"I didn't know you were in the Air Corps."

"I wasn't. I was a plain old doughboy—that's how I got gassed. But nobody wants to read about the Argonne woods any more. You got to know your readers and your markets."

Harold shifted his bony frame in the swivel chair and drew back his lips, showing me not only those store teeth white as his shanks, but his pale-pink gums as well. "You like to think you're sitting up there and writing for posterity. But first you got to get published, right? You know what James Joyce went through with his stories? Here, take this copy of *Writer's Digest* and see what the editors of *Blue Book* have to say."

The worst of it was that when he gave me something to read I was under obligation to return it and so start a whole new round of conversations. Once I tried to outsmart him by leaving the magazine on the mail table in the hall with a note of thanks. All that happened was that next time I passed, Harold called out, "Hey, Tommy, you don't have to stand on ceremony, I'm always here. And you don't have to worry about interrupting me. I can always pick up where I left off."

All through that autumn I lived half in anticipation, half in dread of those sessions in Harold's den. Businesslike and implacable, he went on writing his unpublishable yarns about lean, silent adventurers and red-lipped maidens on the Amazon or the Yangtze, and I struggled on too with my unpublishable college romances that make me cringe when I recall their ineptitude. Night after night I heard his typewriter, and he reassured me that the sound of mine was music to his ears.

Finally it got to be too much for me. Not the writing, but Harold's belief that he and I were engaged in the same kind of enterprise. The more I heard his machine, knowing that when it stopped he would seek me out for what he called "shop talk," the more it graveled me. And so, because I was constrained to leave the rooming house and find another place to write, I regard it as Harold's doing that I went out and fell in love.

The closest campus building to my rooming house was the old music school, which I had had no reason to visit before. Now as I wandered through its seedy corridors in search of a quiet corner where I could write undisturbed, I was charmed by the mishmash of sounds that filtered out to the hallway— fiddles tuning up like cats in pain, cellos clearing their throats, clarinets showing off, sopranos trilling loudly as if terrorized— sounds that happily bore no relation to my work.

I chose an empty practice room, slipped into a chair with a writing arm in front of the piano, and was deep in my work when a girl walked in and said, "I'm sorry, but I signed up for this room for this period." She didn't sound at all sorry.

"You want to practice?" I asked. I was a little stupid not just from surprise, but because she was an excitingly attractive girl, downy, dark and snapping-eyed.

"It's not just that I want to," she explained, zipping open her briefcase and placing a Czerny volume on the piano rack. "I have to."

I persuaded as hard as I could, and finally succeeded in getting her to let me stay on and work while she did her exercises. Elaine was intrigued with my having selected such an unlikely place in which to write. At four-thirty, when she had finished her stint, I walked her to her dorm; then we had dinner together and walked the streets, telling each other about ourselves, until eleven o'clock. The next morning we met for breakfast, and in two days we were in love.

Now we did together what before we had done alone. We embraced on a bench late at night at the edge of town, and I read Yeats aloud to her by the light of the street lamp. Because I had given her *The Tower*, Elaine attuned me to the passions of the Schubert Trios in the record room of the Women's League. We arose early, anxious to come together, and met at dawn where we could hitch a ride from the milk wagon, breakfasting as we clattered along on a sackful of jelly doughnuts and a container of milk sold us by the driver. We walked, walked, walked, alongside the Huron River, through the Arboretum, past the stadium and on out into the country, on the railroad tracks, under viaducts, across golf courses and meadows, stealing pumpkins and, back in town, scuffling through heaps of leaves piled up for burning.

The happy surprise was not only that I was loved (although I could not stop wondering that I, I of all unlikely people, should cause such a girl's face to come alive when she caught sight of me) but that I could still do all I had before, and more. My schoolwork flourished, and I found that, sitting alongside Elaine while she frowned over her scores, I was writing more fluently than ever before.

As winter came on, though, Elaine and I were driven from our meadows, lakeside paths and park benches, and we grew to detest the icy ivy wall of her dormitory, where we ended our days at one o'clock on a Sunday morning clinging not alone but in concert with rows of other gasping, groping, miserable couples. It was then that I began to realize how much more bold and resourceful than I this seemingly fragile girl was; and it was disconcerting to have to admit to myself that worship and awe were not enough, that I simply did not understand women in general and Elaine in particular. I could not reconcile her delicate frame, her narrow bones, and the way she fitted into the circle of my arms, with her cool determination that we find a way to be alone together. She was only nineteen and had been too busy with her music to run around much with boys, but her eagerness for absolute intimacy gave me the uneasy feeling that she must already have had a string of lovers as long as my arm.

A premonitory shudder went through me, and not just because of the danger involved. But the inflaming vision of the two of us alone together in the darkness, warm, safe, locked in a fast embrace, overwhelmed the compunctions of inexperience. I had already told Elaine all about my rooming house, about the fellows on the second floor who knew that I was trying to write undisturbed and never came up to the attic without knocking, about Mrs. Bangs, who always turned in early. And about Harold, always tapping out his yarns at the dining-room table and leaving the sliding doors ajar so that he could collar me for shop talk.

"It's perfectly obvious," Elaine said coolly, "that if you don't want me to slip in behind you and go on up while you engage him in conversation, you'll have to put it to him man to man and see if he'll help us."

Man to man! Even the wicked glance with which she accompanied that cliché could not quite remove the curse from it. Still, it was worth trying to win Harold's support, considering that his wife was a devout Methodist Episcopalian, much involved with the Epworth League when she was not mopping or scrubbing. So, after all those weeks of avoiding him, one day I brought Harold his mail.

He had been wondering, he said, why he hadn't seen me lately and hadn't even heard my portable clacking away. Was I in a dry spell? He had never had that trouble himself, but he did have a book about writers' block, put aside for such an eventuality.

No, I assured him, it was just that I had taught myself to write longhand. "The reason is," I wound up, with none of the dash of Robert Montgomery or Melvyn Douglas, "I've got a girl."

Harold cracked his knuckles and scratched speculatively at his stubble, then flicked a kitchen match across his gritty blackened thumbnail to touch flame to the damp butt that hung from the corner of his mouth. He was not the sort to get his kicks from prying into others' sex lives. "Well," he opined, releasing smoke through his nostrils, "as long as it doesn't interfere with your work."

I hastened to reassure him. And I went on, with a glibness that surprised me, to tell Harold how Elaine had inspired me, and how well we worked together, and what a shame it was that she couldn't keep me company in my room while I typed just as I did her while she practiced her scales and sonatas.

Without changing expression, as though he hadn't been listening, or simply wanted to change the subject, Harold mumbled, "The missus has got an Epworth League meeting this Saturday night, right after supper. Myself, I'll take advantage of the peace and quiet to lock myself in here and get some typing done."

My temples started to pound when I realized what Harold was telling me. The next few days passed in such fevered anticipation that I scarcely noticed how matter-of-factly my sweet Elaine took Harold's clearing the coast. When I think of it, she was not unlike those coeds I hear about nowadays, who move in and out of their boy friends' rooms as casually as if the boys were their brothers. People weren't all that different when I was in school; it was just that love was a little more difficult, and you had to be more circumspect—unless, like Elaine, you were born self-assured and knowing what you wanted.

After the first rapturous nights we grew almost careless, up in our hideaway. Once I concealed Elaine in the shower when Mrs. Bangs suddenly shuffled up the steps bearing soap and a light bulb that she had forgotten to bring up earlier; another time I had to throw on a bathrobe and run my fingers through my hair at eight-thirty in the evening to answer Mrs. Bangs's buzz—two short, three long—summoning me to the telephone.

But we managed to keep our rendezvous all through the winter without being discovered, thanks not only to the tact of my housemates (some of whom were envious, others amused) but even more to my accomplice and accessory in fornication, Harold Bangs. Never once did he become sly or leering when he made his offhand remarks about his wife's comings and goings. All he asked in return was that I continue to acknowledge our literary fellowship, which I could do only in the most begrudgingly reluctant manner.

Neither of us had been having what you might call a smashing success with our respective efforts, unless you were to count the handwritten note of encouragement I'd gotten on a story rejected by *Esquire*. But Harold was unquenchable, and unchangeable in his absolute self-assurance that one day the gates would be opened for him by the elect, while I, if somewhat more prey to self-doubt and occasional despair, was buoyed up by Elaine's avowals of faith in me.

Elaine liked the idea of my being a writer. "I want success for you even more than I do for myself!" she cried one night, and I was transported. When the Michigan *Daily* announced a spring writing contest, Elaine went after me to enter it. I had never gotten mixed up with the campus literary crowd, even to the extent of submitting my stuff to their magazine. To Elaine I explained that they were a bunch of poseurs, big-city intellectuals trying to impose their tastes on us provincials; but in my heart I dreaded the possibility of rebuff. It was one thing to be honorably rejected, no matter how often, by unseen editors in high places, but it would be quite another to be brushed aside as unworthy of publication even in a campus magazine by people of my own age.

I don't know whether Elaine understood the real reason for my hesitancy. In any case, she swept away the ostensible ones, and by repeated assurances of faith convinced me that I should enter the competition, which called not for a short story or a piece of journalism but for a character study, a portrait of someone unusually odd or interesting. The winner was to be awarded a hundred dollars plus publication of his sketch.

If I say that it was Elaine's idea for me to write about Harold Bangs, I hasten to add that I accepted it enthusiastically and gave it all I had. To be sure, I changed his name, calling it "Howard: Portrait of an Unsuccessful Hack"; I changed his habitat from a rooming house to a trailer, in which he wrote science fiction while his wife was out demonstrating kitchen ware at neighborhood parties; and I doctored him up in other small ways that would, I felt sure, prevent his being recognized by anyone but the other fellows in the house, such as giving him a wooden leg instead of bad lungs. But I retained the essentials, the stacks of incoming and outgoing manuscripts, the clattering old typewriter, the glass ashtrays choked with butts, the smell of dead cigarettes and the feel of falling hair, and above all the look of Harold the happy fanatic, with his sleeve garters, dead-white skin, and cadaver's growth of whiskers, tapping out his malformed fantasies at the mahogany table from which he never rose, embedded forever in that gloomy room like a dead dictator in a wax museum.

Well, I won. It was a sweet day, with a girl to embrace me on the street when I told her the news, with teachers and other skeptics to call out congratulations, with the spring air invading even my stuffy attic room while I composed my letter home of pardonable triumph and vindication. Then came word that the *Daily* had sold my sketch to an intercollegiate press association for syndication across the country.

For a day my article was everywhere, and for a little while I was a hero, at least to Elaine and to myself. But then my stories began coming back, seemingly faster than ever, with the same printed rejection slips. And one night as I was sorting through the dismal mail on the hall table, a voice called out to me from beyond the dining room's sliding doors.

"Mr. Harlow, would you come in here?"

It was Mrs. Bangs. But what would she be doing asking me into Harold's sanctum? With the bad news tucked under my arm, I moved uneasily down the hallway to see what was up. To my astonishment Mrs. Bangs was standing beside Harold, her red and roughened hand resting on his rounded shoulder. Before she could say anything, however, he spoke.

"Congrats, Tommy, on the prize and the sale. I knew you'd hit if you stuck at it." For once he was not smoking, and his hand seemed to tremble as he passed it along his bristles. His shoulder blades jutted like a twin hump.

I peered at him across the student lamp, but before I could thank him Mrs. Bangs said, her voice shaking, "You have chosen a poor way to repay confidence and friendship. Harold is too polite to say it, but you have disappointed us both."

I was sick with embarrassment. I stammered, "I'm afraid I don't know what you mean."

"Don't say that," she said, blinking rapidly. "You knew who you were writing about. It would have been different if we had been mean to you, or intolerant. But you never had a better friend here than Harold. Isn't that true?"

What did she know? I stared at Harold. Had he told her? Nothing like that showed in his face. He looked wretched, but not as though he had given me away. On the other hand, how did I look? Fortunately his den had no mirror.

"Yes," I said to Mrs. Bangs, "it's true. Harold has been very loyal."

"And you made a joke out of him for your own gain." Mrs. Bangs had tears in her eyes, but she wouldn't stop.

Oh God, I said to myself. Aloud I said, "Honestly, I didn't think of it that way."

"Well, you should have, because I do. I work hard to keep this house nice, and quiet for my husband so he can concentrate on his writing. And you come along and treat it all like some kind of dirty joke. My husband is nobody to laugh at, Mr. Harlow." Now she was weeping openly.

"Harold," I said miserably, "I didn't mean—"

"It's all right, kid." Harold cracked his knuckles. "The missus just got upset, what with me not having any luck lately with my own stuff. But I'll hit one of these days, just like you did."

"I know you will," I said. "I'm sure of it."

"It's just a question of time. Maybe I won't make it like you did, but I'll make it. You and I work in different ways, is all. I have to make things up. I couldn't write about what happened to me, or about my family or friends. I couldn't do that."

Even as I backed out of that artificially lit, artificially lived-in room, mumbling apologies to the couple whom I was seeing together for the first—and last—time, my heart was hammering triumphantly in my chest. Harold had put his nicotine-stained finger directly on the difference between us, a difference on which I was ready to stake my life.

For when the chips were down, Harold would never dare; and I always would. Even on his own limited terms, his caution condemned him to failure, since, immured in his dark study and his immature fantasies, he shrank not just from human beings but from the materials of his own life; while my ruthlessness, of which I had not known myself capable, assured me that, with all the failures in store for me on all the hall tables of my future, I was bound for certain ironic petty successes (even though they were to be most gallingly belated), bought at a price Harold would never be prepared to pay.

And so, victory strangely mingled in my heart with self-disgust at seeing that it was Harold and not I who had defined the boundaries separating us, I slunk from his room and from his wife's contempt and despair. I could be bold on paper, I would be bold on paper again, I was certain of it now. But I would always be a coward in other ways.

A few weeks later the semester was over and I tiptoed out of the Bangs house with my two valises and my laundry bag, leaving the final week's rent in an envelope on the accursed table so as not to have to face Harold or Mrs. Bangs again. And that summer, my love affair with Elaine already dying, I returned to the lifeguard's job and to my typewriter.

THE BALCONY

THEIR ROOM had seemed ideal at first sight. High-ceilinged and airy, it had a cool, shabby, clean appearance that was most inviting. Madeline stepped to the jalousies and tugged at them gently, and as the sun came streaming through, outlining her slight figure, she turned to smile at her husband.

"It *is* nice," she said. "It looks out on the street. Very lively."

Brian nodded to the hotel owner's wife, who stood at his side, the huge door key in one hand, a scrubbrush in the other. "*Muy bueno, Señora.* We'll take it."

But they should have known better, for it was hardly their first day in the country. No sooner had Brian lugged their bags up from the lobby, and Madeline shaken the wrinkles out of their folded clothes, than they were stunned by a roar that started at the corner two stories below and seemed to increase in volume and intensity as it blasted through the open window, driving directly at them. They stared at each other, almost frightened. Then Madeline walked to the window and looked down.

"It's one of those trailer trucks—what did you used to call them in Kansas?"

"Semis. But for God's sake, it sounds like he's driving it right into the bedroom."

"It must be because the street is rather narrow and the walls are so high. They almost seem to slant inward, toward the street, as they go up, so maybe it's—" Madeline seated herself in the wicker rocker and rubbed at her ankle— "something like an optical illusion, only for the ears."

"Always the invocation of science. Has it struck you that the Avenida Juarez happens to be the main drag for all the bus and truck traffic out of town?"

"Did it strike you? It was you who marched us up here from the bus station because you didn't want to be right in the town square."

"I wanted to save money. And it just occurred to me about the highway." He was about to say more when the air was filled with a shrieking whine, punctuated with a series of rhythmic rattles. Brian winced. "They're zeroing in on us." He raised his voice. "Madeline! Pack up that stuff and let's blow. I never heard anything this bad in Florence, not even in Rome."

"It never did us any good to move in Italy, either. We could never afford the kind of place that was quiet, could we? Come, let's go for a walk and look over the market. Maybe it'll be quiet tonight, after supper."

But the city, for all its pleasures, was no more quiet than any other Latin town. Children played tag, women bickered in the market, an old Indian hawked noisemakers, a young blind beggar girl moaned from her shawled huddle on the spittle-stained sidewalk.

They bought a pair of unyielding huaraches made from old truck tires for Brian, an impractical comb carved by hand from one piece of wood for Madeline, and a kilo of red bananas that they could peel and munch on as they strolled the musical streets. They tried to figure out the tub of humming insects casually guarded by a yellow-toothed old lady, and what the dignified and distant Indian squatting on his shredded serape could earn even if he were to sell every one of his little pyramid of speckled apples. Then the seasonal afternoon rains came, and they paused, taking shelter under the hospitable awning of a sidewalk café for a leisurely coffee. But there, across the road, under the overhang of a building that hardly protected her from the straight down-driving rain, knelt the blind girl in her black tatters, her rebozo stretched tautly across the narrow curve of her shoulders. At her side a naked baby a year old, perhaps two, a stick of bamboo clutched in his small fingers, dabbled his other hand in the water that gushed furiously from the drainpipe next to him, while his mother continued to move her lips in the singsong whining chant that was now inaudible above the drumming of the summer rain: "*Por amor de Dios, por amor de Dios.*"

In sudden fury, Brian grasped Madeline by the forearm. "Do you see that? She doesn't even stop her pitch in a thunderstorm. Nobody to listen, nobody could hear her anyway, but she keeps right on wailing."

"I'm sure the poor thing was trained to beggary from childhood. It's particularly horrible when you think that there's no need for it any longer."

"I suppose you mean atomic energy and all that crap. Well, in the meantime I take it as a personal affront. If I emptied my pockets into that baby's dirty little paw, what good would it do?" He held up his hand to forestall her reply. "I know, I know, charity isn't the answer. But I don't want to write to my congressman, I just want to paint."

"You might have thought of that before you suggested that we come to an underdeveloped country."

"Logic again. Why is it that your logic is always based on sentimentality? You know, I read someplace that they rent those babies by the day, the beggar women. Very effective with the tourists."

"Brian, you go to the most disgusting extremes to protect yourself from pain. Even if that was true, would it make the baby's plight any the less terrible? Or her mother's? Or this girl's?"

"How would you know? You're worse than your mother, always exhibiting her self-satisfaction by making like a mother. You haven't even got the excuse that she does."

Madeline said, almost inaudibly, "And whose fault would that be?"

"All right, I shouldn't have said that. But you know, I think if you lived in a world without misery, you'd have to invent some in order to be happy."

"I'm getting out of here. The rain's stopped."

Brian folded some bills under his saucer and hastened after Madeline, who was already striding up the street. He took her arm and slowed her pace as they crossed the Zocalo. There was noise there too, but it was more what they had hoped for, the rattling soulfulness of a strolling mariachi band, and with the help of the players the time passed more pleasantly until the late dinner hour.

After they had eaten, however, they were both very tired and ready for bed, and there was no excuse for them to stay away from their room. The hotelkeeper barely inclined his bald dome away from his vacant contemplation of the evening paper as they passed before the desk and mounted to the second floor. At the head of the broad stairway they came abruptly upon the hollow open square off which opened the dozen rooms of the second story. The emerging stars and the wedge of moon, riding slowly through a soft bank of clouds, illuminated the begonias and cactuses in their terra-cotta pots on the margin of the open square.

"Be careful, Brian," Madeline murmured. "The tiles are still slippery from the rain. A cactus spike can really hurt if you fall on it."

"It isn't the rain that worries me, it's the noise." Brian closed their door behind them. "I know you've heard this routine before, but if they're going to be pounding at us all the time, what kind of work can I get done in the next couple of weeks?"

"Sometimes I wish that we could trade places. I wish that you had to listen to those seventh-graders snickering while you were trying to show them color values, and trying to think what to make for supper, and where to go that would be cheap on our vacation. If you had to, you'd do it, that's all." Madeline turned back the bedcovers and began to step out of her skirt.

"That's what you said in Mexico City, and I still couldn't draw a line, with all that racket. The difference between you and me is that you love what you do, *especially* when it's unpleasant. But I hate to paint, I admit it, it hurts. I welcome any little distraction."

"Haven't I always done my best to protect you from distractions?"

"Yes, you have, baby, and I love you for it. Now do you mind if I read for a while?"

"The light won't bother me. But I do need my sleep."

"Of course you do. How else could you have the strength to take care of me?"

Somewhere below, the doors of a cantina swung open, and a roar of laughter, followed by a tenor raised in romantic song and a bellowing protest, floated up to their window. Madeline raised her head from the pillow to stare anxiously at her husband. His lips were set in a thin line; his large pale eyes stared unseeingly at the book before him.

"It'll surely stop soon," Madeline whispered. "After all, they need their relaxation too."

"From what? You don't have to whisper—*they* can't hear *you*."

"Do you really believe that rotten propaganda about them sleeping in their sombreros all day? Because if you do I—" She could not finish; at that instant a semi came blasting up the highway and shifted gears at the corner beneath them with a grinding clatter and a rising howl that seemed aimed deliberately and directly at their hearts.

They stared at each other, united in despair.

"Maybe if we closed the windows part way . . ."

"Part way won't do."

"Then let's—" Madeline raised her voice as a motor scooter

howled and howled higher and higher, straining as it swung around the heavy truck.

Brian hauled himself out of bed and clopped to the window. "If I close these jalousies we'll stifle."

"We can open the door."

It was a bad night. They tried everything, but in the end it was useless. If they barricaded themselves they could not breathe; if they allowed air in, they were engulfed by the shock waves of the street noises. Only toward dawn did the sounds subside at last, so that they could drop off finally with nothing but the calls of the awakening songbirds to punctuate their fitful slumber.

Early in the morning two small girls began to play with an inflated rubber ball in the open patio beyond their door. The ball smacked sharply each time it struck the terrazzo, with a loud report like gunfire, and the voices of the little girls were shrill.

"Those damn brats. Let's get up and have breakfast."

"Brian, I'd try to find us a place in the country, but where? What will you do? You claim you can't work without stimulation."

"I claim. How about you? Don't you like to see different faces sometimes too?" Tugging at his trousers, Brian stared red-eyed at his wife. "Are you going to start in on me before breakfast? Are you going to tell me what I know better than you, that I ought to be painting all year instead of just trying to sketch in the summer? Are you going to put in for a medal because you haven't saddled me with kids and a mortgage?"

Madeline replied in a very steady voice, "I am going down-stairs to see if they can't give us a quieter room."

"The idea being that we could fight better on a good night's sleep, is that it?"

"If you like. I'll see you at breakfast."

Somewhat abashed, Brian temporized. "I'll order breakfast while you negotiate. Would you like *huevos rancheros*? Papaya?"

"Lime with the papaya, please."

There was a vacant room on the far side of the court, the quieter side; its small balcony overlooked only the local street. After breakfast they packed up and hauled their stuff across the sunny patio to the new room.

The morning sun, streaming in through the open windows and throwing the intricate shadows of the wrought-iron balcony across the woven-fiber rug, made everything seem at least bearable, and hopefully even pleasant.

"I guess this might do, don't you think?" Brian asked his wife.

Madeline replied, a bit doubtfully, "The movie house is just across the way."

"At least it doesn't open until four o'clock. Then I think you get a triple feature for your four pesos and you go home."

What they did not know was that the blind beggar woman was in the habit of stationing herself with her baby on the sidewalk in front of the movie theater every afternoon.

It was several days before Brian himself had this brought to his attention. He and Madeline did in fact sleep better in the new room and in consequence were in a good humor to explore the city at leisure, to sketch and read in the parks and plazas, and occasionally to swim.

One afternoon, when they had returned for a siesta in the shade of their high, dark, airy room, Madeline stepped onto the balcony to hang their bathing suits out to dry. As she glanced across the street, she uttered an involuntary cry.

"What's the matter, Madeline?"

"Oh, nothing. There's a blind woman in front of the Teatro Alhambra. She looks just like the one that's always at the entrance to the public market."

Brian jumped to his feet. "Let's see." Wrapped in a towel, his bare feet slapping on the tiles, he joined his wife and peered down, following the direction of her finger. "That's my girl friend. And there's the baby. He sits there sucking at that damned sugar cane as though he'll never have a care in the world. Dopey little bastard."

He took his sketch pad and pen from the round wicker table and dragged the armchair forward so that its front legs hung out onto the little balcony. Then he sat down and began at once to draw.

Madeline watched over his shoulder for a moment as the figures began quickly to emerge from the blank pebbled paper. She touched her fingers tentatively to her husband's sparse, wind-ruffled hair, smoothing it into place, and said almost shyly, "You'll get arrested if you don't put something on."

"Later, later," Brian muttered impatiently, and continued to sketch swiftly, whistling almost soundlessly through his teeth as he worked.

Pleased, Madeline tiptoed back inside, picked up an orange-backed Penguin novel, and stretched herself quietly across the bed.

Every day thereafter Brian took up his post on the balcony, sometimes sitting, sometimes leaning against the wobbly wrought iron, staring down at the lively panorama below him and occasionally, but less and less frequently as the days slipped by, trying to draw: brown women with pale-green woven baskets on their heads, barefoot children slapping at flies and at one another as they ran laughing around carts and burros, sunglassed and sombreroed tourists staring impatiently, pink-faced, at the unconstrained life around them—and always, shortly before the movie opened its doors to the townsfolk and peasants, the blind woman squatting in her tatters with the nude infant at her side and her terrible empty eyes upraised, keening softly her dreadful demand.

"My window on the world." Brian extended his arm in a grandiose gesture. "I envision myself as an old man here, complete with pipe and slippers and sketch pad, jotting down my observations on those still climbing the hill."

"How about the meantime?"

"You couldn't resist that crack, could you? It's easy to be demanding when you're safe yourself—there's never been a lady painter who wasn't a second-rater. Yet I don't see you even trying to sketch, and you went to art school just like I did. What's the matter, are you so worn out from baby-sitting those seventh-graders that you can't even pick up a Conté crayon?"

"I wouldn't want you to feel I was competing." Madeline spoke between pinched lips. "All the best handbooks say it unmans an American husband."

"You want to know what unmans me?" Brian tore the topmost sheet from his sketch pad, crumpled it and threw it over the balcony railing. "It's that goddam blind female, scrunched up there, mumbling about love and God. She won't let me work, she sits there daring me to ignore her or to love her and help her—and I can't do either."

"I suppose that's as good an excuse as any. It's better than the ones you had in Perugia and Cagnes and Torremolinos. Poverty should be as challenging to an artist as to a social scientist."

Brian swore. "It must be wonderful to be so liberal-minded that you can wipe out the smell of misery with one of those little cliché catchalls that you carry around with you like a spray deodorant. I wish I had your faith in progress. I could explain to that flea-ridden, half-starved bag of bones over there that her underdeveloped nation must make the leap into the industrial age. That she should petition for increased participation in UNESCO and bigger grants-in-aid from Uncle Sam. It's so much more reassuring to pin a label on her wretchedness than to give her the price of a handful of *garbanzos*, isn't it?"

Madeline replied in a trembling voice, "I never stopped you from giving her charity. If it would make you feel better than painting her—which is what you've been trained to do—you could wrap up your dinner in a napkin and give it to her every day."

"You know what I'd like to give her? A swift kick. I'd love to give her a boot and say, That's for tormenting me. That's for rolling those blind venereal eyes and blaming me that nobody put drops in them when you were born. That's for picking the busiest corners in town to do business, but not having the guts or the strength to raise your voice to the customers above a whining whisper. Then I'd give her one last shove, for borrowing a lousy little brat that hasn't even got sense enough to cry, but just sits there in the dirt all day like a corny prop for a proletarian movie." Brian sighed, shudderingly, and fell back in the heavy chair. "Now you know what I say to myself every day when I come out here and look."

"I'm sorry. Maybe we ought to go home, Brian. It was a good idea up to a point, but—"

"But we've passed the point? Or missed it? Well, even if we have, the apartment is rented till Labor Day, remember?"

"All right, then. We'll continue to sun ourselves and stare at the beggar girl—is that the program? If only I could convince you that I've never lost faith in you! Wouldn't that mean anything? Wouldn't that help?"

"Not as much as a little honest skepticism. Have you ever thought of trying that?"

They might have continued as Madeline had indicated, save for a rather ridiculous accident. The next afternoon, after Madeline had gone shopping, Brian padded over to the balcony to bring in his plaid bathing trunks from the railing. He felt a drop on his bare shoulder (he was wearing only dungarees and huaraches) and glanced up; yes, the rain was beginning a little early. He was about to turn away to push the armchair back into the room where it would be safe from the rain when it seemed to him that from the corner of his eye he could espy the blind woman feeling her way along the rough stucco wall of the movie palace, inching forward to her post with the infant wrapped tightly in the shawled crook of her arm.

Brian leaned forward to make sure and accidentally brushed his trunks from their resting place, straight down to the sidewalk two stories below. He peered down through the bars at the little particolored bundle lying like a discarded rag on the sidewalk, then shoved the armchair back into the room, slammed the long windows closed, and hastened across to the open patio, which was already slick with rain and darkened with the reflection of the metallic sky above.

Rather than cling to the shelter of the wall and its little over-hang, he decided to cut across the patio to the main stair-way. Halfway there, he felt the drizzle quicken to a downpour; Brian spurred his gait to reach the sanctuary of the covered staircase, but instead his foot suddenly went flying out from under him. He landed in a wet heap on the slimy smooth stone, his right leg bent grotesquely beneath him.

He twisted himself into a sitting position, but when he attempted to rise, his leg flamed with pain. Huddled weakly under the pounding of the tropical rain, he began to sob aloud.

As he sat, soaked and trembling, his head against his knees and his arms wrapped tight about his calves, the two little girls who had disturbed his sleep on the first day of his arrival stuck their heads out of their room and regarded him curiously. He raised his head and glanced at them, only half recognizing them and so only half acknowledging their existence, but they came all the way out onto the patio, wrapped from braided hair to ankles in plastic ponchos.

They approached him warily, one on either side of him, as if his injury might have made him dangerous. Chattering with soft rapidity in Spanish, they knelt and took him firmly by the arms. He could not say to two small children, Leave me, I want to be left alone, so he allowed them to help him to his feet. His right leg buckled under him, but by bending the knee deeply in a kind of swoop and at the same time stepping delicately on the ball of the foot, he found that he could make his way with their assistance through the blinding rain to his bedroom door. With mature dexterity they maneuvered him over the ledge and through the door, which they worked open, to his bed, where they held him gently while he lowered himself to a prone position. Then, before he could protest, the older one had knelt at his side and removed his soaked huaraches, while the younger sister, whose front teeth were still missing, brought him a towel from the washstand to mop the rain and perspiration from his bare skin.

"*Gracias, gracias,*" he mumbled as they stared down at him

unsmilingly from either side of the bed, their dripping ponchos falling away from the braids that hung to their shoulders, the delicate gold hoops glinting below their pierced earlobes.

He leaned over to the bedside table and took from it the paper sack of huge, sugar-sprinkled cookies that Madeline had bought to indulge a bedtime sweet tooth. But when the girls reached, tentatively, each for a single cookie, he tossed the entire bag to them. *"Tómate esa!"* They accepted it gravely, without protest, executed a funny little bow, as though they were retreating from royalty, and backed out of the room almost at a run.

After that Brian lay there, without moving, listening to the sounds of the moviegoers filtering up faintly through the closed windows. for what must have been several hours. When Madeline returned at last, the rain had stopped; the sun had returned too, and it sparkled through the windows onto the chair where his sketch pad lay abandoned.

"Hello," Madeline said. "I almost got caught in the shower. But there was this crazy parrot—" She stopped abruptly. "Why are you so wet?"

"I fell, with my leg under me. Now I don't seem to be able to move."

"Oh my God, I'll get a doctor. Are you in pain?"

"Not as long as I lie still. Those two little girls next door practically carried me back in. I was going down to get my swimsuit—it fell off the railing. Did you happen to see it on your way in?"

Madeline laughed a trifle hysterically. "You're the one who's always calling me naïve. If you dropped a washrag, it would be gone in two seconds."

"Take a look out the balcony," Brian insisted. "Humor me."

Madeline peered through the window. "No," she said after a moment, "there's nothing down on the sidewalk. Nothing."

"Now see if you can spot the blind one and the baby over by the box office."

"Why?" But, not waiting for an answer, Madeline craned

her neck. "No, no sign of her. Does that make you feel better?"

"Worse. Don't be malicious."

"I'm sorry. I didn't mean it that way. I'm going down now to see about a doctor."

"Which we can't afford."

"Don't be ridiculous. Can I get you anything while I'm downstairs?"

Brian shook his head. "Unless you want more cookies. I gave the bag to the kids for helping me in."

Madeline stammered something incoherent and hurried out. It seemed hardly a moment before she was back, breathing hard and looking a little peculiar.

"The Señora says the girls told her about you, and she took the liberty of calling a masseur. He is supposed to be here any minute."

Brian started to laugh. "If he can't help, maybe they'll send a voodoo doctor."

"Do you suppose," Madeline asked nervously, "we could explain to him that it was a mistake, when he arrives? Otherwise we'd just have to pay him and start all over again. You ought to have an X ray—we don't know if you sustained a fracture."

"Sustained?" Brian laughed again. "I sustained worse than that. But I didn't break any bones. Sometimes I think I don't have any to break. I could use a good rubdown, though. As a matter of fact, so could you. When he gets here, let's ask him if he has a special rate for aching couples."

"Please don't make any more jokes. It's no better than seeing a chiropractor, or a naturopath. What'll we tell him when he gets here?"

"I don't know about you, Madeline, but I've had a bellyful of science. I'd like the touch of a healing hand for a change, instead of just a diagnosis and a prescription."

"Oh, Brian . . ."

There was a knock at the door. Brian said politely, "Please let him in, dear."

Madeline opened the door to a big-bellied, jovial man of fifty, with a wrestler's neck, a gold tooth, and a large black bag, which he gripped in his muscular brown fist. In the other hand he held a panama hat, as immaculate as his white blouse, which was delicately embroidered at the cuffs, the throat, and along the front and back panels.

"Good afternoon, I am sorry I am so late." He spoke a heavily accented but very rapid English. "I am mostly retired. My wife takes the messages when I go out. You have trouble with the leg?"

"The right one. Madeline, would you get a chair for Señor—?"

"Call me Tony, I am known widely as Tony." He flashed a smile. "No chair is necessary, Madam."

"Can you tell," Madeline demanded tensely, "if the leg is broken?"

The masseur bowed. "I am thirty years in the business, eighteen years at the Chicago Athletic Club." He manipulated Brian's leg tentatively but tenderly. "If there is a break, we have to have splints, no? But I believe not here. How you fell?"

"In the rain. I was starting to run." Brian went through the ludicrous episode again, keeping his gaze on the masseur, away from Madeline.

"And it hurts here."

"Yes!"

"And here."

"Yes. Not as much."

"But not here?"

"No. You see, I can walk on it, if I keep my leg bent." He glanced at Madeline. "I can limp around quite rapidly, and without any pain at all, except that I must look like some godawful freak, a Quasimodo or a boogeyman from a nightmare."

Madeline closed her eyes. Her fists were clenched.

"I know what you mean." The masseur nodded sympathetically. "Lady, will you leave us alone, please."

"Alone?"

"I must remove his garments so to examine and to give him the treatment."

"Oh. Yes, of course." She picked up her purse. "I'll go down to the corner and have a coffee."

"Make it a tequila," Brian advised her. "You could use it."

The door closed behind her and the masseur set to work. Removing his embroidered shirt, he proceeded to don a short-sleeved white blouse which buttoned up the side of the throat and gave him the look of a dentist, a Latin tooth-yanker with big biceps. Then he took a bolt of unbleached muslin from his bag and unrolled it alongside Brian half the length of the bed.

"Now we take off the trousers." He gentled Brian out of the dungarees and out of his shorts as well, and then rolled him onto the muslin and covered his loins with it, exposing the length of his leg. Brian lay back with his arms tucked behind his head.

He asked lazily, "Can you tell what it is?"

"You know the anatomy?"

"I used to know the name of every goddam bone and muscle."

"How come?" The masseur regarded him solemnly, almost with suspicion. "You studied?"

"That's right. I'm an artist—of sorts."

The masseur's broad face cleared. "You paint the nudes."

"Once upon a time. Then I did their insides, but I wasn't very good at the essence either. Then . . . Never mind. What does it look like to you?"

"I think is a ligament, a muscle sprain. Bad, hurts like awful. You know what they call? A Charley horse. Hurts, but is going to be better. Now we use the pressure."

He opened a bottle of liniment and poured some into his clean cupped palms, then proceeded to work the fluid slowly into the soft parts of Brian's leg. The insistent pressure was almost voluptuous. Brian closed his eyes and responded willingly to the masseur's directions to turn, flex, lie still.

Slowly, painstakingly, methodically, he worked over and over the area, stroking, rubbing, pressing with his large, bent thumbs, coaxing away the pain. As he worked he chatted, softly, smoothly, in a liquid, slurred English as soothing as his moistened hands.

"You know Chicago? Art Institute, lots of paintings? Eighteen years I work there. Brr, I freeze in winter. Terrible town to be broke in wintertime, no friends. But then I meet rich men at the Athletic Club. Soon I got money in the bank."

"Are you married?"

"Sure. Not to American girl. Too flashy. How I know they want me, not the bankbook? So I come home for vacation, I marry a girl from here, I take her back to Chicago. Seven years we live there. You know what? Little by little she gets like a flower when you take it out of the ground. Finally she says, Tony, I can't stand the snow in the face on Michigan Boulevard, is not for me. So I take her home. Now I'm retired, but they come down from Chicago, they pass the word. Still I'm in demand, still the services are requested. You got responsibility, people ask for you, you got to go."

"I suppose so. I wouldn't know." Brian raised his head from his arms. "Tony, do you think it's a bad thing, having a wife make sacrifices for you—so that even when she doesn't remind you of them because she knows you can't stand it, you can still see them in her eyes?"

The masseur's vigorous brown hands paused above Brian's leg for an instant, then resumed their hypnotic rhythm. "I can do good for the leg. Maybe when you move around better, you can do good for your wife."

"It's a little late for that."

The masseur showed his gold tooth. "Never too late."

"Didn't your wife look at you cross-eyed, those winter nights in Chicago?"

"*Look* at me? She cried!"

"So you gave in. You took her home."

"Only after I saved up enough money, so we wouldn't live poor in my own city."

"But doesn't it bug you to have the poor all around you, pleading for help—" Brian gestured toward the balcony— "when you know that even if you gave away all your loot, it wouldn't do a damned bit of good?"

The masseur continued to work, and to talk, in the same high good humor with which he had begun. "Nobody can do everything, not even Jesus. Everybody can do a little. I make you feel better, maybe you paint better, you make your wife feel better. Then she make babies."

Brian sat up abruptly. "Are you almost through?"

"Couple minutes more. You like it here, before you hurt the leg?"

"It's more beautiful than Chicago. Nicer people, too."

"But poorer too, huh?"

"You ought to know."

"That's right. You and me both. It's good for us to know."

"Why?" Brian stared at him curiously.

"The better men think about the poor ones. Okay, we're all finish for now." The masseur reached into his hip pocket for his heavy tooled wallet and drew from it a small engraved card. "You want me tomorrow, next day, I come again or you come to me. Maybe we have to strap, but I think no."

Brian accepted the card and struggled into his trousers. "I'm very grateful. How much do I owe you?"

"We make it forty pesos, all right? And don't put weight on the leg yet. Stay still, make the wife work." He smiled, almost secretively, as he rolled up the muslin and the blouse and tucked them away in the bag with the liniment. "When she gets mad, you jump up and run after her. You feel better then."

"I seem to have only a few pesos," Brian said in embarrassment. "Would you mind stopping at the café opposite the movie house and asking my wife to pay you? And would you tell her that I need her?"

"Sure. Let's open the window, give you lots of fresh air."

When the masseur had closed the door behind him, Brian turned his head to observe the setting sun throwing its last beams against the blank plaster wall of the cinema across the street. Already the neon sign had winked on; and although from his prone position he could see nothing of the life on the street below, he could hear quite distinctly the sounds of the motors, the sidewalk vendors, the excited children, and a supplicating mendicant woman. Closing his eyes, he lay back against the pillow and waited for his wife to return.

MY

CONEY ISLAND UNCLE

I NEVITABLY our parents are the bearers of our disillusion. After they have ushered us into the world, they must bring word that Santa does not exist, that camp is out of the question, that Grandma is dying, and that they themselves are flawed by spite and unreason. Sometimes it falls to another grownup to renew in us for a time, through disinterested kindliness, that original seamless innocence, the very notion of which can otherwise become a sour mockery. The lucky ones among us can be grateful for a childhood graced by an unencumbered relative—a bachelor uncle, perhaps—who enjoys us not for what we may become, or may one day owe to him, but simply because we exist. I had such an uncle.

We lived, my parents and I, in a small frame house not far off Main Street in Dunkirk, New York, which is on Lake Erie about halfway between Buffalo and Erie, Pennsylvania. My father had inherited a hardware and agricultural-implements store to and from which he walked every day, and where my mother joined him to keep the books and wait on customers during the hours when I was in school.

My mother was a good sport, I think now, about a life that she could not have foreseen when she fell in love with my father on a summer vacation at Lake Chautauqua. She had been a New York girl with musical ambitions; she often exercised her light and agreeable soprano voice of an evening during my boyhood, accompanying herself at the Aeolian Duo-Art piano father had given her on the occasion of the arrival of her first-born—me, Charley Morrison, who also turned out to be her last-born. Mother solaced herself with introducing me to "the better things" (Friday-night poetry readings at her Sorosis Club, piano lessons with Miss Letts, and reproductions of the Great Masters), traveling to an occasional concert in Buffalo, and taking me to New York every year to visit her three brothers, my uncles Al, Eddie, and Dan.

Uncle Dan was the one who mattered. I can't remember why he happened to be visiting us when I entered kindergarten on the very morning of my fifth birthday. What I do remember, so vividly that the sunlit-noonday thrill of it is still almost painful, is the sight of Uncle Dan coming toward my mother and me on the cracked sidewalk before our little house, which sagged, a bit askew, like my father, as we returned from that terrifying first day of school. He was leading an Irish-setter puppy by a braided leather leash.

Aside from our family doctor, who had bad breath and wore high-top shoes, Uncle Dan was the only real doctor I knew. He might not have been an outstanding physician, but he did know, even though he never married or fathered a son, what could turn the trick with a small boy. As I ran up to him, still trembling from the strange lonely newness of the classroom, he unwound the leash from his fingers and flipped it at me.

"Here you go, Charley boy," he said. "Here's a puppy dog for a good student."

And he stood there, stocky and self-possessed, smiling around his cigar, ignoring my mother's shocked surprise and nudging amusedly at my bottom with his toes as I dropped to my knees to caress my new dog. "Just treat him right, Charley boy," he said, "and you'll have a real friend."

I didn't know how to tell Uncle Dan that he was my favorite.

The other New York uncles were all right, but they had wives and children of their own; he was the one who I felt belonged to me. People said that I looked like him, which was beyond my understanding—he was a burly man with an impudent mop of reddish-brown hair (my father had almost none that I can recall even from my earliest childhood, and I couldn't even tell you the color of the fringe around his ears), and an even more unlikely mustache, full, square, and bristling. How could I resemble a middle-aged man—he must have been in his thirties at that time—with a big thick mustache? It was enough that he would give me a dog, and an occasional boot in the behind, to show me that he appreciated what I didn't dare to tell him.

As the years passed, I came to believe that he would have understood, had he been around, far more than my parents. Not that they didn't try, in that dull and drowsy community. But in the cruel way of children, I often felt, particularly as the depression invaded our lives like a prolonged state of mourning, that they—immured in their dark semibankrupt store that smelled of iron filings and bird seed—had no notion of how they ought to treat me. Else why would they have lied to me after they had my dog put away when he went into distemper convulsions? And why did they take it for a kindness to let me oversleep the grand opening night of the circus, the only half-way exciting event of the year in Dunkirk, after I had worked to the point of exhaustion for a pass, a ticket which they could never have afforded, in those lean days, to buy me?

I was going on thirteen that summer, sullen and rebellious after the circus fiasco, when my father informed me with clumsily evasive tact that, as a reward for having done well in school and helped out at the store, I was to be sent to New York. Alone.

I was old enough to know that my parents could not have come to this decision by themselves. Mother's family had to be consulted, if only because they would have to put me up. My mother had already forgone her annual visit home, but this, as well as the matter of who was paying for my ticket, was something that simply went unmentioned in our household; to bring it up would have been like asking if you were going to get a Christmas present, and how much would be spent on it.

Besides, I had a strong hunch that it was my Uncle Dan who was footing the bill. He was the one with the fewest responsibilities, and it was he who scrawled me the postcard (he never could manage a whole letter) asking if I'd like to batch it with him for a while.

If they had fixed it up not with my Coney Island uncle but with the Manhattan uncles, Al or Eddie, I probably wouldn't even have wanted to go at all. Not that I was spoiled or blasé about New York. But mother and I had always stayed with Uncle Al and Aunt Clara, mother sleeping on the studio couch, me bunking with their boys.

They were all right, but as far as I was concerned there was nothing glamorous or big-city about them. Uncle Al was seldom home except Sunday evenings, when he'd slump down morosely before the radio to listen to Ed Wynn, and Aunt Clara was in the kitchen baking all day, gabbing with mother. She wouldn't let my cousins own bicycles, they didn't even know how to ride, and they never ceased needling me monotonously as a hick. We'd stand around in the concrete courtyard of the apartment house, not a blade of grass in sight, bouncing a sponge-rubber ball back and forth in the little clear space to one side of the corroded green fountain of a nymph with jug that never worked anyway, and taunting each other out of boredom and aimlessness.

"Is this all you guys ever do?" I'd ask. "Isn't there anything else to do in New York, except follow the horseballs in the bridle path in Central Park?"

"Horseballs yourself. Is it true you still got Indians running around loose in Dunkirk? Aren't you afraid of getting scalped? Why do you always say faw-rest and George War-shington?"

And then my mother, with her relentless passion for intellectual improvement, would haul us off on the bus to the Museum of the City of New York to look at dolls costumed as dead mayors' wives, or to the Museum of Natural History to study the pasted-together bones of brontosauruses and tyrannosauruses. After five or six days I was more than ready to go home.

I just knew that it would be different now, staying with my Coney Island uncle. From the moment that father bade me goodbye in the unwashed bus depot that smelled of depression and defeat, stowing his rusty Gladstone in the rack over my head, shaking hands with me shyly, and smiling a reassurance that did not conceal his perpetual somberness, I settled into the new mood of freedom and adventure. All through the long ride down across Pennsylvania, Erie to Warren to Coudersport to Towanda to Scranton to New York, I pitched and rolled on the torn leather seat with the stuffing oozing out, exalted as though I strode the deck of a Yankee clipper. Even the discovery that my uncle was not at the Manhattan Greyhound Terminal to meet me, as he had promised, was exhilarating. I kept a good grip on the valise, as father had advocated, and while I was looking about for Uncle Dan, a lady from Travelers Aid came up and asked if I was Charley Morrison.

"Your uncle is tied up in an emergency. He says to come right out to his place. Now you can take any line of the BMT, can you remember that? Don't take the IRT, you'll get all mixed up."

It was like Uncle Dan, I thought, not to send some stooge relative after me, but to trust me, even though it was already well into the night, to find my way out to Coney Island. I got there without trouble, hauled the valise down the steps of the elevated into the street at Surf Avenue, and walked straight up the block, milling and restless as Times Square, even at midnight, to the corner where Uncle Dan's signs hung in all his second-floor windows. Just as I was reaching out to punch his night bell I heard my uncle's familiar voice behind me, deep and drawling.

"Charley boy! Have a nice ride?"

I swung around. Uncle Dan was standing there smiling,

medical bag in his left hand, cigar and door key in his right. His hat was shoved back on his head, and his Palm Beach suit was wrinkled at the crotch; he had put on some weight and seemed tired, but otherwise he looked the same.

"Let's just throw our bags in the hall, so we can go out and grab a bite."

He led me around the corner and up the ramp, gritty with sand, to the boardwalk. Above us the looped wires of bulbs drooped like heavy necklaces, the neon lights of stores and stands slashed on and off, some hurling their arrows hopelessly after each other, others stabbing into the sky like red-hot sparks, and the night was so illumined by them all that you could follow the smoke from the skillets of the hamburger joints high into the air before it disappeared into the darkness, along with the hot steam of the coffee urns. Amidst the acrid smell of burning molasses, before salt-water-taffy machines swaying rhythmically as they pulled the fat, creamy ribbons to and fro, girls opened cupid's-bow mouths to receive huge wobbling cones of cotton candy extended eagerly by their sailor boy friends. The ground shook beneath me with the thudding of thousands of feet on the wooden boardwalk, stained in spots from the wet footprints of late bathers and the spilled soda pop of boys my age who shook up the open bottles and released their thumbs to aim the spray at the unsuspecting before they fled. And over it all the intermittent roar of the plunging roller coaster across the way at Steeplechase Park, its electric controls rattling as it raced down below the horizon like an express train to hell.

Uncle Dan led the way to Nathan's hot-dog stand and said to a Greek counterman, "Two franks well done, Chris, for me and my nephew." He turned to me. "You take yours with sauerkraut? I forget."

I said boldly, "I like mine with everything." Mother would never have let me eat a spicy hot dog in the middle of the night, much less with all that junk smeared, rubbed, and squeezed on it.

"That's your nephew, hey, Doc?"

"Come in from the West to keep me company for a while. We're going to have some fun, us two bachelors." My uncle took a huge bite; I had never before seen anyone handle a hot dog, a cigar, and a toothpick all at once. "And listen, Chris, if this boy comes by with a hungry look during the day, his credit is good."

"I got you." The counterman extended his bare arm, hairy as a gorilla's. "Have a knish, kid."

We washed down the hot dogs and knishes with big shupers of root beer. The glass mugs were heavy as sin, frosty, with foam running down the sides; Uncle Dan blew off some of the suds at me as if we were drinking beer, which was just what I had been secretly pretending. As we strolled on he asked, "What time do they make you go to bed back home?"

I hesitated. I wanted to add thirty minutes to my weekend late limit, but then something made me answer honestly.

Uncle Dan screwed up his face. "That sounds awful damn early to me. At least, it is for Coney Island. Tell you what, if you promise not to snitch to your mother, we'll just forget that curfew stuff while you're staying with me."

I could hardly trust myself to reply.

"Your mother's a good woman," Uncle Dan remarked, in a thoughtful tone that I had never heard him use before. He took me by the elbow and led me to his apartment through the midnight crowds, thicker than we had even for circuses back home. "She's got her troubles, you know, like all of us. But she's my favorite. I mean, your uncles are all right, they're not bad fellows, but they've made a couple mistakes. Number one was when they got married."

As he threw away his cigar, he added, "Number two was when Al and Eddie left Brooklyn. In Manhattan, you don't even realize that you're living on the shore, on the edge of the ocean, the way you do here."

He fell silent, and I, matching my step to his, could not remember when Uncle Dan had ever talked to me so much all at once. After a while he went on, "This is a good place to live. You'll see."

In the two minutes that it took me to fall asleep, I observed that Uncle Dan came to bed beside me in his drawers. It was a practice that my mother condemned as disgusting, but I resolved to put my pajamas back into father's Gladstone next morning. Mother thought too that you couldn't get really clean in a shower, and at home we had a monstrous old claw-legged tub that we filled part way with kettles of boiling water from the kitchen stove, in a bathroom so drafty that we stuffed the casement with rags and plugged in two electric heaters from the store ten minutes before bathtime. But Uncle Dan's shower stall, into which I leaped when I awoke, with Uncle Dan already halfway through his office hours down the corridor, had a ripply-glass door with a chrome handle, the first I'd ever seen outside of the movies, and water that kept coming out hot, forever.

I did get a rather haphazard tourist's view of New York in the days that followed—waiting in line with the other out-of-towners on Sixth Avenue to see a Marlene Dietrich movie about the Russian Revolution at Radio City Music Hall, riding the elevator to the top of the Empire State Building to peer down at the tiny pedestrians who might be Uncle Al or Uncle Eddie ("from up here your uncles look like ants")—but what entered deep into my being was a sense of the variety and richness of possibility in the city, a sense of how one could, if one only wished, enter any of a number of communities, each as unique as the single one in the small town I had left behind.

Uncle Dan did this for me, and without even realizing it. All he knew was that it might be fun for me to tag along with him for a while. It never occurred to him that just by exposing me to his daily round, which to him was not particularly exciting but pleasant enough so that he had no deep incentive to change it, he was presenting me with motives for persisting in this confounding, fascinating world.

If my father knew everyone who came into his store, everyone knew Uncle Dan when he stepped out onto the street. But there was a difference. On our way to his Buick, which he kept garaged a few blocks away, on Neptune Avenue—I cannot remember whether it was the first or the second day of my visit, for by now everything has blended into a generalized memory of that liberating week, as if the revolution I was experiencing was far more than the sum of its insurrectionary incidents —we were suddenly stopped by a pleading woman.

"Doctor, doctor!" she cried, gasping for breath, holding out her empty reddened hands as though she were extending something precious and hot, like a freshly baked cake. It occurred to me that if she had been carrying something, anything, even a little purse, in those swollen hands, she wouldn't have looked so wild.

"Let's take it easy," my uncle said. He addressed her by some Polish or Slavic name. "Is it your husband? Casper?"

She nodded, trotting alongside us as we approached the car. "He beat up on Mrs. Polanyi. He knock her down, he try to kill her."

"I warned you it was going to happen, didn't I?"

"What I can do? I can send him away? How we going to eat?"

"Well, now you'll have to do it. No two ways." He held open the front door of the car. "Hop in."

She shook her head vigorously. What was this? Why wouldn't she get in? My heart thumping, I stared at the frightened woman, who stood there with her chest heaving, refusing to sit in the front seat.

But Uncle Dan understood. With a sigh he yanked open the rear door. "OK, let's not waste time."

She crawled into the back, and as I settled myself beside my uncle, he muttered, "She thinks it's not polite to sit up front next to the doctor. It's a wonder she'll ride with us at all."

In a few minutes we had pulled up in front of her house, a red-brick tenement indistinguishable from all the others on the block except for the crowd gathered before it. Uncle Dan leaned on the horn with one hand to clear the way as he reached back with the other for his satchel. "Come on, Clara," he said to the woman, who had been crouched on the edge of the seat as if afraid that she might soil it, "we'll go take care of Mrs. Polanyi. Charley boy, you keep an eye on the car."

I couldn't just sit there on that baking Brooklyn street, not with the neighborhood kids staring at me. So I got out and thrust myself into the crowd.

In its midst a girl of about my age, one of her twin braids half unwound, was crying against the bosom of a gray-haired woman.

"What happened?" I asked boldly.

A boy answered wisely, "It was her mother." "Huh muddah" was the way he pronounced it, and it took me a second or two to understand. "The nut stomped on huh. He's a real nut. You the doctor's son?"

Before I could answer, a thin-faced sallow man came out the front door and sauntered down the stoop, pausing only to light a cigarette with a wooden kitchen match. Although he was tieless, he wore a sharp striped suit with a grease stain big as a campaign button on his left lapel; his fly was open. The crowd moved off even while the flame of the match still flickered, before he blew it out. He came directly to me, placing his face so close to mine that I could see the pores on his fleshy nose, and fixed me with his very pale, almost colorless blue eyes. I had the feeling that he was looking through me, at something just behind my head, rather than at me.

"You the doctor's boy?"

"I'm his nephew." I heard mutters from the crowd, which had drifted back to either side of us.

"He's a great man. Man of science. You know science?"

"Not much."

"It powers the world. You know science, you got hidden power. Mrs. Polanyi, she was tuned in. She was wired for sound. They send her messages against me. Man, she could have destroyed everybody. You know Mrs. Polanyi?"

I shook my head wordlessly. I knew, suddenly, who he was, and what was wrong, but I was not frightened. I was simply curious and fascinated. After a few moments of odd disjointed talk my uncle tramped out in his heavy, solid way, lugging his satchel and blowing on a prescription blank. He beckoned to the crying girl.

"Hey, Jeanette! Take this to Rudnicki's drugstore and get it filled. Your mother'll be all right—I'll stop by tomorrow." He winked at me as he shoved a fresh cigar into his mouth, then turned to the man who had been talking with me. "Casper, you got to go for a ride. You met my nephew already?"

"Sure. He's a smart one. Science, like you. It powers the world." His pupils were the merest pinpoints; his jaws were clamped as if with a wrench; when he smiled it was like a dog baring his fangs.

"Amen. Come on, Casper, let's go. Here comes your wife."

Her handkerchief to her face, she stumbled down the steps and through the ranks of the curious.

"I'm going to need you to sign the commitment papers, Clara. . . . Close that door, will you, Charley boy?"

And we were off to the hospital, my uncle making easy talk with the wife, and me sitting beside the demented husband who had almost murdered a defenseless woman. It did not take long for him to be removed to the barred retreat where for all I know he still paces, hunting for the secret wires of science.

After we had finally left his wife, in the charge of a sister, weeping in terror at the prospect of feeding her family without her husband's wages, Uncle Dan took me into the precinct house, where he had to make out a report. Then we drove across the length of Coney Island, from the hump of Sea Gate, sticking out into Gravesend Bay, over to Brighton Beach, to that corner of it which encloses Sheepshead Bay, and there, on a street of bay-front cottages smelling not of traffic exhaust, dumb-waiters, and dark metallic elevators, but of clams, salt marshes, oakum, and rotting bait, I met a sword swallower.

Mr. and Mrs. Alvarez might have been, superficially, custom-ers of my father's. She was a childless but motherly woman with the bosom of a pigeon, but her flashing eyes were those of an opera singer. When we arrived she was just removing a sheet of cookies from the oven. While her husband, who greeted us in his bathrobe with the *Daily News* dangling from his left fist, was squeezing my hand so hard that it brought tears to my eyes, Mrs. Alvarez was already pouring me a glass of milk and setting the cookies before me.

She stood over me and stroked my hair while I ate and drank, saying, "You come from a nice part of the country, kiddo. Many's the time Alfredo and I played the fairground circuit all in through there."

"What did you do?"

She laughed, her bosom shaking. "You wouldn't think it to look at me, but I used to be a bareback rider. Since I got too heavy, we settled here, and Al works the shows on the island."

Her husband, the examination of his throat and chest completed, returned to the kitchen from the bedroom without bothering to throw his robe over his undershirt and trousers. I was impressed by his shoulders, which were embroidered like tapestry with writhing tattooed dragons, their tails looping up around his wiry corded neck.

"How you like it here, kid?" he demanded.

"I like it fine."

"Doc says I'm going to live for a while," he announced to his wife and to me.

"Not if you don't change jobs," my uncle grunted, but that seemed to make no particular impression. Mr. Alvarez stepped jerkily to the closet and fetched out a long package, a broom handle maybe, wrapped in flannel.

"You didn't take the boy to the sideshow yet, did you, Doc?"

Uncle Dan shook his head. "Give us a chance. He hasn't even been to Bedloe's Island yet, to the Statue of Liberty."

"Aw, the Statue of Liberty. Let me show you something, kid." He unwrapped the flannel with a flourish and exposed a glittering sword, wonderfully filigreed all along the blade.

Before any of us could say a word Mr. Alvarez snapped to attention as though he were presenting arms at court, then raised his walnut-brown sinewy arms and brought the point of the sword to his lips. He bent his grizzled head back farther than I had ever seen anyone do and slipped the sword into his open mouth and down his gullet, inch by inch, then foot by foot.

You could actually see it going down from the outside, his bare neck working and swelling as it contained the cold steel.

Mrs. Alvarez sat at the kitchen table, placid and proud. "Pretty good, huh? Here, take along some cookies in wax paper. You'll get hungry later."

Mr. Alvarez brought up the sword as deliberately and delicately as he had slid it down, clicked his heels, and bowed. "You get the point?" he asked, and laughed with a hoarse bark.

"That's the most amazing thing I ever saw," I said honestly.

"I can do that with almost any type sword. Except one that's too curved, like a scimitar." Skimitar, he pronounced it. "I can do it with a rapier, even with a saber. You got to keep a straight passage, see, the head has got to be straight back. It's all in the head, am I right or wrong, Doc?"

Mr. Alvarez gave me the sword to examine. "You come to the show, kid, and you'll be able to see right through me. I swallow an electrified sword, it's got little bulbs on it. I stand in front of a black curtain and you can see the bulbs inside me just like my backbone was lit up."

He was chuckling all the way to the door. "See you in the freak show."

In the car my uncle sighed, his hands hanging over the steering wheel for a moment before he stepped on the starter. "Nice people, aren't they?"

"You bet."

"He's got an ulcerated throat. It's a precancerous condition, really. You can't go on insulting the body indefinitely, Charley boy. But his wife can't work anymore, and he doesn't know how to do anything else. Well, I thought you'd enjoy meeting them."

We did visit the freak show a few nights later. I gaped at the tattooed lady's bluish hide, blurred like an old map, and stared in uncomfortable awe at the seminude form of the half man, half woman, not wholly convinced by Uncle Dan's explanation of glandular pathology. My parents would never have taken me there, either as a favor or an object lesson, and I did not dare to ask Uncle Dan what he had in mind, if anything, besides entertainment.

The Fat Lady was off that night because of a toothache. But since she too was a patient of Uncle Dan's, next morning I found myself riding with her and my uncle in an old panel truck from her flat in Brighton over to the dentist's, on Linden Boulevard in Flatbush. Uncle Dan and I sat in front with the driver, her brother-in-law, who was all business; Smiling Sally herself was spread out, like some giant growth, all over a plank fixed to the bed of the truck for her. From time to time a groan would issue from that vast heap of flesh, and her massive arm would rise slowly, alarmingly, reaching out to my uncle for comfort.

Uncle Dan was to give her the anesthetic, but before the extraction we had to get her into the office of his colleague, Dr. Otto Reinitz, whose first-floor office fortunately had French windows. No sooner had we begun preparations to transport Sally through the window to the dentist than the envious neighborhood kids began to gather, picking their noses and pointing at the groaning circus queen.

First we had to rig up a kind of staging with a block and tackle, like the bos'n's chair used by sign painters, and then, supervised by her sweating but experienced brother-in-law, we hoisted unsmiling Sally aboard and on into the office of the waiting Dr. Reinitz, a skinny man with an eyeshade and the biggest Adam's apple I had ever seen. We pushed the sofa from the waiting room into the office so that Sally could recline on it within reach of the dentist's forceps.

When the job was done and Sally came back to life, she became a person for me. I had no idea how old she was, maybe twenty-five, maybe forty-five, but beneath all of that fat there beat the heart of a flirt. She smiled winsomely, bravely making light of her pain, she looked sidelong at me, she squeezed my hand.

"That's some assistant, Doc," she said to my uncle. "A regaleh doll. How old are you, sonny? Old enough for the girls?"

I knew the answer to the first question, if not to the second, and she rewarded me with an inscribed postcard photo in a glassine envelope, displaying her in a grotesque tentlike puffed-

sleeve party dress, bobby socks, and Mary Janes, which she took
from the purse that dangled like a toy doll's from the rings of
flesh at her wrist. SMILING SALLY, 649 LBS. OF JOLLITY, it said.

"I get a quarter for these at the freak show," she told me.
"For you, nothing. Someday you'll grow up to be a big doctor
like your uncle."

That morning, I thought maybe I would. There were others
my uncle attended whose lives had also been tarnished, some
in ways I would not dare to mention when I returned home. In
Greenpoint, just across the East River from Lower Manhattan,
on Noble Street (the name has stuck in my mind), I waited in
a candy store while Uncle Dan administered sedation in the flat
upstairs to a screaming woman whose son's body had just been
brought back from Red Hook, where rival mobsters had put
three bullets in the back of his head. From there we drove in
silence, around the Navy Yard, over to a portion of Sands Street
which no longer even exists, teetering shacks aswarm with prostitutes.

I waited in the car, my face on fire, trying not to stare back at
the bored, gum-chewing girls waving at me from behind lace-
curtained windows. When my uncle came out, he tossed his
satchel on the back seat and gave my bony shoulder a squeeze.

"The more trouble I see," he said, "the hungrier I get. Let's
grab a bite in Borough Hall before I get stuck with my office
hours."

He had to file some papers and pick up vaccines in downtown Brooklyn too, so we parked on Montague Street and had
a businessman's lunch in a real bar, where I watched salesmen
matching each other for drinks by rolling dice from a cup.

"Nothing like that in Dunkirk," I assured my uncle.

"Charley boy," he laughed, "you could say the same thing
about Sands Street, in spades."

On the way back to the car, cutting across the open square in
front of Borough Hall, we came upon a circle of lunch-hour
loungers listening to a sidewalk speaker. I thought at first that
he was selling razor blades or carrot slicers, the kind of pitch-
man that my father always referred to as cheap, cutthroat com-

petition, but then as I pushed my way through I saw that he was black, and that he displayed nothing but a stick of yellow chalk.

He was a skinny, solemn man, conservatively dressed, but with eyes bulbous and roving like those of a rearing stallion. The bony, imperious hand that held the chalk slid occasionally to his mouth to wipe the spittle from his lips.

"*Ich bin a shvartser id!*" he cried.

Out of the corner of his mouth Uncle Dan explained, "He's telling them he's a black Jew."

"I do not preach the New Testament," the orator shouted in English. "Let us speak only of the wonders concealed in the Old. Let us confine ourselves only to the Pentateuch. Those of you who paid attention in *heder* will recall where it says . . ." and he lapsed into Hebrew.

His accent brought grins from the crowd; but suddenly he squatted and began to print characters on the street, in the space before us. His calligraphy, stark and sharp and yellow, stood out on the black street like the brilliant mysterious border of an Oriental rug. Drawing with nervous rapidity, he continued to scream at us as he stooped over his chalk, lecturing in English, quoting in Hebrew. Swiftly a pattern emerged as he whirled and twisted on his haunches: The mysterious phrases intersected at their center to form—"Inevitably!" he cried out, enraptured, the sweat of persuasion dripping down his cheeks—a cross.

"What I tell you?" a tubby man beside me demanded of his companion. "He's a *meshummad*, like I said."

"To be a *meshummad*, you got to be a Jew to start out. Otherwise, how can you change over? Nah, he's a missionary, an agitator. He comes downtown to convert."

Some of the crowd were muttering angrily, others turning their backs in disgust, a few (like Uncle Dan) chuckling, as the black orator called after us, flailing his long arms, white cuffs dangling over his wrists, "It is written in our own Book! We must admit the Christ to our hearts!"

And in the course of that week I saw signs and portents, cabalic symbols chalked on the city streets and tattooed on the shoulders of beings who ate cold steel; I rode with lunatics, moved from murderers to fallen women, accepted an inscribed photo from the fattest woman in the world, and one morning Van Mungo, the great Dodger pitcher, my hero long before I had come to Brooklyn, and my uncle's friend, rumpled my hair and autographed a baseball for me to take home, where I could varnish it to protect his signature and display it to the doubters of Dunkirk.

What is more, during Uncle Dan's office hours I lolled on the beach with *Official Detective* magazines from his waiting room that were forbidden me at home, surrounded by the undressed throngs come in their thousands from every stifling flat in New York, from every darkened corner of the world, actually, to sun themselves at my side; I learned the sweet subtleties of bluff and deception, kibitzing at the weekly session of my uncle's poker club, attended by the cadaverous dentist, Dr. Reinitz, and three Coney Island businessmen; and I was not just allowed but encouraged to stay up practically all night for the great flashy Mardi Gras parade, blinking sleepy-eyed at the red rows of fire engines rolling glossily along streets sparkling like Catherine wheels. It was the greatest week of my life.

But if my uncle graced my childhood, he also—one bitter wintry evening some ten years later—illumined my adulthood. When the destroyer escort on which I had been pitching miserably through the North Atlantic on wartime convoy duty paused in the dead of night in Gravesend Bay before nosing on up through the Narrows to the Navy Yard, I wangled my way ashore and hurried directly to my Uncle Dan. After all those black nights blinking at meandering merchant vessels groping toward their own destruction, Coney Island was startling, even in the dimout. But it had changed. Icy and inhospitable in the off-season, its faded invitations to dead pleasures creaked in the winter wind, and its empty, empty streets were rimmed with frost and frozen grime.

My uncle was not at home. "But you go on over to the Turkish bath," his housekeeper said to me. "You remember where it is, right down the block. He's playin' poker there with his club, Dr. Reinitz and all of them."

Already a little let down, I shivered along the barren streets and shouldered on into the hot, dank sanctuary of the bathhouse. There, seated around a card table messy with poker chips, sandwich ends, French fries on wax paper, and beer in paper cups, were my Uncle Dan and his fellow bachelors, their bare skulls and shoulders shining wetly under the brilliant light of a hundred-watt bulb that hung straight down from a cord. The cadaverous Dr. Reinitz was naked save for clogs and a Turkish towel across his lap, but I recognized him at once by his Adam's apple and his green eyeshade, which apparently he never discarded; instead of his swiveled drill he held three cards in his hand, but he had changed in no essential aspect.

Uncle Dan was half draped in a bed sheet, roughly like a Roman senator, except that you don't think of Romans as clenching cigars. The fringe of hair on his chest had turned white, and his paunch was twice what I had remembered it to be. He glanced up at me coolly, with a weary casualness more startling than the collapse of his looks.

"Look who's here. How are you, Charley boy? Gentlemen, you remember my nephew. Otto, Oscar—"

I nodded.

"Here, pull up a chair." The one named Oscar extended his hand and showed me two rings. "Hey, Jake, bring another corned beef. And a beer. Never saw a sailor didn't like beer."

"You been overseas?" Dr. Reinitz inquired incuriously.

"I've been back and forth," I muttered. "On convoy duty. Halifax. Scotland. Murmansk."

"You don't say. I was in Archangel once myself. Very drab. You could see daylight right through the chinks in the log cabins."

"Well," said Uncle Dan, "main thing is you're back in New York safe and sound. What are you going to do with your leave —paint the town red?"

"Paint the town red?" I cried, hoping desperately that he

would do for me, one last time, what he had when I was thirteen.

I had been seasick and frightened for a long time. I had been
knocked off my feet by depth charges, I had been nauseated by
the twilight farewell of a helpless wallowing Hog Island vet-
eran of the first war, flaring briefly against the horizon like a
struck match and then pointing its bow at the sky like an accus-
ing finger before sinking beneath the sea, leaving nothing but a
few screaming men and the junky debris of war.

Now I was appalled by these civilians and their unrationed
self-satisfaction, and most of all by my uncle himself. I was
heartsick with disappointment. Like a boy crudely misunder-
stood by a girl he has romanticized, I wanted only to flee. Then
I saw that my uncle wore a queer expression that I would never
have identified with him, and so found incomprehensible: At
that moment I took it to be a look of envy, embedded in the
puffy used-up features of one seemingly beyond anything but
an evening of cards with his similars in a Turkish bath. And I
could think of nothing to say except to repeat, "Paint the town
red?"

He shook his head slowly. And slowly, as he turned the cigar
between his lips, an old glint came back to his eyes. Passing his
index finger across his whitening mustache to brush it into
place, he murmured, "I know what you mean, Charley boy. But
I wasn't worried about you for a minute. You're bigger now
than I ever was. I'm the one that's been going down, here, little
by little, and with no lifesaver either." Ignoring those about us,
who had suddenly ceased to exist either as his friends or my
antagonists, he paused for a moment in order that the words
that followed, more shocking to me than his appearance, might
bar the door forever to my childish demands on him. "I'm the
one who could use some help now."

THE TREE OF LIFE

IN THE SUMMER of my thirty-first year, I found myself living alone in a rural slum, in a Mexican village outside Oaxaca called San Felipe. My wife had left me in Taxco and I was having a bad time of it, what with self-pity and lack of funds. Although I had failed to persuade her, I was still trying to convince myself that I had a distinct talent as a potter. What was happening to me was that, with no wife, no children, and no great originality, I was slowly being overwhelmed by the terror of growing old to no purpose, of gradual annihilation by the meaningless declension from a life that in my heart I despised but still feared to let go of. In between throwing and firing pots, I played dominoes with a Mexican linoleum salesman I knew, at the sidewalk café in front of the Hotel Marques del Valle in the main plaza of Oaxaca.

One afternoon, as I was washing down my tequila with a swallow of sangrita, a perfectly enormous American automobile, its windows ablaze with Mammoth Cave, Blue Ridge, and *turista* stickers, rolled to a stop at the curb, over at the far end of the plaza. There was no one in the car but the big-bellied driver, who wriggled out slowly, like a snake easing himself free of his skin.

"Good God," I said.

"What about him?" Julio glanced at me drowsily. "Jus' one more tourist, no?"

"No," I said. "It's my Coney Island uncle."

And as I sat there, all but paralyzed, watching my uncle make his way gingerly around the square with that blind, groping uneasiness peculiar to the American away from his homeland for the first time, I saw not this aging man, with the outsized cigar and dark glasses, the outrageous Hawaiian sport shirt over the great soft paunch that spelled lassitude more than stateliness, but rather the stocky, self-assured bachelor who had been the favorite uncle of my boyhood. How I had admired him! And how good he had been to me!

Although more than ten years had passed since he and I had been in close communion, what I remembered now was not our last, wartime encounter, when I had been a frightened sailor back from Murmansk and he a philosophical civilian physician, relaxing with his cronies over a poker game in a Coney Island bathhouse; nor even the wonderful week I had spent with him on his medical rounds as an adolescent in flight from my parents' failing hardware store in Dunkirk, New York, during the depression. No, what I would always associate ineradicably with him was the healing visit he had paid me during a terrible period of childhood disillusion.

One summer afternoon when I was seven or eight, my Irish setter Ryan and I had gotten caught in an unexpected rainstorm on our way home from the lake. At the front door I knelt to wipe him off and discovered that the dog's eyes and nose were running and that he was breathing jaggedly through the mouth, his sides heaving as though he had run all the way. Mother refused to listen to my pleas. She threw the dog out of the house and threw me into a hot tub.

Next day the vet told us that Ryan had pneumonia. My mother was contrite and let him into the house, but it was a little late, for the pneumonia was simply a secondary result of distemper, about which we could do nothing but wait.

I wrote, or rather printed, a letter to Uncle Dan in Brooklyn, since I thought he ought to know what had happened. He was the one who had given me the dog for a present, on my first day of kindergarten; and besides he was a big-city doctor. Uncle Dan sent me a picture postcard of the Hotel St. George (World's Biggest), and advised me to hope for the best.

We all did, but one sultry afternoon Ryan went into convulsions. Mother ran to the hardware store to get help while I called the vet. I had been feeling queer for some hours, almost as if I'd had a premonition; by the time the dog was taken away I had a raging fever and was aching not just in the region of my heart but all over, as if I were being squeezed in one of the steel vises in the back of Father's store.

Mother's hair, usually coiled so neatly at the nape of her neck, was coming down; as she bent over me a hairpin dangled limply, like a worm from a leaf; and as she unbuttoned me tears were running down her cheeks, leaving shiny tracks in her face powder. I was crying too, but I couldn't even tell whether it was because poor Ryan, his hindquarters quivering uncontrollably, had been taken from me, or because I myself was suddenly in such pain as I had never known before.

It turned out that I had rheumatic fever. As I lay fretful and languid in my sloping-eaved little room at the back of the second floor, mesmerized for days on end by the coffee-colored stains where the chimney flashing had curled back and allowed the snow to seep through the wallpaper, I sipped juice through a straw and whined for my dog who could have comforted me at the foot of the bed. But I did not rage against my parents, or even blame them, until Ronnie, the big kid from down the block, came to bring me some Don Sturdy books and laughed in my face when I told him about my folks putting Ryan out to board in the country.

"Put him away is what you mean."

I stared at him and his grinning buck-toothed superiority.

"The vet chloroformed him. They always do. Ryan is dead, that's what."

"Mommy!" I cried. "Mommy, come here!"

Frightened by the anguish in my voice, my mother hurried into the room. She collided in the doorway with Ronnie, who mumbled something about having to be going and left her to cope with the terrible suspicion he had aroused in my heart.

Yes, she said, reaching across the bed for my hand, which I withdrew and hid, clenched, under the covers, it was true. Ryan was dead. They had had to put him away.

"But why did you lie to me?" I sobbed. "Why did you lie?"

"We didn't mean to." She tried to stroke my hair, but I turned my head aside. "We didn't want to hurt you, when you were so sick. If you'd been well, we'd have told you. Your father was just waiting—"

I pulled the pillow over my head and refused to listen to any more.

Instead of getting better, I grew worse. By the next day I was out of my head, and I thought I heard Mother discussing me with Uncle Dan, who was almost five hundred miles away. But I was not wholly mistaken, for in her fright Mother had turned to her brother the doctor, calling him for advice on the long-distance telephone, which was something we did only in extreme emergencies.

It seemed to me only moments later, although I suppose it was the next day, that Uncle Dan was standing at the side of my bed, his cigar drooping beneath his big mustache, his watch chain glinting in a double arc across his vest. He hauled out the gold turnip watch that had been his father's, my grandfather's, and took firm hold of my wrist.

"What do you say, Charley boy?" he demanded. "Giving the folks a hard time?"

"They killed Ryan," I whispered.

"That's right. They did. But it had to be done. It's my business, you can believe me when I tell you. It would have been cruel to keep that dog alive. Even a miracle wouldn't have saved him."

"They should have told me."

Uncle Dan smiled, showing me his discolored teeth that were

supposed to be shaped like mine. "They should have. But people don't always know what's best for a sick person. Not even parents. Come on, swallow this, and I'll tell you something." He waved his fat cigar at me as though it were a wand. "You turn around and go to sleep, and in the morning there'll be a different kind of miracle in the yard, right outside your window. Is it a deal?"

I could barely nod, for already I was slipping off to sleep.

When I woke again, I was alone in my room, it was morning, the sun was already hot and bright on the patchwork quilt folded at the foot of my bed, and a whole flock of robins were talking to one another in the old apple tree, a branch of which brushed my windowpane. As I came awake I remembered Uncle Dan's promise, of a miracle outside my window, and I squatted on my knees by the casement to see if it had happened yet.

For a moment I was disappointed. Through the thick foliage of the tree which my father's father had planted at the turn of the century, all the familiar objects in our yard—the hollyhocks, the red pump set in the concrete lid of the well cover, the bird bath bordered with petunias, my little two-wheeler lying on its side rusting in the damp grass—looked just as they had when Ryan and I had chased each other round and round the doghouse Father had built for him.

But then, as my eye was distracted by the birds whirring about their nests in the twisted arms of the apple tree, I realized that it was not just the ripening Baldwins among which they fluttered and sang. No, there were oranges hanging from the tree too! And lemons! It wasn't possible, but why else were the birds crying out so passionately?

"Plums," I said aloud, "and pears. And there's a whole bunch of bananas!"

"That only makes six different kinds, counting the apples," remarked my uncle from behind me. "There must be more than that. I promised you a real miracle, not just a plain ordinary one."

"Uncle Dan, how did they *get* there?"

"Just go ahead and count."

"There's some grapes over there, and a bunch of cherries. That's eight different kinds of fruit. And what are those little green things?"

"Look like quince, but I'm no expert, Charley boy. In Coney I buy my fruit from Giuseppe at the corner stand. You spotted nine, now what about the other branch? Take a good look."

"I see a cantaloupe, and some tangerines, a lot of tangerines. That makes eleven different kinds of fruit. Eleven! And there's even some tomatoes, down there near that nest. Except that tomatoes are vegetables."

"Wrong again. Don't they teach you kids anything in Dunkirk? Tomatoes are a fruit, they're a member of the berry family, like grapes or bananas. And that makes twelve fruits, and that's your miracle." Uncle Dan's eyes were glittering, blacker than I had ever seen them, and the flesh around them was unusually dark and shadowed. "That plain old apple tree turned into a tree of life."

"A tree . . . ?"

"Sometimes I think you don't know anything at all, Charley boy." Uncle Dan pushed open my window very wide. "Reach out and pick yourself a fruit."

I glanced at the doorway behind him, at Father in his dangling suspenders and collarless shirt, at Mother wiping her hands tremulously on a dish towel.

"Go ahead. If I say to do it, it's okay."

My parents made no move to stop me, so I scrambled onto the sill, leaned far out, and picked myself a plum. As I bit into it, after rubbing it on my pajama sleeve, my uncle gave me a tremendous squeeze.

"There," he said. "Now. You've eaten of the tree of life. If you read your Bible, Book of Genesis in the Old Testament, Book of Revelation in the New Testament, you'd know what that means."

"My father claims you said the Bible is a pack of lies."

My father's face flamed. He had always supported Mother's insistence that I attend Sunday school regularly, and I had heard him charge his doctor brother-in-law with being a heathen.

Uncle Dan said easily, "We're not going to get into a discussion about that now. It's a known medical fact that when you eat of the tree of life, regardless of what you think happened in the Garden of Eden, it makes you immortal. I promise you, you'll be here long after the rest of us are gone. So why not start getting well, Charley boy?"

I did, of course. My uncle might not have been an outstanding physician, but he knew, even though he never fathered a son, what could turn the trick with a small boy. He must have been up the better part of the night in that old Baldwin apple tree, teetering wearily from Father's extension ladder while he fastened all that fancy fruit outside my window, but it was good medicine, because the next thing I can remember, he was gone and I was well and pumping my box scooter through the streets of Dunkirk.

And now here he was, an old man, peering up and down the streets, while I—I had to force myself to raise my arm and call out, "Uncle Dan, here I am," for I was ashamed of his seeing me. My chinos were stained with clays and glazes, my leather sandals were torn, I needed a shave, my hand shook. What could he think, if he too remembered me from those dead days as the fresh-faced boy who could be solaced for the loss of a pet with fairy trees?

But he strolled up to me with his old equanimity, as if it were only since breakfast that we hadn't seen each other. He waved the cigar confidently, as though it were the old magic wand with which he could change me back to what I had once been.

"How've you been, Charley boy? Had a feeling I'd find you here."

"I bet you did," I said. "Word gets around. But what brings you down here?" I could not get used to him in this context, or in any outside of that which I had always associated with him —it was like meeting your barber, out of uniform, at the movies.

"It was time," he said vaguely. "It was time. Am I interrupting anything?"

I introduced him to Julio, whose English was not good, and

over a bottle of dark Mexican beer he explained to us leisurely that it was hotter than the hinges of hell in Brooklyn, that his poker partner Oscar ("You remember Oscar, Charley boy?"), with whom he had planned to go on a cruise, had died, and that he had simply closed the office and started driving.

"I may just keep right on going to Guatemala, if my tires and my spirits hold up," he said, smiling.

But I knew that wasn't so. I felt that he had come to see me, although I wasn't sure why, and I observed that beneath the heartiness his skin was worse than white; it was yellowed and greasy.

"I hear there's some nice ruins around here," he said. "I'll just go on inside and check in—figured I'd stay for a couple days?" His voice went up on the last words, as though he feared that I might discourage him or indicate my unwillingness to have him around.

"I live out of town a ways," I said, "and it's just a dump, or I'd invite you to stay with me."

"Oh, I didn't mean—"

"But I'll be happy to take you to Mitla and Monte Alban, and any place else that appeals to you. I'm not very busy these days."

"Me either, Charley boy." Uncle Dan flashed the old smile as he arose. "Nice to have met you, Julio."

When we drove out to the great ruins in Uncle Dan's air-conditioned monster the following morning, I began to think that perhaps I had been reading things into his appearance that weren't there. He poked around dutifully, asked me to photograph him blinking in the bright sun with his arms around a pair of ragged Indian kids, and haggled over some fake Mixtec relics with the women who peddled them in baskets outside the church at Mitla; but he said nothing to indicate that he wanted anything other than this.

What was more, he displayed no curiosity about my personal situation, after he had made sure that he wouldn't be putting me out by making me his guide. We did not talk about our relatives, as we used to occasionally when I was a boy, except that in the town of Mitla he did shop for rebozos. "I've got to bring something home for your aunts. Let's pick out a couple nice quiet ones, not too loud."

In the home of a family of weavers, standing spread-legged on the dirt floor with his cigar stuck in his mouth, trying out his Brooklyn Spanish on an old crone and a mostly naked youngster, Uncle Dan pointed at a small placard tacked to the door, below a faded movie poster of Cantinflas as a comic bull-fighter.

"Say, Charley boy, translate this for me, would you?"

"This is a Catholic home," I read. "Protestant propaganda is inadmissible and unwelcome here."

"I'll be damned." He thought for a while. "All my life I lived in New York, and I never once saw a sign like that."

The next day Uncle Dan asked, almost shyly, if it would be possible for me to drive to the coast with him. I suppose the fact that I was somewhat taken aback must have shown in my face.

"Not Acapulco," he added hastily. "Too far. Besides, everybody says it's Miami all over again. I was thinking, It would be fun to see an unspoiled place before it gets taken over. Someone told me Puerto Angel is like that, not like Coney, just a quiet beach, with palm trees and tropical fruits, and hardly anybody there. We could make it in less than a day from Oaxaca, they say."

"I've never been, myself." I paused and stared at him, but he looked back at me blandly, expectantly. "Sure, let's go."

We made it to Pachutla in something like five hours in that monstrous car, with me driving and Uncle Dan relaxing, ignoring the hairpin turns and enjoying the wild landscape, the ravines and chasms that gaped on either hand. From Pachutla we had maybe another half hour to reach the Pacific, and I hesitated to press on to Puerto Angel, filled suddenly with a queer foreboding.

But Uncle Dan was a good traveling companion, uncomplaining about discomforts that he had surely never been exposed to in all his life. He ate wretched food and red-hot food, filthy chicken wings and ulcerating tacos, he laughed at indescribably dirty toilets and no toilets at all, he didn't mind the heat that boiled up as we descended, for he was eager to get to the sea. So we jounced over the potholed road that was an insult even to jeeps, and at last we swung round the last bend and beheld the blue body of the Pacific.

"Like stout Cortez, that's how I feel," laughed Uncle Dan, patting his belly. "Just like stout Cortez."

"Except that it was really Balboa."

"Well, whoever. You know something, Charley boy? I never saw the Pacific Ocean before. Come on, let's hit the beach."

But when we got there I could have wept for my Uncle Dan. His tropical paradise consisted of a modern school, a few stone buildings, and for the rest a row of wobbling wooden shacks tenanted not only by human beings but by cats, dogs, chickens, and pigs. The beach was strewn with refuse, alive with litters of squealing piglets slithering back and forth, and black with their excrement. And the heat fell on us as though it had been waiting, venomous and smothering, for us to emerge from the air-cooled car.

"Buck up, Charley boy." Uncle Dan rapped me lightly on the biceps. "Don't feel guilty. Imagine how *I* feel, dragging you off to this."

We made our way around a corner of the village and cut across a dried-up stream and a bend of hill to what had looked from the distance like a mirage but turned out to be exquisitely real. A heavenly beach, curving away from the midden of the village, where we undressed and lay on our backs, utterly alone, with our feet in the bluest, most caressing water anywhere in the world. We were wary, paddling through the water, of sting rays, and an occasional shark, but no matter. There were no pigs, there were no people. We might have been the first human beings ever to trace our toeprints in that crystalline sand.

"I want to tell you something, Charley boy," my uncle said

at last. "I imagine that when you were a kid, you used to envy me."

"Well, I admired you. You were good to me."

"But I wasn't to myself. I should have married, I should have —oh, done any number of things. We're all cowards in one way or another. And then, you know, these last few years, after all the old urgencies were burned out, the chasing after women, running to make a buck, wishing for things that weren't going to be, like eminence in the profession or adventures away from home, I found that just being alive was like finding a treasure every morning."

He rolled over on his big stomach and spoke with his mouth inches from the fine white sand. "The trouble was that just when I thought I had it made, a new fear came at me—the fear of death, something I'd never understood in all my years of practice. You remember, when you were a little boy I told you that you were immortal . . . well, I never really believed it myself, maybe because I wasn't a small-town kid and I'd never tasted of the tree of life the way you did. Or maybe because when you grow up in New York there's no innocence for you to lose."

He paused. I said, as casually as I could, "And now?"

Uncle Dan startled me with his loud, almost raucous laugh. "I'm glad I came down here, that's all. I got caught up a little. You can't have everything, but what a shame if you never get to reach for it! That's the only thing I'd regret. There's really nothing to be afraid of in the reaching, you know? You strain your engine to reach paradise, and when you get there, all sweaty and out of breath, you find that the little piggies have beaten you to the beach. And there isn't a damn thing wrong with that—it's all part of the game. Don't you think it's worth a lot to find that out? Life is great, and you've got to grab for it every morning. But what good would it be if you knew it was going to be yours forever?"

Next morning, after a crazy night barricaded against the invading pigs in a cubicle of one of the beachfront shacks that called itself a hotel, Uncle Dan and I crawled into his car and headed back for Oaxaca. We drove in silence all the way, both of us staring into the green depths of the ravines and breathing more deeply as we climbed into the pure mountain air. I knew that my uncle was dying, but I wasn't sure that he had come, as he had claimed on the beach at Puerto Angel, just to find out certain things for himself.

Now that he is gone, though, I feel fairly certain—even though he never asked me about myself, either to commiserate or to condemn—that Uncle Dan made his last trip as much to communicate with me one last time, to show me another path, as to please himself or to assuage his own yearning heart.

Shortly after he drove away, leaving me to stare at myself in the cracked mirror of my Mexican lodging place, I threw off my self-pity as you would cast away a soiled and worn-out coat, and returned to the United States, to a better and more reasoned kind of life. And when I visited his resting place in a crowded and unlovely corner of a Queens cemetery—for one morning before my return Uncle Dan had died quietly in his office, without making any particular fuss—I took along a small arborvitae, and when no one was looking I planted the tree of life quickly and gently on his grave.